Night Dragon

The Rise of a Shadow Warrior

R. O. McCray

To order additional copies of this book, contact:
Bookwhip
1-855-339-3589
https://www.bookwhip.com

DEDICATION

For all the unsung heroes and those never seen as a hero. Everyone is a hero to someone. For my Babies: Kameron, Dwaun, and Remii. You three are my heroes. You are my reasons to keep writing. Thank you.

Thank you, God for the pen and my babies. My Blessings are the ultimate blessing.

Contents

THE BEAST IS UNLEASHED

As the rain poured down, the eyes of a shadowy figure watched his latest work. The pain from battle was building and the blood flowed freshly. With the smell of burning rubber and flesh in the air, he sheaths his sword and begins to move to higher cover. Any moment the police would be coming, and his work would be seen.

Last night was too close and they almost had him cornered. The sounds of justice could be heard, and he had to disappear. Detective Steele would be there definitely and to be sure, he reached into his utility belt for a flash bang grenade. With one motion, he activated the grenade and flung it into his work two hundred feet below. The flash was huge and sparked a chain reaction of flames.

As the fire began to chase the liquid accelerator, a form started to take shape. The dark figure saw his signature signed and disappeared into the night. The first police car on scene pulled up to the carnage. The officer got out and immediately realized the design in the flames. He got on the radio and called into police headquarters.

"H.Q. this is Lincoln 56," he called in, "It's that beast thing again. Better get Steele on the all call."

"Thanks Lincoln 56," the operator responded before performing an all call, "All units be advised, we have another siting. Please respond to the shipping yard district and await Detective Steele. I repeat we have another Night Dragon siting. Detective Steele in route."

More officers appeared within minutes as well as the fire department. They cornered off the area and arrested what was left of a small war. As the police began to make sense of what happened, the man leading the investigation finally arrived. Once on site, he quickly looked around and began to put the pieces together. He ordered the arrest of the know thugs and hired guns hiding in the crowd watching the scene.

After searching the warehouse, he and his fellow officers found a little girl locked away in an office. He began to question her to find out what really happened.

"Hi," he said in pleasing voice to ease the shock, "I am Detective Steele. Can you tell me what happened here?"

"Yes sir," she replied with tears, "They tried to hurt me. They hurt my dad bad...Daddy! You have to help him."

"Where is he?" Detective Steele questioned.

"He is in the trunk of that black car," she said as she pointed.

Without a thought, Steele ran to a nearly destroyed sedan and tried to open the trunk. He wasn't sure if the man was okay, so he listened to hear breathing as he knocked on the door. All he could hear was moans of pain. He called the firefighters over, and with a couple minutes the injured man was free. Forgetting his duties, Steele rushed the injured man and his daughter to an ambulance...

"I want a guard with them 24/7 until I say so. Keep them safe and wait for me to get there with further orders," Steele ordered a few officers, "Get choppers in here. The Dragon is still here."

"How do you know sir," an officer asked.

"He maybe a smug bastard, but he is not the one to leave a little girl unattended," he pointed out, "Get exits blocked and boats in the water now."

As officers sprang into action, they began searching every inch of the area. They only found bodies and bodies of unconscious men. The weapons found beside each man were either in pieces or empty of ammo. The entire scene looked like a war zone. As arrests were being made left and right. Steele grew more and more irritated by the minute. After a final sweep, the police started to load prison buses. The Commissioner of Police finally arrived along with news vans.

"Steele, what do we have here?" the Commissioner asked.

"It looks like an arms deal was interrupted by Night Dragon," Steele said boldly, "We are still looking for him."

"Didn't I say that Night Dragon is a myth," he scolded the honest police detective, "I said we don't use myths to solve cases."

"Well, Sir, if he is a myth, then why is there a dragon burned into the pavement?" Steele asked as he pointed at the symbol.

"Do you want to keep your job?" the Commissioner returned, "I suggest that you get your story straight before the news crew interview you. And if I hear that name one more time, you are fired."

"Then you talk to them, I have a crime scene to process," he told his boss as he returned to avoid the rushing news anchors.

While the Commissioner began to answer questions, Steele proceeded to look around the scene. He knew the truth needed to get out, but the politics were clouding his duties. He was now more determined to bust the faceless vigilante no matter what. He continued walking away when he saw another piece of the mystery man. Like times before, he grabbed a plastic bag out of his coat and placed inside a throwing star with the dragon emblem. He quickly hustled the item into his coat and went back to processing the scene.

"I am getting too close," he told himself as he rushed to question the man and daughter at the hospital.

It was just before dawn again, and he was finally getting in. Tired and spent, he began the task of recharging his armor and himself. As he placed each item into a charging station, he tried to not focus on the pain. This was the first time in a long time that his armor and powers failed him. As his mask was finally charged, he took a closer look at the video of his battle. He was fortunate that his skills with a sword and Bo staff were beyond measure. For with the loss of his strength and agility, he would have been killed with all those guns against him. He saved that man and daughter from death, but he lost his chance to track down the Grandmaster. To him the tradeoff was worth it. The idea that he was close to the prize put a smile on his face. Honor for his family would finally be restored and revenge for his parents would be delivered.

Revealing his true face to only a mirror, the shadow warrior began to follow his usual routine. Opening a book on his desk, he began to further his research. The answer was in front of him as he and his fore fathers have always suspected. After an hour of reading, his mind began to race. Words and images began to blur. Feeling the urge grow strong, he left his work aside and proceeded to hit the punching bag. He could feel his powers returning but could not understand why. Then with a blink of the eye, the answer finally came to him...The Final Trial.

Fading back into time, the story of the Night Dragon is older than the United States. It begins in the home of all life, Mother Africa. Coming from a great distance, a man studied the strange land upon which he stood. He was on an official mission from the Emperor, but he took this as an opportunity to see the world outside of Japan. He loved his home land, but the death of his wife and son left him lost in his heart.

As he studied the land and resources, he made notes and tried not to be noticed. He traveled under the story of a lost sailor looking for his brother. He was there to study a star that fell from the sky. A story that made its way to his emperor and now his best warrior was on the trail for truth. As he traveled deeper into Africa, he learned the history and the culture of this untapped world.

While he learned and continued to count the endless wonders of this new land, he also witnessed many of the shameful acts of outsiders. The slave trade was new and booming. He knew the truth of slavery coming from Japan. He also knew of the Honor among men. The respect given to a man could free him of the chains of society and bondage. However, he was duty bound and could not interfere. That was the case until he happened upon slave traders marching their newly acquired cargo from the burned remains of a village. The urge to attack was unleashed at the site of children shackled and beaten.

Suddenly, one small child attacked a slave trader then freed himself. Before he could escape, the small boy was shot in the back. The foreign traveler stood there in shock. He watched in horror as the boy fell to the ground. Flashes of his family's violent death filled his mind. Before he could unsheathe his sword, a warrior in black leaped from the bushes with his army. The slave traders didn't have a chance as they faced true justice that day.

The foreigner quickly moved towards the boy without a concern for his own well-being. Finding him barely alive, he quickly used what he could find in his bag to help him. To his surprise, the warrior in black appeared before him. Not a word was spoken as they looked at each other eye to eye. The truth was shared in that stare. The warrior allowed the foreigner to continue.

Once he bandaged the boy's wound, he picked the injured child up and carried him to the warrior. Removing his war mask, the tears of pain rolled down his face. The Foreigner wanted to talk but did not know the language to speak. He picked up very little of the native tongue in his travels. The Masked Warrior grabbed the boy and invited the Foreigner to follow. Taking him back to his village was the beginning of the journey that would change and unite them forever in an amazing bond. Upon his arrival, the Foreigner realized that the Masked Warrior was the Chief of the village.

Staying with the Warrior and his people, the Foreigner lived among the people and was accepted as one of their own. The longer he stayed in their village, the more he could understand and felt at home with the people.

The Foreigner gained a new life and passion from his stay. In time, his visit turned into his home. The only thing keeping him from enjoying a new life was his wife and son. He wished they could be there with him. It had been almost three years since their deaths. To mourn, he focused on his work. Being one of the Emperor's trusted men, he focused his lost love on his country.

Being who he was, the Foreigner turned his pain into his power and weapon. He focused on his duties to country and Emperor. He was a warrior and true patriot to his country. He eventually found an ally and new wife. She was a widow herself and knew the pain of lost. She helped him mourn and work on his projects. Within their time together they found love and a kindred connection. He saw her as his equal unlike the men of his country. He began to see how his country differed from him and his new bride.

The class system among his people broke his heart as well as his wife's. The way the lower classes were treated would drive him mad. His own status among his people was in question. Shamefully, he lived his role in his society. To the public he was a swordsmith and skilled warrior. As former samurai general, the Foreigner became more important to the Emperor for his mind and skills with hammer. His past accomplishments earned the honor of being the Emperor's advisor. However, this title came with a hidden agenda.

To his people and fellow statesmen, he was just a royal blacksmith and goodwill ambassador. He may have been a great warrior in the past, but the Foreigner was just a fancy craftsman. However, there was a secret he held from everyone in the land. Only his wife and the Emperor knew his secret. The former warrior was now a silent assassin and spy…a ninja.

Coming home from another successful mission, he was immediately summoned by the Emperor. While away, a star streaked across the sky as if the heavens were falling to Earth. Fear and power drove the Emperor to seek out the fallen star. However, it had to be done in secret.

The foreigner was summoned immediately to search for the fallen star. It was the Emperor's opportunity to gain more power. A great prophecy foretold of the power of the Heavenly Dragons would fall to Earth and give the ultimate power. The journey to study the star that fell from the sky was a perfect chance to get away. The poor broken warrior needed to leave his home land to find himself. At first, he was reluctant, but his new bride assured him that he needed to get away. She knew he was not the man in his heart. The man in his heart was the man she fell in love with. That man was the man she wanted to return home.

As the Foreigner lived in this strange new land and among its people, he began to see things clear. Ever since his arrival at the village, he and the leader grew close. Plus, the little boy he saved became his own ward. Caring for the little boy, he made sure to feed and spend his time with him. The boy knew and treated the foreigner warrior as his only family.

The Foreigner fell in love with him and the village. As time went on, he began to call the village home. The boy, he proudly called his son. He even learned the native tongue and spoke it fluently. The only thing missing from his new life was his new bride. He knew in his heart that she would love the village and all of Africa.

While time went on, he and the Masked Warrior built a deep friendship and brotherhood. He introduced the Foreigner into his inner sanctum. It was there the Foreigner admitted his mission to the Chief and friends. It was at that moment the two shared all the secrets they held. Their bond became stronger that day. Not only did they share their thoughts and agendas, they also shared skills as warriors.

That was the beginning of his training as new warrior. It was two years before the Foreigner finally finished his training. Both men grew in strength and knowledge. They forged a bond that was stronger than anything. They saw each other as equals and brothers. They also took those new abilities and skills and trained the men of the village.

The day of completion was finally upon them when word finally reached the foreigner. The Emperor ordered his return and to report his findings. He did not wish to return to his homeland. Africa was now his home. The boy was his son and a sign of good fortune. He wanted to send for his wife and build their home there. Being duty bound, he knew that could not happen.

While the Chief and Foreigner trained each other, they both trained the boy to be the warrior that was in his heart. The three of them spent those two years together training, learning, and building the foundation of something that was much greater than anything any man could do in the world.

Upon the news of his new father leaving, the boy made his mind up that his place was not with his people. He knew in his heart that his place was with his father. With a huge and great smile on his face, the Foreigner embraced his adopted son and happily helped him prepare for his new home. He knew that the people of status would demean and discourage his new son.

However, his love for his adopted son was far too great. In his eyes, he was the second son he, his deceased wife and son always prayed for to complete their family. The journey home was long and dangerous. The father and son traveled with the Chief and the village elders. They chanted most of the way a song of a hero's farewell. The entire village made it clear that they miss their brother and his son.

When they finally reached the African coast, the Foreigner looked at his son and smiled. He knew that the life for his child would be difficult, but his faith was in his son. His son had the strength of a thousand warriors. The boy had the ever-growing mind of the wisest of sages. Most importantly, his dear son had a heart as vast as the world itself. His only fear was his countrymen. The Foreigner knew that the people of Japan were not ready for his son and his leadership.

After a while of thought, the Foreigner pulled his son to the side. He spoke his fear openly to his son. He was ready to disobey orders and defy his Emperor. With the knowledge given to him in training, his son gave his father the perfect idea. Before their journey to a across the seas and oceans, the Chief presented the Foreigner and his son a parting gift.

It was the gift of Emperor's desire. The gift was not of this world. It came with a duty to protect the world from those seeking its great power. It came with the awesome responsibility to be that warrior and protector of all people. They all knew of its' capabilities from their training, but they also knew of the dangers if it fell into evil hands.

Father and son agreed to protect the innocent and the world from those who would misuse the power of the fallen star. This began a family legacy that has span centuries and countless lifetimes. As Night Dragon began to wake from the memories of his family's past, he began to think about her again. She was the other half of the family legacy of secrets.

Created to be his anchor in this world, her mind and teachings were corrupted by the lies and treachery of his enemy. She was once his reason to avoid this life of endless fighting. The goal of every Night Dragon since creation was to settle down and just focus on family. Promising to only carry his sword as a method of justice without shedding life, Night Dragon kept his vow to protect the innocent and to always serve fair justice.

As he opened his eyes and looked around his lair. He could hear his trusted assistant coming and quickly put his mask back on. Adonai was more than his assistant, he was his only family left in the world. To protect him, he wore his mask and voice changer even in front of him. His father and fore fathers always kept that rule to protect Adonai and his family throughout the years.

Even as a child, he and his family wore mask to protect their identity as well as Adonai's family. They knew if anyone linked them to Adonai's family, innocent blood would be spilt. Keeping all secrets but the one mystery, they were trained in the many arts of life just like Night Dragon. Helping him to grow in his abilities and powers, they were his public face as his identity remained in the shadows.

Adonai gathered his gear up to be sharpen and repaired if needed. Night Dragon quickly showed Adonai the footage from the battle and the data from his gauntlet computer. The two confirmed that the fear of the clan was approaching. It was time of the Ascension, and the three pieces of the Dragon were still missing.

Adonai grabbed a huge old book from a self of books in a small library section of the lair. Placing the book in front of Night Dragon, he passed a pen over and prepared the super computer to continue his studying. Before long, Adonai had disappeared to complete his duties.

After working for an hour, he was sure that his plans would work. He only had one concern. She was the only loose end. He swore to protect her by any means necessary. He needed her not only for the Ascension, but to also to have a chance to live a regular life. Night Dragon had to get back to his life unknown to the world. He was getting tired of the back and forth. His ability to multitask two different lives was amazing, but it was eating away at his mind and body.

Fortunately, His lair was under his building. He had to get back to his other reality. Opening a secret elevator, Night Dragon quickly climbed inside to go back to reality. Once in the elevator, he removed his mask and dressed back into his street clothes. Once he reached street level, he exited the elevator eagerly. He had more work to do. He had to get to the hospital and check on the victims. He didn't expect any innocent bystanders. Night Dragon always put the innocents before the mission.

The site of the poor man trying to deliver his shipment and collect the money worried Night Dragon. When he saw that there was no intent to pay the driver, Night Dragon knew he had to stop the murder. Then he spotted the little girl. His heart broke when he saw her. He had two innocent lives to protect. Night Dragon rushed from his position, but he could not get to the little girl in time. She was discovered and placed into an office. The girl became priority. Rushing into the shadows, he used all his skills to rescue the girl.

When he appeared before her, he tried to keep his mask in the shadows, but she ran to him due to the many stories of his actions among the streets and other children. He assured her that she and her father would be safe. He found a car away from the upcoming fight. He pointed the car out to the little girl from the office window. Night Dragon promised that he would rescue her dad and put him inside the trunk. The told her to remember the car because she would have to direct the Police to help her dad. He promised her to stay in the office and remain hidden until the Police came.

Night Dragon disappeared into the shadows. The little girl watched from the window as the man from the stories she heard kept his promise. He took on everyone and showed no fear. Within minutes he arrived with a beaten and broken man pleading for his daughter.

Opening the trunk, he put the man inside and told them not to say a word for until it goes quiet. He slammed the trunk and broke the lock. With the image of a family almost destroyed in his mind, his rage was his fuel and focus. In his town, the innocent were off limits, especially the children. It was time for the Night Dragon to teach a major lesson to the evil of New Peak City.

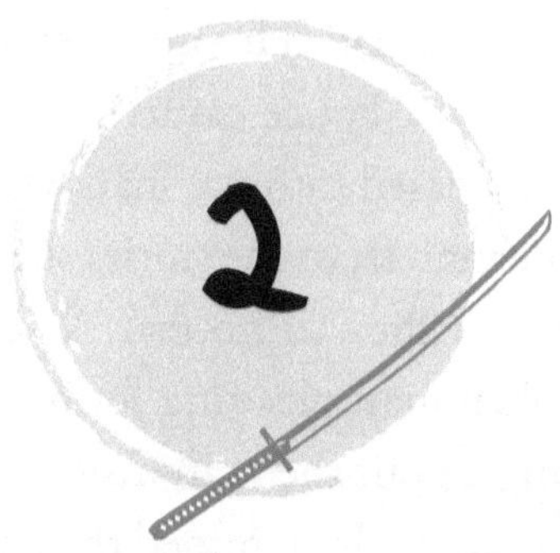

RICK STEELE, MAN OF HONOR

Rick Steele was a man of honor, and he believed his job was a way to make a difference. Although he kept to himself, he always stood out. He was six-foot one, well-built and looked like an ebony male model. Growing up, his parents raised him to be strong, smart and flexible.

The fact his parents were an interracial couple raising a child during a time when it was still taboo. With his mother being half Japanese, half black and his father black, he had to learn to embrace both cultures. He spoke multiple languages, and he was well travelled. Steele was also a trained solider serving as a Marine and a master of several martial arts. Being a part of a military family, he knew the importance of disciple, hard work, and honor. To him Night Dragon stood for everything that the justice system was created for.

After last night's events, he didn't know how much more he could stand. He had been a lead detective for five years and Night Dragon had been doing job the whole time. Confined to a desk, Steele had been trying to show his worth since his promotion. He honestly saw it as a demotion.

Every day when he sat at his desk, Steele saw the look of his former partner and mentor. The picture on his desk was his bittersweet reminder. The very first and only victim to die by the hands of Night Dragon was his partner and father.

Steele had to deal with his partner and father was labelled corrupt. The fact he died on his watch haunted him still. As he laid in his bed, Steele couldn't stop tossing and turning. With everything going on around him, he also began to miss the one thing that completed his life, Mya Wollert.

She was the one that he pushed away because of his thirst for justice and revenge. They first meet as kids but drifted apart. Mya was also the beautiful best friend of his current partner. They met up five years ago. Once again, they drifted apart due to schedules and their own ambitions.

Every night he looked at her picture that was next to his bed. His mind thought back to the perfect curve of her hips and breasts. She was mentally strong as her body. A gymnast and martial artist, Mya was a force not of this world. The many hours they spent together were the sweet memories of their youth. Of all the many traits of Mya it was her hair and her skin his missed the most.

The natural curls and locks in her hair was always his favorite thing to fiddle with as they watch TV or read together. The feel of her mocha latte skin was always on his mind. The last thought of her was the kiss goodbye when he told her that he had to focus on work.

Over the years, they barely kept in touch and only saw each other in passing or certain functions. However, Rick kept his distance as he thought it would be the only way to protect her. He tried to go back to sleep, but everything continued to swirl around in his mind. It was an hour before he had to be back at work. The alarm clock started to ring as he groaned to the lack of sleep.

Steele was still in his clothes as he walked into the bathroom like a newly created zombie. He was walking out the door refreshed and brand new, when he realized he was missing his ring. Finding it on his desk, he put on his ring with a small grin. It was his only reminder of his late father. As he wore the insignia ring of his family crest, he walked out of the door with the hope of a new day.

As walls began to close in on him, Detective Steele continued searching through files and video footage of the previous night' events. Security cameras captured everything. Once again, more proof that the Night Dragon exists. It also proved the fact that he was a law man.

Of all the years as the Night Dragon roamed the streets at night, the evidence of his presence was locked away to hide the truth from the public. Steele had been searching for answers for the cover up. The evidence he gathered could explain everything including the murder of his partner and father. Rick had to get the truth out. The Night Dragon was his obsession and his reason to keep going.

He knew the Captain would be in his office this morning after last night's incident. After a final warning, he knew his job would be in danger after crossing the Commissioner. In the eyes of the department, he had become the nut-job cop that was too close to a straight-jacket.

Night Dragon became an easy out in the eyes of the other cops. If he was doing their job, it didn't matter if they could hide his actions. However, for the cops that loved their job and cared about justice, Night Dragon was a criminal as well.

Rick Steele led that small group of honest cops. The powers that be were building a case against Steele to remove him from the force. Somehow nothing they used could stick. Steele was always aware and in complete control. He always kept his head and emotions in check.

However, after last night, Steele knew he had to hand over his badge. His actions at the hospital last night would meet retaliation any minute now. He started thinking back to his decision and wondered if it was worth it. The more he thought about it…it was more than worth it.

After processing the scene last night, he rushed over to the hospital for the victims' statements and check their well-being. He knew he had to hurry before the Commissioner had a chance to corrupt their statements. Luckily, he made it there in time and gathered all the information he needed. He warned them both that they could not mention certain information.

Winning over their confidence, the man admitted that he was hired to make a delivery to the docks. He brought his daughter with him as he always did for night deliveries. When Steele was finished, he gave them his card and told them to be on the lookout. There was no doubt that Night Dragon would be coming back to speak to them. Detective Steele wanted the information to be untarnished before the Commissioner arrived to twist the truth of Night Dragon. When he walked out of the hospital room, the devil himself was walking to the room followed by his goons.

"What did they say? What did they see?" the Commissioner asked, "And how did you beat me here?"

"My witness statements are now in the right hands," Steele said with a cold stare, "And if you pulled your face out of the camera, you could actually be a cop again."

"Watch your mouth, Steele," he fired back, "You are still on thin ice. Now give those statements to Thorton before you find yourself back on the beat!"

"That piece of trash lackey is not ruining my case," Steele refused, "Thorton can't even find the toilet let alone a clue."

"Hey, you better watch that mouth or end up like your father!" Thorton ordered. Without a second thought, Steele threw a haymaker that knocked Thorton two feet back into the wall. While everyone was checking on Thorton, Steele simply walked calmly away. Now thinking back, Steele smiled because it was more than worth it. It was a precious memory he would cherish.

Looking at the clock, he knew the Captain would be coming into his office soon. He loaded a flash drive and removed his files the computer. The moment he relinquished his badge, he would then become a marked man. Steele was not only investigating the Night Dragon, but the criminal figure only known as the Grandmaster. This mysterious figure was connected to Lieutenant Thorton as well as the Commissioner, himself.

But just like the Night Dragon evidence, it would either disappear or it never existed. If Steele was taken out of the equation, the idea of justice would finally die for the entire city. Realizing an opportunity, Steele grabbed another flash drive and hid his away. Just as he was loading the empty flash drive, Captain Kenzensho walked in slamming the door.

"What the hell were you thinking?!" Kenzensho yelled, "You hit the Commissioner's son and in front of the Commissioner!"

"Captain, you know Thorton will ruin the evidence and cover everything up," Steele told him straight.

"Look, I don't want to hear that conspiracy bull in my department!" Kenzensho interrupted, "I want your gun and badge now! You are suspended indefinitely."

"I got a better idea," Steele fired back. Pulling out an envelope from his desk, Steele took a deep breath as he passed it to the captain. "Tell the Commissioner, you have my resignation in hand." He handed the envelope over and began to grab his prepared box of personal effects. As he started to walk out, he reached for the flash drive.

"Steele, don't take the job with you," Captain Kenzensho said in somewhat calm voice, "Just get away from this mess and live. It is what your dad would have wanted."

"No, he would have told me to stay and punch Thorton again," Steele replied, "Cap, I need to find answers and I can't get them here."

"Look, if I take this to him," Kenzensho told him, "He wins, and you will never get the answers you want."

"Good-bye Captain," Steele replied as he turned and walked away from his life.

As he made the long walk out of the station, everyone just watched in shock and amazement. Corrupt and honest cops stood in awe as they all watched a brother walk away from the family. When a good cop leaves the job, every cop feels the lost. For the New Peak City Police

Department, Steele was the heart that kept them going. He saved half of their lives countless times just because it was his job. He earned and deserved their respect. Steele would always be their brother in arms.

As Steele continued to walk away, a smile grew on his face. His plan was working to the letter. He would finally get the answers he wanted. Now he had to sit back and wait for Night Dragon to bring the truth to the light. Making his way to his car, he looked up to his office window and saw the captain holding the flash drive. He climbed into his car and started the engine. He began to pull out of his parking space and away from the life he loved so dear.

Suddenly, the car locked up completely and the engine shut down. A look of fear appeared over his face as smoke began to fill the car. He looked up at the Captain, whom wore an evil grin as smoke began to engulf the car. Steele began banging on the windows and coughing violently. His fellow officers watching tried to get to Steele but were prohibited by raging flames. With one final look, Steele received the answers he had been searching for. Seconds later, he was swallowed up by the smoke and fire. Before anyone could try another attempt to save him... 'Boom!'

Pieces of the vehicle began to rain down and cops were scrambling to try and save their brother. As the fire raged and grew stronger, all hope was gone. They stood back as firefighters tried to control the blast. As the station cleared out to the bombing, Captain Kenzensho gave an Academy Award performance. Fighting back tears, he took control of the scene and played the part of a sadden leader. The truth was finally come into the light, but Rick Steele would not be around for the final acts of his plan.

Working away at his super computer, the mysterious warrior watched the news footage of the car bombing. He had been following the story since it hit the evening news. The attack was foreseen but the time was too early. His plan was working, and the power play with Steele went off like clockwork. However, with the death of the lawman, doubts and problems were created that he would have to deal with.

Night Dragon decided to deal with those details and focus on the end play. He took out a burned flash drive and began to search the records and data. The information continued to add up, but what he was searching for could not be found. It seemed hopeless until he noticed an address. His clue was found, and now it was time to connect the dots to the Grandmaster.

It was time to unleash the Dragon once more. Heading to a key pad on a wall, he entered his code to unlock armored case connected to the wall. Revealing the Dragon Armor and Weapons, he prepared himself for another night out on the town. His mind began to fade back to the battle the night before. He was worried his powers failing again. He shook the idea out of his head and continued to prepare.

Tonight, Night Dragon was going to make his presence felt throughout the entire city. Justice will not die on his watch. He placed his mask upon his face and synced his on-board computer with his gear. He made his way to his motorcycle and revved the powerful engine. Before heading out, he took a final look at picture next to his computer.

With just a simple nod, he rode off down a dark corridor. Pushing a button, he opened a door hidden behind a stone wall. Using a hidden ramp, he launched himself into the air. Landing perfectly on the road, he rode into the darkness. As he sped off, Night Dragon knew that he was beginning the end of his journey and would proudly avenge the lost a great law man. He only had one other concern. The news of Steele's death would be under his name. Night Dragon would now shoot to the top of a kill list that would ruin his plans. He knew that his name was now on the list to receive a white rose.

ENEMY AND PARTNER

As the rain began to fall, a shadowy figure appeared on the street. Waiting for the moment to emerge from the alley, the figure moved calmly across the street. Revealing her face and hair in the light, Detective Layla Lopez walked up to a cornered off section of the police headquarters parking lot. She stood there staring at the burnt remains of a car frame. The thought that Rick Steele was gone, plagued her mind.

A single tear began to fall as she remembered their last conversation. He was supposed to meet her tonight. Now she stood at the very place he drew his last breath. The sight sickened her. This was important evidence left to the elements to be destroyed. She knew Steele was on the verge of catching the Night Dragon. He often talked to her about the vigilante, and from time to time they called each other for back up.

Lopez stood there mourning when she heard something. She turned and noticed something next to a manhole cover. She tried to refuse from disturbing the crime scene, but with it being destroyed already there was no reason not to act. Steele's thoughts of corruption were truer than ever with the handling of his own murder. Throwing caution to the wind, Lopez retrieved the item with a plastic evidence bag she always made sure to carry. A habit she picked up from Steele, himself. The tears began to really flow when she realized it was Steele's ring.

Lifting her head to allow the rain to erase her tears, she noticed someone on the roof. She locked her eyes on the figure, realizing it was Night Dragon. Lopez took off racing inside Police Headquarters. Rushing to the elevator, she noticed no officers were at the front desk. Something was wrong, and she was going to find out exactly what. Lopez made her way to the roof access door with her weapon and flashlight drawn. Steele may have been gone, but his work had to be finished. She reached the door and found it unlocked.

Lopez knew he was in the building. She walked in stealth as she checked each office on the top floor. Just as Lopez was about to give up, she saw a light go off in an office. She moved closer and notice wet footprints leading into that very office she saw a light on. With gun still drawn, she turned off her flashlight. At that same moment, she heard footsteps.

Rushing into the office, she took aim at an empty target. Lopez searched the office for the Night Dragon. As she moved towards the desk, she saw footprints coming to the desk but none leaving. Feeling the lamp, she found that it was still cold. That meant that whatever he was looking for was not a hard copy. Touching the computer monitor, her suspensions were proven correct with a warm temperature. Night Dragon had to be in the building...in that office. Turning on the monitor, she found the computer was still on with certain files left open. The files consisted of her fellow detectives. High ranking officers and detectives were or had been under IAD investigation. As she continued to read, her eyes got wider as names were named. She broke out into a shocking gasp as she started at the last file. Internal Affairs had launched a major investigation. She was in shock as she read the list of complaints and the leader of renegade cops. It was the file of her dear friend and partner...Detective Rick Steele.

"Shocking information, I take it," a deep electronic voice said from the shadows.

"Freeze, you murderer," she exclaimed as she tried to find out where the voice was coming from. Grabbing her gun, she just took aim towards the shadows. "Come near me and I will put a major hole in your chest."

"Detective Lopez, please lower your weapon," the electronic voice said as Night Dragon revealed himself. "I mean you no harm. I am here to find out what happened to the Detective. Just like you, I want answers."

"I already know," she responded as she took aim, "You killed him."

"Detective, please don't believe those lies," Night Dragon interjected, "It was a setup to protect the real murderers. I was working with the Detective. His murder was an attempt to stop justice."

"I don't believe you," she snapped back, "Rick would never work with a criminal. He would never allow you to get within five feet of him without putting handcuffs on you."

"If you want to go off false beliefs, then continue to read that bogus file," he told her as he pointed at the computer.

"I don't have to!" she yelled at him, "I know my partner."

"If you know him," Night Dragon started, "Then you know that he believed in honor and lived for justice."

"Which is why I am going to arrest you for his murder," she returned as she cocked the trigger back.

"Lopez, I suggest you lower that weapon and sit down," he told her with an extended hand.

"I don't think so," she responded, "Now put you hand up slowly."

"Okay, I warned you," he said as his hand turned into a fist, firing a dart from his gauntlet. The dart hit her thigh, causing instant paralysis.

As she began to fall, he grabbed her and her weapon. He sat her up in the desk chair and put the safety on the gun. Placing the weapon right in front of her on the desk, Night Dragon checked her vitals.

"Detective Lopez," Night Dragon began to explain, "You are temporarily paralyzed. You gave me no choice, so listen close. Detective Steele found out about something that made him a target. Look at the screen." He grabbed the monitor and continued to explain. "He and these other cops were too close to the truth. Now that dart will wear off in 69 seconds exactly. If you want to honor him, be at this address tomorrow at midnight."

And with that he dropped a card on the desk and threw a smoke pellet on the ground. Before she knew it, her limbs had mobility. Lopez quickly grabbed her gun and tried to give chase. However, after looking around, she could not get a sense of his direction.

As she went back into the office, her emotions were building into a raging fire. She needed answers and revenge. Lopez grabbed the card and read the address. She recognized it and knew what she had to do. Determined and focused, she knew tomorrow would bring her both of her desires. Exiting the building, she paused just before stepping into the rain. She pulled out Steele's ring and took a final look.

"I will make them all pay for this," she vowed. Lopez stuffed the ring into her pocket and disappeared into the rain and shadows.

The night life of New Peak City began to pick up and the rain finally stopped. The shadow of a man began to appear on the side of a building. Crouching over the edge of a high-rise tower, Night Dragon watched and waited for his prey to finally make an appearance in front of the Duke Hotel. The hotel served as a meeting place and a safe house for all the major crime figures.

The Duke was their refuge from each other and the law. Criminals and the Law knew the rules of the Duke. Many peace treaties were brokered there, as well as many calm surrender arrangements. Business was never conducted there, but there was one man that broke that rule. Security was increased and upgraded constantly due to the actions of Night Dragon.

If Night Dragon wanted to get more information, the man to find was Hollywood Jones. Jones was a flashy old-school pimp and numbers runner. Hollywood claimed to be retired, but everyone knew that he kept his hand in everything. He owned and personally managed the Duke. It was because of the Duke, that Hollywood got out of the business and focused on the hotel and its special services.

As he sat out in the elements, Night Dragon tried to be patient and wait for the opportunity to arise. He had been trying to get a hold of Hollywood for a while and knew that time would eventually lead him into his hands. However, after the day's events, he knew he had to strike now in order to get leverage. After dealing with Lopez earlier, he was in serious need of information. His patience was wearing thin. Night Dragon stood up and leaped off the edge.

While is a swan dive, he kept is eyes focused on the street. With a flick of the wrist, he fired a line from his gauntlet and swung into a controlled flip. Landing perfectly in front of the door, he stood boldly in front of the armed doormen. Stunned, the guards stood back at the sight of the urban legend. The head doormen took the risk of trying to block Night Dragon's entry.

Smirking through his eyes, Night Dragon quickly and quietly grabbed the doorman's out stretched hand. He snapped the doorman's wrist and flipped him into a parked car window. Spinning around he cut off a sneak attack with a back punch to the face of another guard. The remaining three guards paused before attacking. Thinking quickly, he grabbed his retractable Bo staff and showcased his skills. Somewhat phased, the three guards reluctantly moved in only to be hit repeatedly by the spinning and whirling Bo staff. With one powerful kick, he sent the last standing guard through the hotel front doors. The expensively extravagant door and frame was in complete shambles.

Stepping over the downed guards, Night Dragon walked through the remains of the door frame. Once inside, he was greeted with more guards. Putting away his retractable Bo staff, he decided to enjoy a workout. Using his hand to hand skills, he took on the lobby full of guards. He went through eight men before the armed guards arrived with their heavy artillery.

Pulling out his sword, he was able to dodge and reflect bullets away. Once their guns were a proven failure, the guards rushed Night Dragon. However, they were met with his sword, slicing them down to size. After two minutes, the floor was covered with wounded guards. He put his sword away and made his way to hotel restaurant and night club.

Walking to the great hall, everyone partied the way as Night Dragon walked inside. There he found an army waiting for him. Looking around the room, he noted the weapons and range to his target. If he wanted Hollywood, then he would have to show all his skills.

In one smooth motion, he threw his dragon shaped shuriken and smoke pellets at the feet of the first wave of attackers. Using the smoke as a shield he flipped behind a pillar for cover. He whipped out his twin Shi and crept his way to an unsuspecting guard. Stabbing the blade through the weapon, he greeted the guard, as he turned around in shock, with a sharp powerful kick.

With the attention now focused on his new position, he quietly disappeared and only to take out the guards who investigated their fallen buddy. With nerves on edge, the armed thugs were terrified of the situation. Night Dragon knew that he could play the hide and seek game all night, but he wanted his answers ASAP. Setting off a loud flash bang grenade, he revealed himself in the middle of the dance floor.

Rushing him blindly, the guards were easily put down. Taking out at least fifteen men without breaking into a sweat, Night Dragon finally made his way to Hollywood's personal table. Heavily guarded by four huge bodyguards, Hollywood sat back calmly in his chair. Motioning for Hollywood to come to him, Night Dragon stood his ground quietly, but firm.

"Who the hell do you think you are dealing with, fool !?" Hollywood yelled as he refused to move, "This is my place. Get this lightweight out of my sight."

Night Dragon didn't say a word. He simply waved his finger, signaling the wrong decision on Hollywood's part. Before the four mountain size guards could pull their weapons, Night Dragon threw throwing knives right in the hands of the guards. Following those knives with his fists, he knocked the guards down like the rest of the hired guns. One by one they all fell to the ground from his fists.

Turning his attention to Hollywood, Night Dragon walked slowly up to the scared crime boss. Flipping Hollywood's table across the room with only one arm, he picked up the pleading crime figure up with his other arm. Just before he could speak to Hollywood, more guns began to fill the room.

Thinking quickly, he fired a line from him his gauntlet and shot up in the air like a rocket. Still holding on to his target, he zoomed up to the balcony. He dragged Hollywood along with him as he battled more guards blocking his escape. Fighting his way to a nearby elevator, he flung Hollywood Jones into the elevator. Using a Shi as a door wedge, he already had his escape ready.

As more men rushed towards the elevator, Night Dragon knew he was on borrowed time. Pulling out his sword once more, he began to put away as many men as he could. Before another wave could attack, Night Dragon threw down a flash bang grenade. Blinding his attackers, he retrieved his Shi and entered the elevator. The doors closed, and Night Dragon could breathe a sigh of relief. Hollywood was out cold from his head hitting the wall of the elevator. As they made their way to the roof, a smile through his eyes was revealed. It was time to play his favorite game..."Truth or Fly".

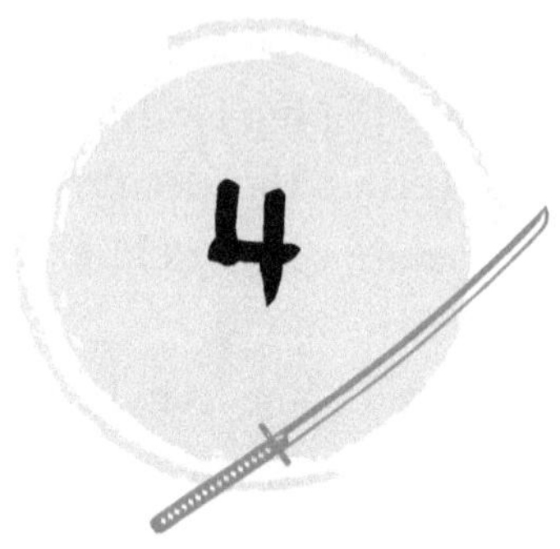

THE MASTER'S FURY

Standing in his penthouse, he awaited the arrival of much needed news. The captain had been on pins and needles since the bombing. Now he wanted the final word of the investigation. As Lieutenant Thorton finally arrived, he lowered his head to hide all emotion.

"What is the final word?" Captain Kenzensho asked, "Is he dead?"

"No remains, sir," Thorton told him after bowing to his knees, "The crime scene techs found sword marks on the floor and bottom of the frame. I had a team sweep the sewers underneath. They found traces of blood underneath the manhole cover under the car. It was Steele's but no sign of him. It appears the Dragon has him."

"I want both found and at my feet by dawn," Kenzensho ordered, "Tell your father to begin the man hunt for a cop killer. We have two days to get the final pieces. I don't want the Dragon to Ascend!"

"Yes, Master," Thorton replied, "I do have some good news. The Dragon is at the Duke. He is going after Hollywood. I have units on the way."

"No, hold off on that," Kenzensho ordered, "I want Hollywood to tell him everything. I have a special surprise when he goes for the Shadow Ring. Then head in with your men to arrest him on camera.

Call our newest "asset" in and let her know it is time. Let your father know he is on borrowed time. He has twelve hours to get the location of the Mystic."

"Master," Thorton cut in, "I want the Night Dragon. I lead your Samurai Army. Let me have the honor of killing your enemy."

"I have bigger plans for you my student," Kenzensho assured him, "But for now follow my orders and honor the code of the Jade Samurai."

"Yes, Master." Thorton told him, "We will not fail your ascension, Master. Here is your new helmet and mask."

"The Samurai Code will rule once again," Kenzensho said as his eyes began to glow a Jade green light. "And this mask will not be necessary. Now head to the Duke and make sure the Night Dragon is introduced to the press as a cop killer. I don't want him to gain any supporters or fans."

Leaving his master alone on the roof, Thorton pulled out his phone. Following his master's orders, he called the special guest for a party in Night Dragon's honor. He began his descent to his awaiting squad car. The thought of becoming the next in line sent chills down his spine. Once the Grandmaster ascended, he would be the new General of the Jade Samurai Army.

Exiting the luxury condo that served as the Jade Samurai headquarters, Thorton was shocked to find his former protégé waiting at his squad car. A smile popped onto his face as he walked up to the stunning beauty leaning against his car. Before he could get a word out, he was greeted with a sharp slap to the face. As rage filled from within, he turned to return the blow. However, he was stopped with the barrel of her gun in his face.

"Did the Grandmaster have Steele killed?" Layla demanded, "And if you lie, I will empty this clip into your face."

"You think you can roll up on me in my house!" Thorton yelled, "Besides, the Grandmaster's business is none of your concern. Snapping his fingers, red dots appeared on Layla's forehead and the center of her chest. "I suggest you leave now, or I will resend his orders against harming you."

"I will find the truth," Layla vowed, "And I will make every one of you pay. I still owe you for that night in the Squad Room."

She lowered her weapon and backed away. Layla slowly walked to her car while watching the shadows surrounding her. Just before getting into the car, she took a final look up towards the penthouse. There she saw the silhouette of the Grandmaster with green glowing eyes. She had never seen his face nor been in his presence. However, Layla could always tell when he was watching her or when he was around. She drove off quickly and decided to get out of Jade territory. It was not her time to be there until her true Master took his place.

Racing away, Layla heard the call about the gun fight at the Duke Hotel. She remembered it served as Hollywood Jones's business center. Turning on her siren and lights, she began to race to the scene. The way the call came spoke of Thorton's doing. All units were told to hold back and do nothing until Thorton reached the scene.

All though she hated Hollywood Jones, she still had to do her job, for Detective Steele's sake. No matter what else she did, Layla still was a cop. Like a flash of lighting, Layla realized that Night Dragon was there. It was now time for her to welcome the assistance of her enemy to honor the memory of her fallen partner.

Back in the Grandmaster's penthouse, he sat at his desk. Pondering his plan, he watched the events of the fight at Duke. He secretly had cameras in dance hall to monitor all the deals brokered there. It was his way of knowing everything in his empire. Hollywood knew nothing of the cameras and was under the impression that he was in the Grandmaster's inner circle. As he watched his nemesis destroy the army of bodyguards, the idea of an equal match was put into his mind. He continued to study his enemy while a mysterious and monstrous figure stood behind him.

"Master, why do you hold on to the fool and his father?" the beast asked, "They are the reason your enemy has continued to postpone your ascension."

"Simple," the Grandmaster began to explain to his loyal and faithful servant, "to ascend to check-mate, you must place all pieces, not just the pawns, into position as perfect bait. Soon my friend, I and Jade Samurai will be whole again. And I will rule what is rightfully mine. Make sure you and our unstoppable warriors are ready for travel. Once Night Dragon is dead, we will remove the rest of the weak from my empire."

"Yes, Master," the monster said as it bowed down in honor and respect, "It shall be done as you wish."

Waking up blindfolded, Hollywood knew that he was in trouble. Feeling the breeze, he heard the city. He was hanging upside down and in no position to bargain for freedom. Feeling the cold steel of Black Dragon's sword against his neck, Hollywood began to plead for mercy. In one smooth motion, the sword sliced the blindfold into pieces revealing his true predicament. Hanging by his feet, Hollywood was tied to the top of the flagpole hanging over the streets below. Strategically place between the two elevators motors, Night Dragon tied the rope to both elevator motors on top of the building. One move in the wrong direction, he could drop onto the cars parked on the street. Standing on the roof of the elevator shaft, Night Dragon held his sword to the rope with the intention to cut the rope.

"No!" Hollywood screamed, "I'll tell you whatever you want to know. I promise I will tell you everything. Please just let me go free."

"Where is the Grandmaster keeping the Shadow Ring and Armor?" Night Dragon asked with the help of his voice scrambler. "And be quick about it. Your men should be coming up in the elevators any minute."

"It is on the way to New Peak City now," Hollywood admitted, "It will arrive tomorrow afternoon by plane. Once it lands it will be transported to police headquarters. Lieutenant Thorton will be locking it up in the evidence vault."

"What about the armor?" Night Dragon snapped back, "I know it came in last night by boat. Now where is it?"

"The Grandmaster has it," Hollywood answered quickly, "He has it and I don't know where he is. I swear."

"I know you don't," Night Dragon told him boldly, "But you answer to him. So, when Thorton comes, tell him I am coming soon. And you better pray that he doesn't use the elevator." With that said he climbed out of the shaft through a roof access door. As his screams echoed through the shaft, he could hear the elevator motor begin to turn on. Fear began to swell from within as both elevators began to move. The cars moved closer with great speed. Then the access door opened, and Hollywood watched as Night Dragon sliced through the rope. He began to fall only to fall a few feet to the ground. Realizing that he was looking at a projection, he stared back at Night Dragon.

"You work for me now," Night Dragon declared from his perch. "You better come up with a good lie. Thorton will be here any moment." With that said, Night Dragon revealed their true location was the Duke Hotel boiler room. Hearing footsteps, Night Dragon climbed out of a window. Within a minute, the door opened to reveal Swat members with guns drawn. Thorton immediately followed. He released Hollywood from his binds and quickly questioned him. Hollywood admitted what he told Night Dragon. Then he was greeted with a jab to the face.

"You better not have told him anything else," Thorton threaten, "Or you will feel my special toy. Better yet, take him to the "Yard" for some questioning.

"No!!" Hollywood let out a blood curling scream as the Swat members drugged him out kicking and screaming. It was time to tie up loose ends. Ordering a gurney, he had Hollywood placed into a straitjacket. Once he was locked up, an orderly gave him a shot to put him to sleep. As the ambulance drove away, Thorton had a grin of pure delight as he thought about future torture session with Hollywood Jones. However, his smile turned into a confused frown as he witnessed the arrival of another ambulance from the mental hospital.

"What are you two doing here?" Thorton asked as he stopped them from entering the crime scene, "I just sent the bus I asked for back to the mental hospital."

"We are the one you called for," the driver told him, "We just got the call and rushed right over."

"If you are the bus..." Thorton paused to think, "Then who...." He reached for his radio and called for his men. "Night Dragon is here... He just left with the witness... All units converge on the bus that just left the scene of the Duke Hotel!"

Waking up to find himself freed from the straitjacket, Hollywood slowly sat up in the back of the ambulance. Looking around, he was puzzled at the scene. He opened the back door to find himself at the waterfront. Confused, he rushed over to the front cab only to find two medics tied up and the mask of a human face.

As the fear began to overwhelm the once feared crime boss, he tried to turn to run. When he turned around, Night Dragon was there removing the rest of his disguise. Revealing himself to Hollywood, he stood firm as he reached out for his hand. He barely got his mask on in time, otherwise, his identity would have been revealed as well. Hollywood hesitated but returned the act of peace.

"Like I said," Night Dragon began to explain, "You work for me."

"I work for no one," Hollywood stated boldly, "Especially, when you killed a friend of mine. I want revenge for his son's sake. After I get rid of the Grandmaster, you and I have unfinished business."

"Trust me," Night Dragon assured him, "You don't want me as an enemy, especially when I am innocent. I am not guilty of the murder of Sgt. Steele. That was your current employer. He was the one behind everything including your fall from your throne."

"He needs me," Hollywood snapped back, "I am the one that gets the info, the weapons, and anything else he can't get."

"No," Night Dragon corrected him, "You are the escape goat to take the blame."

"You play a lot of mind games," Hollywood declared, "How do I know if you are playing another trick on me?"

"Be at this address at midnight," Night Dragon said, "A former associate of yours will also be there. Both of you are going to see the truth. I suggest you leave your goons at home. They belong to the Grandmaster now."

With that said he threw a smoke pellet at the feet of Hollywood and disappeared as it cleared. There was no trace of the Dragon anywhere. Their conversation weighed heavily on his mind. He quickly began to walk away before anyone found the ambulance. He knew that his life was endangered if Thorton got his hands on him. Hollywood found it quite strange that Night Dragon left him in a part of town where he could be safe. Hollywood was in his own territory with plenty of safe houses. It was there he decided to take Night Dragon up on the offer to meet. He wanted the truth and revenge for the betrayal.

SECRETS REVEALED

The feelings in the air screamed tension. As Layla Lopez made her way across town, she couldn't shake the doubts in her mind. Driving to the address Night Dragon gave her, she kept her gun ready just in case. Pulling in front of a rundown brownstone, she still questioned the motives of the masked man.

Looking around she, didn't see anything out of the ordinary. The only people around were prostitutes, pimps, dealers, and junkies. Lopez climbed out of the car and began to scan the environment. As usual, everyone began to scatter or hid their faces at the presence of the law. Lopez walked up to the front door and proceeded to enter with gun drawn. The building was pitch black. With the light of her mini flashlight, she examined the room. Before she could begin to search upstairs, the front door opened. Lopez quickly rushed to hide and switched her light off.

Hoping it was the masked man, she wanted to make sure it was not a trap. The moment the mysterious figure entered the brownstone, she waited for the perfect moment to spring from his position. Just as the figure began to climb the stairs, Lopez leaped from behind a grandfather clock.

"Freeze NPPD!" Lopez yelled as she took aim and switched her flashlight back on. To her surprise, a gun and light were both pointing back at her. Looking at his face, she lowered her gun when she recognized her former mentor to the street life. "Hollywood, what are you doing here?"

"Hello, Princess," Hollywood returned as he lowered his weapon, "I see you still can't speak to family like normal people."

"Drop it," Lopez cut him off, "We ain't friends and we ain't family. Now what are you doing here."

"Same thing as you," Hollywood admitted straight out, "Just coming to the meeting. Didn't you get the same invite?"

"I don't know what game this is," she said boldly, "But I am not sticking around for this."

"Scared of the reunion," a digital voice said from the top of the stairs, "Enjoying the get together? I did put a lot into setting this up." With that said, they both pointed their flashlights towards the voice to reveal Night Dragon standing proudly.

"What is this?" Lopez asked, "What is he doing here?"

"Just like you he is seeking the truth," Night Dragon told her. "Now both of you, follow me quickly. We don't have any time. Company will be here in least than three minutes." With that said he took off towards the roof. The two quickly followed him upstairs to find him on the roof. Night Dragon quickly waved them over to his position. They rushed over to the edge to see the street flooded with Thorton's personal thugs.

"I thought we had at least three minutes," Night Dragon said, "But I guess we will have to move ahead of the schedule. Quickly, take the fire escape to Hollywood's car in back. I will distract them while you two get away. Follow this GPS signal, I will meet you there."

Without a second thought, Night Dragon took a leap off the building. Landing onto the top of Lopez's car. Crushing the roof and windows in a loud crash, all eyes and weapons were pointed directly at him. Without hesitation, he drew his sword and leaped into action. Taking on all comers, each thug ended up thrown back with little resistance. Finishing off the last man, he stood boldly as samurai warriors began to converge onto him. Thorton brought the true Jade Samurai out to finish Night Dragon.

While he continued to hold off his attackers, he hoped Lopez and Hollywood made it. Out of the corner of his eye, he saw them pulling off into the opposite direction. To save his energy and make his next appointment, he launched a smoke grenade from his gauntlet. Leaping over a car, he quickly made his way to his awaiting motorcycle. Riding out of an alley to the street, Night Dragon wanted to make sure he was followed.

Allowing the Samurai to surround him. He allowed them to believe he was pinned down. Roaring his engine, he tore off with great speed into the brownstone. They followed with the idea of trapping him inside. Once inside, he turned the building and the motorcycle into his weapons. He used the bike to climb the stairs and fight off attacks. Making his way to the roof once more, Night Dragon finally appeared to be out of options. However, his number of attackers dwindled from twenty men to six.

Standing boldly with devilish grins, the Samurai withdrew the weapons. Moving slowly, they began to move towards their trapped prey. Night Dragon simply began to laugh as he retrieved a small remote from his belt. The Samurai stopped dead in their tracks when he showed the remote and pointed to the ground. His gesture highlighted the fact the roof was covered in small bombs. He pressed the button cause a chain reaction of explosions.

While the building began to cave in, the Samurai became trapped prisoners. Night Dragon took off at top speed, using the falling roof as a ramp. Leaping off the collapsing building, he landed safely onto the street and made a perfect getaway. The Samurai were imprisoned in the rubble and his plan was back on track. Disappearing into the night he made his way to a safe meeting place. The only thought in his mind was, "It's time for the game to begin".

Looking over her shoulder, Lopez continued to make sure they were not followed. Hollywood continued the path set by the GPS. He didn't want to say a word. The last time he spoke to Lopez was four years two years ago when she worked for Thorton. Their last encounter revealed a terrible secret hidden between them. Lopez didn't want to even be in the presence of the man that taught her everything about street life. As they made their getaway, they heard and felt a power explosion rock the city blocks. Lopez looked back again to find two SUV's following. She instantly recognized them as Jade Samurai foot soldiers. She pulled out her gun and began to open fire without warning.

"What are you doing?!" Hollywood yelled over the gun fire. "Can you ride in a car without shooting your gun?"

"Just shut up and drive," Lopez demanded, "try to lose them".

"Look here, little girl," Hollywood snapped back, "Remember who is driving. I will send both of us off the road."

"Just drive before I shoot you," she told him while firing few more rounds. Dealing with their current problem, they were both confused when both phones began to ring. They ignored their phones which continued to ring simultaneously. The GPS began to ring next. Stunned, they were about to ignore the incoming call, when the unit automatically answered. Their meeting turned into a conference call.

"What are you two doing?" Night Dragon asked, "Cause if you are trying to lose your tail, you are not doing so well. Lopez must be shooting I take it."

"If you know how to get rid of them please go ahead," she snapped back.

"I am but you keep missing them and hitting me!" he yelled over into the communicator, "Now put on your seat belts. I will be there in a few seconds. Hollywood give me a count down from ten."

With that said Hollywood began to count down from ten. When he reached five, Night Dragon was in his rearview mirror with sword drawn. Whizzing by the second SUV, he sliced the entire right side with his blade. Passing by quickly, he made it smoothly by as the SUV split apart and began to flip repeatedly until it crashed into a newsstand. Moving on to the next SUV, he met serious resistance as the Jade foot soldiers turned their sights towards him. The only thing on his mind created a devilish smile in the eyes of the midnight beast... "Time to be unleashed!"

Putting his sword away, Night Dragon stood up on his bike. With ease he gained balance as his bike continued a straight course. He showed no fear as he leaped off the bike and almost flew into the air. Curling into a ball, Night Dragon rolled through the air over the remaining SUV. Bullets shot past his hurling body without touching him. Unfolding himself, Night Dragon braced him as he landed on his feet while forcing his fist into the front end of the SUV. Upon impact the truck went flying into the air.

In one smooth move, Night Dragon jumped to the side and grabbed his bike as it rolled up to his position. He landed perfectly onto his bike and sped off to the awaiting Hollywood and Lopez. He pulled up next to them and shot a nod. Taking the lead, he took off into the night with them right behind him. The look in their eyes spoke of true shock and amazement. They were both wondering what they were about to step into with Night Dragon in the lead.

DANCE OF DEATH

Night Dragon, Hollywood and Layla made their way deeper into Downtown New Peak City. With sirens and witnesses all around, they blended into their surroundings like chameleons. Night Dragon parked his bike behind another brownstone. However, this one was in a well-to do area of the city. Without a thought he shot a look inviting them over. They exited the bullet ridden town car and proceeded to follow Night Dragon on foot. Without a word, they kept close to the masked warrior while looking for more of the Jade Army.

Walking over to a tool shed, Night Dragon unsheathed his sword made a quick swipe at the pad lock. Opening the doors, he revealed his new toy. Night Dragon motioned them to stand back. A low roar exited the shed, then headlights shined through the darkness. Pulling out of the shed, Night Dragon drove his black on black Shelby Mustang GT. Leaving the car running, he hopped out.

"Hollywood," he ordered as he handed him another GPS unit, "Take my car. Follow these instructions. A friend is waiting for you at this address. Do not stop or pull over. If you are spotted, push this button. And everything will be taken care of."

"Who is this friend? And what will happen when I hit the button?" Hollywood asked, "Will I blow up?"

"No," Night Dragon stopped and looked back, "You will blow up if you press the buttons next to that one. Now get going because they will be here soon."

"How did they find us?" Layla asked, "I thought we lost them."

"We did," Night Dragon responded as he pulled a small remote from his belt, "But they will be responding to this" .... 'BOOM!'

Night Dragon stood in the shadows as flames exploded into the air. He destroyed the town car and his motorcycle. He quickly began to make his way to the fire escape while Detective Lopez and Hollywood watched in pure shock.

"Are you trying to get us killed?" Lopez asked, "They will be here soon after that move."

"That was my car!" Hollywood shouted.

"The car already had a tracker," Night Dragon explained, "Now the Jade Samurai will have to deal with the fire department and police. Now drive off and blend with the traffic."

Without further delay, he climbed into the car and drove off following the directions of the GPS. Night Dragon began to lead Lopez up the fire escape just in time before a crowd grew. The fire department arrived first. From the rooftop, they both watched the scene. Night Dragon watched to see who was in the crowd.

After seeing the Jade Samurai give up pursuit, he knew they could move on to the special meeting place. They made their way across rooftops. He wasn't surprised that Lopez could keep up with him. Running, flipping, and leaping from building to building, Lopez performed at almost the same skill level of Night Dragon. He continued along the dangerous path until something stopped him in his tracks. Night Dragon paused and lowered his head. Puzzled, Lopez walked over to him with great confusion.

"What is wrong?" she asked as she walked closer to him, "Are we at the "special" meeting place or..."

Before she could finish her next step, Night Dragon pushed her down to the ground. He caught a flying arrow with his hand just in the nick of time. He had that same grin in his eyes once again. He had been longing for this meeting for a long time. He looked at the arrow and confirmed his suspensions.

The Rose blossom tied to the end was the calling card. This arrow was symbol of the most-deadliest assassin in the world. Now he could see his only real challenge face to face. Night Dragon finally knew how well he was doing to be the newest target for the world's top ninja assassin. To have her hunting you meant was an unfortunate honor.

"Wait here," Night Dragon ordered, "We have a special guest in our presence."

With that said, he took off sprinting like the wind towards the direction the arrow was fired. Lopez could not see the attacker nor anyone else around. She climbed to her feet with weapon drawn, but she decided to hang back just as she was told. Lopez could feel trust in the masked warrior. A feat that she couldn't perform with anyone else but Rick Steel.

Night Dragon knew they were being followed, but he was not sure if he lost them. However, he knew that their special guest picked up the trail six buildings back. Night Dragon knew she had been called into town but didn't know when they would meet.

Unfortunately, Lopez almost walked into his intended calling card. Making his dash towards her, he took a massive twenty-foot leap off the building. Landing perfectly onto the next with great ease. He stood there and grabbed his retractable Bo Staff.

"Greetings, White Rose," Night Dragon called out, "Step over here and deliver your message."

"What makes you think I have a message?" White Rose said as she dropped from a water tower. "It is just a shame that I missed."

"We both know you could have made that shot from 500 feet and not miss the wings off a fly," Night Dragon corrected her, "Now what do you want? Hell, I am surprised you would work for the Grandmaster himself."

"I go where the money takes me," she told him, "Besides, I didn't think the great Night Dragon knew about me."

"Yeah," Night Dragon started, "I didn't think the White Rose would ever work for the man that murdered her entire clan."

"You know very well that you are responsible for that," she corrected him, "I do plan to take my revenge, but not tonight. I just wanted to deliver a message."

"And message is?" he insisted as he spun his Bo Staff ending in a fighting stance.

"Don't worry," White Lotus, assured him, "As I said I am not going to kill you tonight. I just wanted you to know I am here for you and the bounty on your head."

"Well, how nice of you," Night Dragon acknowledged, "But I am not one to keep a lady waiting."

"It's good to know I will be killing the last of the gentlemen ninja," she said with an evil laugh.

"Lady, ain't nothing gentle about me," Night Dragon told her just before attacking her with a powerful swing of his Bo Staff. Ducking the fury of swings with ease, White Rose followed with a fury of her own. Slicing her katana through the air, the only connection she made was with the blocks he created with his staff. Every time one had the upper hand, the other would switch and take control. Losing his balance close to the edge of the roof, Night Dragon stumbled.

White Rose caught him off guard with a jab to the solar plex with the handle of her sword. As he dropped his staff to the ground, he grabbed his stomach, gasping for air. White Rose seized the opportunity by grabbing him by his neck and kneeing him to the face. She then grabbed him and slung his dazed body through a nearby roof shed. Standing over his body, a smile shined through her eyes. Throwing a Rose blossom on top of him, she dropped a smoke pellet and disappeared. Night Dragon quickly stopped playing the possum and climbed to his feet. He wiped the dust off and laughed. He grabbed his retractable Bo

Staff and put it away. Before taking off, he looked back at the White Rose blossom. He picked it up and stared.

"I think I am in love again," Night Dragon told himself. Then he took off into the night to rejoin Detective Lopez. Rushing back, he found her still waiting on the rooftop. He surprised her as he appeared out of the shadows.

"You okay?" Night Dragon asked, "Are you hurt?"

"Just bruised from the fall," Lopez told him, "Thanks for the save."

"Follow me," Night Dragon ordered, "We are behind schedule."

He moved quickly towards the edge of the roof. Night Dragon guided her down the fire escape. Once they reached the ground, there was another tool shed. Pulling a key from his belt, he unlocked the door to reveal another motorcycle. Unlike the previous bike, this one was customized with his emblem and weapons.

"Why did you blow up your other bike?" Lopez asked with a puzzled look. "Are we going to just jump from bike to bike? I thought you had something to show me."

"That wasn't my bike," Night Dragon admitted as he climbed on, "Besides, why would I blow up my own bike. Now come and hold on, we are late."

With that said, they rode off in the night. She held on tight to him, but her mind was lost in his motives. Ever since she met him, it was an endless rollercoaster ride. Night Dragon was also lost in thought. He wasn't sure the attacks were just decoys, until White Rose appeared. He knew he had to be close if White Rose was called in. It was amazing how Lopez was almost killed by accident.

The White Rose never made mistakes. It was almost like she expected his reaction. Now Night Dragon began to question if the White Rose was riding on the back of his bike. However, he knew the truth about White Rose. He just needed the truth about the woman riding on the back of his bike.

Across town, a figure leaps onto the building and makes their way to a skylight window. As she climbed into the window, she made sure she was not followed. Once inside she closed all the curtains with the push of a button on the wall. Inside the apartment, she removed her mask.

Still hidden in the shadows, she moved gingerly for the medicine cabinet. She grabbed the first aid kit and removed her gear. Her mind was still scrambled from her encounter with Night Dragon. He was everything she heard and more. She was fortunate he lost his footing along that edge. If only she didn't toy with him, then she would be prepared for the Grandmaster's plan. As she began to treat her bruises, she replayed the fight in her mind. She knew what he was capable of, but he was more than she ever remembered.

However, she now thought it was an honor to battle with a ninja master of Night Dragon's caliber. He could push her to the level of a master as well. The more she thought about it, she questioned how he could have lost his balance. Then it hit her like a kick to the face. She rushed over to her gear and checked her chest plate. Finding a tracking dot, a small grin crept onto her face.

"Great move, Night Dragon," White Rose said in admiration as she crushed the dot to pieces, "The next dance will be slow and deadly."

White Rose knew that her true mission was in the hands of Night Dragon. She had to fulfil her training and duties with one fateful battle with him. It had been the tradition of their two clans since their creation in Japan. With the rise of the Jade Samurai Army, she knew their duel was on permanent stand-by until the war was over.

Now she wanted their paths to cross for other reasons. There was something about him that captured her mind. His skills were great, but his spirit energy was new but familiar. She only wished that she was not working the Jade Samurai. Especially, after she overheard the truth of Rick Steele's death. He was a man of honor and an amazing past lover. He was the reason she almost gave up the being the White Rose. However, his father's death and their desires in life were never on the same page.

Kissing him goodbye the day his father died was to end of their time. The more she thought about him, the more she realized that his absence was the only thing that kept him safe from her life. She knew that her life would catch up to her one day. However, she never wanted Rick Steele to be dragged into her mess. It was his job and her secret quest to become White Rose that drove them apart.

Sometimes she regretted her decision of the clan, but she knew she had these amazing abilities for a reason. The reason was unknown, but she would find out. Revealing her true face in the mirror, her jet black and kinky hair could finally flow freely. She loved her beautiful brown skin and her beautiful brown eyes.

As she removed and stored away her secret personality, she climbed into shower to wash the smell of the battle off her body. She emerged from the shower back as her true self... Mya Wells. Grabbing her briefcase, she quickly opened it and removed a huge stack of papers. She was two weeks behind and promised her students that she would grade their essays before the next exam. Here students may be only in middle school, but she drove them to high performance levels. Performing at a twelfth-grade level, Mya's students worked in an environment that didn't mirror the images of public inner-city schools. She allowed them to see the world without limits and boundaries. To her students, she was a hero. If they only knew the warrior within her heart and soul.

DRAGON HEART &
SHADOW DRAGON RING

It seemed like they were on the road forever. Riding at top speed, Lopez clung to him with all her might. She didn't know where they were going but knew she was safe. Finally stopping in front of a housing project, Lopez recognized the area. It was her old neighborhood and her first assignment on the force. The once blue-collar plush area was now the most poverty-stricken area in the whole city. It was there that she met her fallen partner and began to see the crossroads in life.

Climbing off the bike, she was not surprised that no one paid attention to the 6'0 ninja standing out in the open. Lopez followed him inside of the building, which was known as a haven for prostitutes, junkies, and runaways. However, the inside appearance did not match the outside cover. Once inside, Night Dragon was treated like a hero returning from war. Women and men waved in silent respect and smiled. The children were playing in the lobby and cheered as he walked by. One small little girl ran up to him for a hug. Without hesitation or ill will, Night Dragon dropped to his knee and embraced the child.

Standing up, he held onto the child as if she were his own. Night Dragon continued his path to the front desk. As she scanned the lobby, it appeared that the entire building was in the lobby. It appeared that something major was happening. Spotting the large tables and food, Lopez realized it was a building potluck party. She didn't know what they were celebrating. All Lopez care about was her ability to walk right back out of there and catch a cab home.

"Adonai," Night Dragon called out to the man working at desk, "Is everything ready?"

"Yes, Boss," the young Japanese man said with great pride, "Your arrangements are being met and Mr. Hollywood is assisting with his end perfectly."

"Adonai, take this little one and keep track of her until I return later," Night Dragon ordered.

"My Pleasure," Adonai said with a smile as he took the little girl, "Anything else?"

"I am taking Detective Lopez to see him," he told Adonai, "Make sure you turn everything on once we are in the elevator."

"Yes, sir," Adonai agreed with a bow.

Without further words, Night Dragon went to the elevator and entered a special code on the keypad. Lopez followed while still in shock. She was completely blown away by the scene in the lobby. So many people that had nothing were smiling as if they were the richest in the world. As they rode the elevator up, Lopez mind was scrambled and confused. She finally had to break the silence.

"Okay, what the hell was that?" She blasted out, "What is the deal with everything downstairs?"

"Everything will be revealed soon enough," Night Dragon said calmly, "Just enjoy the ride."

"What happened to that special meeting?" she asked, "What is it with you and this craziness?"

"Listen, I am taking you to the truth just as promised," Night Dragon said, "Now calm down before you lose yourself."

"What did you say?" she replied.

Lopez was thrown off by those words. Those were the same words Rick Steele would say to keep her calm in tense situations. Before she could say another word, the bell rang and the doors open. She followed closely to observe his movements and mannerisms.

Night Dragon led her to the only door on the floor. Entering yet another code, the door buzzed, and he led her inside. Once inside, she found his base of operations. Varies weapons and gadgets were everywhere. Surveillance photos covered almost every wall. Looking closely, Lopez found her own photo on the wall. She moved closer and realized that one wall was dedicated to her every movement for the last three months.

"What is this? What is this about?" Lopez protested as she drew her gun and pointed it at Night Dragon's heart. "Tell me what you want from me? What does this have to do with Rick's death?"

"You tell me what this means?" Night Dragon said as he removed a folded picture from his back and opened it in front of her eyes. It was a picture of her attaching the bomb to Detective Steele's car. "For someone that loved you, this is a great way to return the love."

With that said, Lopez fell to her knees, crying. The pain she felt and hid from the world was released. The photo was the reminder of her sin and betrayal. Steele was the only cop brave enough to take on the corruption head on.

"He told me that you could be trusted," Night Dragon admitted, "Now you must atone for your sins."

"Is this why I am here," Lopez screamed, "You're going to take your revenge...Rick. I know that you are the Dragon, so here take my head."

"No, thanks," Night Dragon said calmly, "You should know that I don't take lives. Besides, Detective Steele wants to see you face to face."

Night Dragon walked over to another door and opened it. He stood back and pointed the way for Lopez. Puzzled, she got up from her knees and walked into the room. Her eyes were swollen with shock as her conclusion was blown out of the waters. Sitting in a hospital bed connected to a large machine was the missing, deceased detective. He was bandaged all over with both a foot and arm in slings. Remorse filled her soul as she rushed over to his bedside.

"Ricky, baby. I am so sorry," she pleaded, "They told me it was a tracker. They knew you were getting close to Night Dragon. They thought you could lead them to him. They asked me to put the tracking device on your car. I didn't know it was a bomb." Holding on to his one unbandage hand, she laid her head onto his chest and cried.

"Those tears mean nothing now," Night Dragon said coldly. "If you are honest in your pain, then tell me about the Grandmaster's plan."

"What do you mean?" she asked, "Who is this Grandmaster?"

"Please, even at your lowest," he pointed out, "You're loyal to the one that uses you like a pawn."

"What do you want from me!?" she screamed.

"I want the Dragon Heart and the Shadow Ring!" Night Dragon demanded, "And don't lie about anything else. I have more photos of you delivering them both to Headquarters ten hours ago."

"Fine. He called me the morning of the bombing," Lopez finally admitted as she sat in horror at the sight of her dear friend. "He said my debt to him would be wiped clean. The Master said that I would be free if I planted the tracker and then made sure his package was delivered to Police Headquarters. They were going to use Steele's ID code to store the package in evidence. I didn't hear about the bombing until after I returned from picking up the package."

"Well, I hope your debt was worth it," Night Dragon said.

"All I wanted was for my father to be left alive. The Master is making moves all over town to take over all crime in New Peak City. He put a hit out on every major figure in the city," Lopez admitted. "He may not be worth saving, but he is my father."

"Well, your father works for me now. And I will protect him and you," Night Dragon declared. "I promised Steele that I would protect both of you."

"I don't need it. Besides, your protection isn't worth it," Lopez declared.

"Look, the best way to protect you two is to put you both together," Night Dragon told her, "Hollywood has a better chance of living if he works for me instead of working that devil, the Grandmaster."

"Did Rick tell you that Hollywood was my father?" Lopez asked.

"I am the King of the Shadows," Night Dragon boasted, "I know everything kept in the dark."

"Is he going to be alright?" she asked as she stared at the unconscious Steele.

"He is in a coma," Night Dragon said, "Medically induced to deal with the pain. He will be okay. I am hiding him until I have stopped the Grandmaster."

"What can I do to help?" Lopez asked as she stood up. "Whatever you need done is done."

"Get me into headquarters," Night Dragon demanded.

Before anything else could be said, an alarm rang out. Rushing to a security monitor, Night Dragon was not surprised. It was the New Peak City Police Department, mostly Thorton's goons. Night Dragon had that devilish look in his eyes. He then rushed over to his wall of weapons and replenished.

"That didn't take long at all," Night Dragon said, "They must have finally updated the tracking software."

"What are you talking about?" Lopez asked, "How did they find us so fast? No cop comes to this area."

"You," Night Dragon simply replied. "When you stopped to question Thorton before our meeting, I saw him sliding a tracker into your pocket."

"Do you just like following me around?" Lopez asked.

"I had to make sure my plan was going off without a hitch," he admitted as he typed on the computer.

"You planned all of this?" she asked in shock.

"Just follow me now," he ordered.

"What about Steele and the people in this building?" she asked.

"Do as I say, and we can get out of here without them being hurt," he told her as he opened the door to the stairwell.

Following his lead, they ran down the stairs. Entering the next floor down, Night Dragon proceeded to the end of the hallway where he was greeted with SWAT team members. Before they could fire a single shot, he took them all out with knockout darts from his gauntlet. He motioned for Lopez to follow him. They made their way to an apartment. Once inside, he opened a closet door to reveal a secret elevator.

"Step inside," Night Dragon ordered, "It will take you down to the sewer. From there, you will follow the lighted path to the river. Adonai will be there waiting for you."

"What about Steele?" she asked, "I can take him down with me."

"No," he stopped her before she could head back. "It is too late for him. I will try to get them to follow me. You get away now or he doesn't have a chance."

Before she could argue, Night Dragon flung her inside the elevator and closed the door. The elevator automatically began to move downward. Once she was out of the way, Night Dragon went back out into the hallway. There he found ten more SWAT team members with guns drawn and ready to fire. At the head of the stack was Thorton smiling from ear to ear. Night Dragon knew he was in for a fight and welcomed it. Putting up his fist, he motioned for the first attack.

However, Thorton had something else in mind. Cocking his gun, Thorton shot a grenade towards the warrior. Dodging it with great ease and speed, Night Dragon dove through an apartment door just as it exploded. Rolling to ease the fall, Night Dragon took cover behind a table. Removing his Sai, he prepared for the onslaught. Thorton gave the order to attack. Two men entered the apartment. As they moved inside, they were greeted with Night Dragon dropping from the ceiling. Using his Sai to redirect their guns away from him, Night Dragon missed a hail storm of bullets.

While still holding them back, he used a standing side kick to knock them down in one motion. Just as they were falling back, he flipped out of the way of their still firing weapons. Hitting only one another, the two men fell hard to the ground. The next two in were greeted with flying Sai right through their assault rifles. Leaving their damaged guns pinned to the wall, they rushed Night Dragon only to be stopped by a fury of kicks and punches. Before he knew it, the rest of the SWAT unit was rushing into the apartment. Just as before, they each lost their weapons upon entry. Thorton was the last to enter only to find all his men laid out and unconscious.

"Finally, we have some time to play alone," Night Dragon said proudly.

"My Master wants you alive, but I am sure he won't mind if I leave you on life support when I bring you in," Thorton told him.

The next move was not a shock. Thorton threw down his weapon and removed his head gear. Revealing his own sword, he stood ready to duel. Night Dragon loved the idea and responded with his sword. As they stood across from each other, the only tension in the room was waiting for the first strike. Taking the first strike, Thorton began the fight. Matched evenly with counters, he couldn't deny Night Dragon's ability as a swordsman. Just as he was about to lose, he tossed a fire ball into Night Dragon's eyes.

Temporarily blinded, Night Dragon fell back to the ground. Just before Thorton could plunge his sword, Night Dragon blocked with his sword and flipped Thorton and himself into a dining table. The impact only was enough to lose their swords and injure Thorton's arm. Still slightly blinded, Night Dragon continued his assault. Using only his hands and feet, he continued to flip, kick, and punch punishment to Thorton.

After a vicious right cross, Night Dragon knocked Thorton to the ground. Once Night Dragon gained control of his sight back, he picked up his sword and stood over Thorton, tempted to strike. Looking up from the ground, Thorton wiped blood from his lip and ordered Night Dragon to finish him. Night Dragon had something else in mind.

"Give me the Dragon Armor and the Ring of Shadows," Night Dragon offered at the point of his blade, "I will spare your worthless life."

"Never," Thorton screamed, "My Master will avenge my death and claim the sacred Dragon Powers. The all mighty Samurai will rule this pitiful city and these peasants."

"You fool," Night Dragon declared, "I will never let you arrogant power-hungry monsters harm another innocent soul."

With a sharp jab of his fist and handle of his katana, Night Dragon knocked blood from the mouth of Thorton once more. Putting away his sword, he turned his back and began to walk away. Before he could step out of the door, he was stopped in his tracks by a gun aimed at him.

"Sorry," Lopez said, "But you don't know everything. He has a hold you can't break."

Without warning she closed her eyes and fired three shots point blank into the heart of Night Dragon. He went flying back into a wall and slid down. She lowered her head in shame. Thorton climbed to his feet and limped over to his body. He smiled as he heard the last shallow breathes from Night Dragon. Thorton then began to remove the mask but was stopped by the cocking of Lopez's gun.

"Don't you dare." she demanded, "Leave it on, the Boss's orders."

"Fine by me," Thorton assured her as he backed off, "Now you have to accompany him to the morgue to make sure nobody messes with the body. Besides, Master wanted him alive."

"You just keep your end of the deal and let my mother go free," she scolded.

"You will get your payment when the Grandmaster gets his package," he told her.

Calling for his men only, Thorton gave the order for an ambulance pick up. He led the way as a parade of injured SWAT members exited the building and were greeted by the awaiting press. It was in front of the press Thorton claimed the fame of catching the cop killer known as Night Dragon.

While Thorton dealt with the press, Lopez followed her orders and stayed with the body. Making sure no one disturbed him, she silently cried as she sat next to him. When the ambulance crew finally arrived, she told them about Rick Steele in the upstairs hospital suite. However, when they returned, there was only the report of an empty room. Forcing them to bring Night Dragon's body with her at gun point, Lopez was in great shock at the truth of the report. Looking back at Night Dragon's body, she thought about his promise to protect. A promise he kept even from the grave.

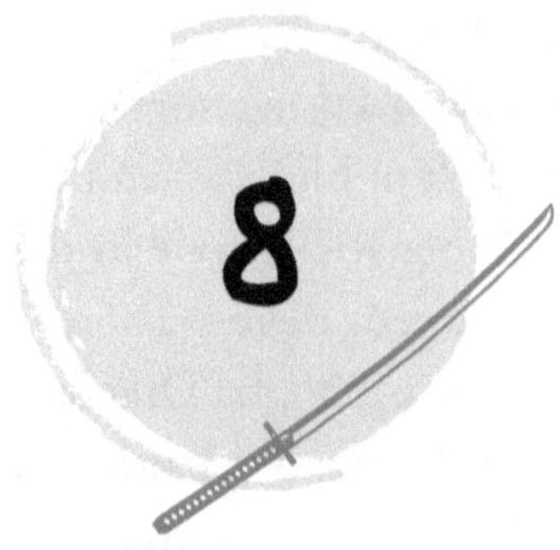

BITTERSWEET REVENGE

Hollywood watched the parade of defeat from a safe distance. He hung his head in disappointment. He began to replay his role in his mind. Once Hollywood arrived at the building, he was quickly ushered inside by Adonai. While entering the building, he introduced Hollywood to the community as a friend of Night Dragon. He was then informed of his role.

While the battle went on below him, Adonai got him out of the building as the fire alarm blared. Holding the remains of his mask in his hands, Hollywood knew that he was just given a special responsibility. He was now a member of the team. He was finally back on the right side of the law. Adonai appeared beside him to direct him to the awaiting car. Once inside, he was blind folded.

"What is this for?" Hollywood questioned.

"The Dragon wants you to rest at his lair until his plan has concluded, and it is safe for you," Adonai explained.

"Night Dragon is dead!" Hollywood replied, "There is no more plan and no more hope for this town."

"Mr. Jones," Adonai began to explain, "The Dragon has planned for everything that has unfolded so far. To keep him on track for his mission we must continue on."

With that said, they rode off into the night. Still holding the mask in his hands, he thought of his ex-partner's son. He wanted to know Rick Steele's role and his whereabouts. He held on tighter to the mask of the only honest cop to serve on the force since the death of his partner. He promised his partner that he we always look after Rick, if something happened to him. Hollywood may have quit the side of law for the treasures of crime, but he remained loyal to his partner throughout the years. When his best friend died, Hollywood made sure to keep an eye on the last honest man left in New Peak City. Now his only concern was to keep his promise and do right by his friend's son.

The ride back to the station was long. Lopez spent the whole time handcuffed to Night Dragon. She wanted to protect her bargaining chip. It was the only way to make sure the odds were anywhere near her favor.

Handcuffing yourself to a corpse was not proper procedure, but neither was anything done with the New Peak City PD. Pulling into the prisoner drop off zone, Lopez ordered guards to stand and walk in tight detail. She knew Night Dragon was dead, but she feared her so called employer double crossing her. Once inside, she rushed the masked body straight to the morgue.

Refusing to allow the autopsy to begin, Lopez removed her handcuffs and locked the body away in the containment refrigerator. Once the key was turned to lock the door, Lopez pushed the attendant out of the way. Kicking the lock, she broke the key on purpose. It was her way of protecting her insurance.

"No one sees or touches that body until I return," Lopez ordered, "Or the rest of these drawers will be filled tonight."

Lopez walked out and placed a heavy detail of guards on the inside and outside of the morgue. She proceeded to head upstairs to her desk and await the arrival of the Grandmaster. Entering into her office, she quickly logged into her computer. She wanted to try and piece to together the information Night Dragon gave her earlier. Her mind was racing since the shooting.

The discovery of Rick Steele being alive confirmed her inner thoughts of Night Dragon being a lawman. Pulling up files, she wanted to understand what the war between Night Dragon and The Grandmaster. She thought back to discussions with Detective Steele. Then she thought about the day he was supposed to have died in that explosion. That is when it hit her.

"Night Dragon wanted to get into the Evidence Vault," Lopez said as she jumped to her feet.

Grabbing the phone, she called the downstairs guards. The phone rung over and over. Realizing that it may be too late, she called for an emergency lock down of the building. She took off running grabbing any cops she could to follow her to the morgue.

When she finally reached the morgue, her fears where made reality. There in the morgue, every guard was laid out on the ground. She went into the cold storage units to find his drawer busted open. Looking inside, she saw a small piece of paper with something written on it. Lopez grabbed it and a small grin appeared on her face. It simply said, "Thank you, Detective."

"Quickly, call in SWAT. Tell them we have a situation," Lopez ordered, "I want this building locked down. Have SWAT meet me at the evidence vault. I need a sealed perimeter around the building and I need men on the roof. I don't want him escaping."

"Who are you taking about Detective?" one of the officers asked, "How many men are we looking for?"

"One," Lopez replied as she rushed towards the elevator, "Night Dragon just used us to walk him into the building to rob us blind. Everyone must converge on the evidence vault now!"

Riding in the back of the blacked-out SUV, Captain Kenzensho held a slight smile on his face. His enemy was in his morgue and his plan was working perfectly. He could taste the power of his ancestors coursing through his veins. He would soon have the treasure his family has sought for ten generations. Soon he could reveal his identity and stand firmly as the leader of the Jade Samurai. The powers of the Night

Dragon will make him invincible. As soon as he ascends to his rightful place, then the Jade Army will rise and take control of the world.

Before he could really enjoy the small victory, his phone began to ring. Thorton was sitting up front boasting of his victorious battle with the fallen ninja. Kenzensho cut him short of his epic story by ordering him to answer the phone. The look on Thorton's face spoke of pure shock and defeat. He raised his voice and began shouting orders into the phone.

Turning in great shame, he tried to deliver the news from police headquarters. The rage that filled that car was enough to be an atom bomb. Giving the order, the driver took off at great speed. Kenzensho knew that Night Dragon's death was too good to be true. The anger inside of him began to emanate into pure energy as his hands and eyes began to glow a Jade green.

"Call White Rose and General Taka," Kenzensho ordered, "He does not leave that building alive. Call your father and tell him to shutdown downtown. This will be the last time Night Dragon will ever disrespect the Jade Samurai. Get me my katana and armor."

Entering the passcode without error, the vault opened and revealed his prize. He stood there with his hidden smile. Night Dragon took out his katana and stabbed it into the floor. He walked over to a huge crate and began to pry it open. Ripping the lid open, Night Dragon revealed a locked chest. After pulling the chest out of the crate, he placed the chest in the middle of the vault floor. He took a key from his belt. He opened it and stood back in amazement.

Night Dragon knew it would be difficult to get it out of there. Removing the cache of weapons, he began his true search. Night Dragon found a Dragon emblem on inside lid. Recognizing the handy work of his grandfather, he took his dagger and popped the emblem off to reveal a hidden compartment.

Inside the compartment, there was a piece of parchment. He took the parchment and stuffed it into his armor. He quickly replaced it with a folded piece of paper. Night Dragon then took the fake weapons and added them to his arsenal. Just as he finished arming himself, he went over to his sword and yanked it out of the ground. When he began to head towards the vault door, the SWAT team made their approach. All he could do was grin through his eyes.

"It's play time," was his only thought.

He could hear the SWAT team preparing to breach the outer vault door. Hiding in the shadows, Night Dragon prepared for his great escape. He waited and watched in silence as they all rushed the evidence lock up. As they made their way to the vault, Night Dragon made his way towards the exit. He was almost out until the presence of his enemy stopped him dead in his footsteps. He stood in true shock as his nightmare turned into reality.

Captain Kenzensho stood surrounded by his guards and loyal samurai. The urge to attack began to build inside of him. However, he held onto his duty to protect the world from the Jade Samurai Army. He watched as they entered the vault. Ripping the chest open, Thorton immediately went for the dragon emblem and the note.

Night Dragon knew something had to be up at the sight. Reporting his findings to the captain, he waited his approval for his next move. With a slight grin, he nodded towards Thorton. Thorton then extended his hand to Layla, who gave him a small remote. Pressing a button, Thorton began to laugh.

"Night Dragon, Night Dragon," Thorton called out, "Come out and play. Die like a man. You are no Samurai, but you will die like a Samurai."

"Thorton, enough games," Captain Kenzensho ordered, "Bring my foe to his knees."

"Yes, Master," Thorton replied with a humble bow.

With a push of a button, an electric current shot through the body of Night Dragon. He let out a painful scream as he fell from the rafters to the ground. His body was consumed with pain as Thorton hit the button over and over. Kenzensho walked over to his fallen enemy with an evil laugh.

"Night Dragon," Kenzensho gloated, "It is an honor to finally face an enemy as formidable as you. You have hindered my plans and business many times. But like the peasants you protect, it is time to learn your place in the world."

"I know my place," Night Dragon replied, "Standing over your cold dead body."

"Oh, don't you remember," Kenzensho laughed as he spoke the truth, "Night Dragon doesn't take a life, he protects all life."

"Yeah that is a vow I may have to break," Night Dragon admitted.

"Remember your place peasant!" Kenzensho shouted, "You have no honor or even the right to live."

"You fool," Night Dragon said as he began to rise, "You have not right. I promise before God and the innocent, you will be looking at me from ground."

"Not true peasant," Kenzensho said as he gave the order to shock him again. "Do you like my surprise for you. I knew that you would attempt to take the chest. I just didn't have enough time to get to the sacred scroll. But those weapons make a perfect conductor for electricity."

"Man, you just think of everything," Night Dragon replied sarcastically as he fought off the electric shocks, "I guess I should be surprised for your next move."

"Yes, you should Night Dragon," Kenzensho said, "I am finally ready to answer the question that has haunted my family for generations... Who is Night Dragon?"

"Tell me," Night Dragon asked Layla, "What is the price of betrayal? Cause you are great at it?"

"I didn't betray anyone, criminal," Layla replied, "I had to do what I did for the sake of my mother."

"Yes, don't blame the detective," Kenzensho scoffed, "She is a loyal servant that knows her place. You should learn from her. If only Detective Steele did the same, he would probably be here on my side as well."

"So, you did order his murder?" Night Dragon asked,

"Of course, I did," Kenzensho answered, "He refused to live in his place and status. Just like you, he believed in fair and equal justice, but could not understand that justice only comes for and from the rulers and masters."

"I swear to you, Kenzensho. You will pay for your crimes against the innocent. You will pay for the sins of this city with your life," Night Dragon declared.

"You will learn your place, even if it is the last thing you do on Earth," Kenzensho demanded.

"I am so glad you showed your true form," Night Dragon said, "It makes it so much better for the courts to punish you for your crimes. Do me one favor?"

"I don't know how you will do this from the grave. But what is your last request?" Kenzensho asked.

"Ready the note and you will have your answer," Night Dragon said as he stood perfectly to his feet.

"What is the peasant doing? Why is he stalling? Thorton bring me the scroll!" Kenzensho demanded as he opened the note Thorton retrieved.

    - You don't hide secrets in the shadows from the King of the Shadow Warriors.

    -Night Dragon

Pure rage filled his eyes and face. Ripping the paper apart, his eyes and hands began to glow a green glow. "Lopez and Thorton, take him now!"

Springing into action, Thorton cranked the voltage to the maximum capacity. However, Night Dragon stood strong and proud with his sword drawn. With his anger building, Thorton threw the remote into the ground, smashing it to pieces.

With a boastful wave of his katana, Night Dragon stood proud as he invited the oncoming attack. Thorton called in his personal guards that carried katanas as well. One by one, Night Dragon took them down with one slash. Only wounding them, he invited the next wave as he stood strong over the defeated. While Night Dragon took on the multiple attackers with ease, Kenzensho watched in rage. Once the last of his men was knocked out, Thorton took out his favorite toy, his electric Kusarigama.

Lopez was standing there, witnessing everything. Her mind was racing. She wanted to help Night Dragon, but the fate of her mother was in the hands of Kenzensho. As she stood back, Lopez tighten her grip on her gun. As the fight between Night Dragon and Thorton intensified, Lopez watched as the corrupted cop finally met his match.

Unleashing skills and speed not seen in their first fight, Night Dragon proved to be the better warrior. He barely used his weapon, but when he did, each strike was precise and perfect. Thorton thought he finally took control when he wrapped his chain around Night Dragon katana and broke it into two pieces. He continued to attack Night Dragon only to be humiliated with his hand-to-hand defense.

Night Dragon unleashed a fury of punches and kicks. Crippling Thorton's arms and legs, Night Dragon ducked a last-ditch fury of punches and then delivered a powerful Superman punch that sent Thorton flying back into a shelf of evidence. Falling apart from the crash, the shelf imploded onto the knocked out Thorton. Watching in horror, Kenzensho ordered in his secret weapon...General Taka.

Standing seven feet, five inches tall, the vial, ugly monster entered the room. Holding his oversize battle ax, he looked demonic and deadly. Fear entered the room at his arrival. For this General was more than massive, he was also the walking undead. Standing firm, Night Dragon had to hide his concern. He had heard rumors of Grandmaster's dealing with black magic. Now he had the proof before him. Looking at his sword, Night Dragon knew that he had to find a weapon to stand a chance with that war ax in that monster's hands.

Spotting his retractable Bo Staff across the room, he made a break for it. However, he was stopped by the near fatal slash of Taka's blade. Back flipping out of the way of deadly slashes, Night Dragon used every trick he had to avoid the monster. Combining smoke pellets and shuriken, he avoided and threw off some attacks.

Sadly, he could see that his attacks were only upsetting the undead general. When he saw a way to escape through the ventilation shaft, Night Dragon tried to use the momentum of an oncoming attack. Just as he could reach the vent, Night Dragon felt the massive hand of Taka wrap around both his feet and flung him through a wall. Upon impact, the entire wall caved in on top of Night Dragon.

Laughing a deep and evil laugh, Taka stared at the rubble with great pride. Before he could turn away, the pile began to move. With a great rage filled yell, Night Dragon emerged from the pile. Standing there, he tried to gain his composure. His battle gear was in shambles, and he was out of weapons and tricks.

His mind was a mess, and nothing made sense. He could feel his armor shutting down as well as his natural powers were weakening. Night Dragon had to regroup, but how could he get away. Looking for anything he could use to get away, Night Dragon could see the front door wide open. He had one trick left that he regretted to use. Reaching into his belt, he pulled out a small remote.

"What now, little fool?" Taka laughed, "Hoping to walk right out of that door with that little thing."

"No," Night Dragon laughed in return. He laughed as hard as a jolly menacing Santa Claus, "I hope I hooked the bombs up right."

Pressing the button, explosions began erupting through the evidence vault. The floor gave way and began to swallow everyone in that vault. Moving quickly with the last bit of his strength, Night Dragon made a last-ditch effort of freedom. Avoiding the falling floor, he still ran into resistance from Taka. Using his mind, Night Dragon use his enemy's own power against him.

With a crumbling floor, the weight of Taka and his powerful strikes were working against him. However, he continued to push Night Dragon back away from the door. To his surprise, it was all Night Dragon wanted. With one final attack, Taka backed Night Dragon against the chest. Ducking a decapitating swing, Night Dragon saw Taka's War Ax crumble to pieces when it struck the chest. Filled with rage, Taka unleashed a fury of punches that only connected with the air. Night Dragon used Taka's own momentum to force him to stumble and fall off the edge of the now crumbling floor.

With the rest of the vault falling apart, the ceiling began to come down next. The entire floor was collapsing. Thinking quickly, Night Dragon leaped into the chest and slammed it shut just as the rest of the floor caved into the next. While the floors began to cave-in, everyone in that building began to scatter in panic.

As the evacuation began, Lopez was outside with the rest of the department, watching their headquarters fall to the ground. Looking through the crowd, she tried to find her boss or Night Dragon himself. She spotted Captain Kenzensho making a quick get away with Thorton in tow. It was there she made up her mind. Night Dragon was not her only hope of saving her mother.

A large crowd of angry cops and bystanders began to watch as Police Headquarters began to implode on itself. All watched in shock and awe of the beautiful destruction. The sun began to rise as firefighters were finally able to gain control of the civic disaster. Everyone watched in amazement as a huge portion of the building collapsed.

When the rubble finally settled, Lopez led a team into the remains of the building. With the help of Ladder Trucks and cranes, she, her team, along with a few armed SWAT team members made their way to the remains of the evidence vault. Her mind was blown at the damage that one man could do in one night. They used ropes and pulleys to climb down into the pit in the middle of the building. While the front of the build fell to the ground, the explosion created a crater that was hidden to the outside world. It appeared that there was more than just the few bombs that Night Dragon planted in the vault. Lopez could tell from training that those bombs were just the fuse to an even large bomb. She automatically realized that the crater was his escape route.

Leading her team into the bottom of the building she found that they were deep past the foundation of headquarters and in the sewers. From the looks of it, Night Dragon may have made the explosion too powerful. They examined the sewers to find the remains of the chest. With guns drawn, they approached the it. Lopez gave the order to hold and approached the chest alone. She took a deep breath before opening the lid.

Once the lid was opened, she held a look of frustration and relief. She ordered the men to search the rest of the sewers and cover all potential exits before returning to the surface. When she finally was alone, she checked to make sure before reopening the lid. Reaching inside, she retrieved a note left in the center of the chest addressed to her.

"Lopez – Now is the time to choose. Bring this chest to our favorite place. And I will promise that I can set you free from Kenzensho. – Night Dragon"

Before long, her men returned with a negative report. She gave the order to return to the surface before the building shifted. Ordering that the chest be taken for evidence, Lopez could tell that something was wrong as one man lifted the chest with ease. When she first brought the chest to the evidence vault, it took four men to carry the chest. And that fact alone was after Kenzensho swapped out the weapons. She knew that something was different.

Remembering the fight in the vault, she ordered the chest to be put down and for the men to stand back. Firing at the chest, five shots enter in to the chest with ease. Night Dragon pulled another one of his mind games. With an evil grin on her face, Lopez silently agreed to play his game. When they made their way back to the surface, Kenzensho was waiting for the news of Night Dragon's death. The fury and rage could be seen on his face when Lopez delivered the news. With all the witnesses around, he had to keep his composer, especially when the news camera arrived. It appeared that his efforts to keep his secrets were fighting a losing battle.

The building was quietly evacuated moments before the alarmed was triggered. Kenzensho gave the order as soon the General arrived at the loading dock. It was a precaution he took to avoid any witnesses not on his payroll. While the rest of the force evacuated the building along with prisoners due to a gas leak, he made sure to bring only his men in to protect his public identity. His rage at the destruction of his cash cow and storage space was well hidden but fire was in his eyes. The evidence vault served as his bank and weapons vault. Its absence would drain his profit and supply stock.

Kenzensho held in his fury for during the day. Dealing with the Mayor and other officials, he had to play the role of a mere Police Captain instead of his true self. He knew that his hand could not be shown until his plan was completed in order. Returning to his luxury penthouse apartment in the heart of Downtown New Peak City, Kenzensho finally unleashed his rage in the privacy of his workout studio.

With sword in hand, he ordered his men to attach him. However, this was no sparring session. Piece by piece, he took apart the ten men assigned to the Vault Detail. Each man was to pay for their failure to keep Night Dragon away from the chest and scroll.

As the last man stood with sword in hand, fear began to creep into his eyes. Kenzensho could smell the fear oozing out of the disgraced guard. An evil laugh and menacing stare took over Kenzensho. His evil powers feed and grew off the fear. His power over the weak minded was his only true source nourishment. His eyes began to glow an evil and hate-filled Jade green. His rage began to morph his physical appearance. His muscles and frame doubled in size. His skin turned to a zombie pale. He looked as monstrous as General Taka.

Channeling his rage, Kenzensho raised his katana for one final attack. He waved the disgraced guard to make the first move. The guard knew his failure was assured. However, the honor he desired was at stake. He rushed his Master with all his might and was greeted vicious slash that shattered his sword and ripped apart his throat. Blood began to gush out.

As the body laid out on the ground, bleeding out at Kenzensho's feet, the Grandmaster began to unleash his true being. As the guard laid there dying, Kenzensho kneeled next to him and looked deep into his eyes. He opened his mouth and sucked the remaining soul out the dying man. He devoured the guard's soul and began to turn back into himself. That was the price of the Jade Samurai.

As life began to fade away from his latest victim, his mind began to fade back into time. Leader of the Jade Samurai was an honor pasted down from father to son since the feudal era of Ancient Japan. The power he now possessed was always forbidden. The family would only use the power to bring back those whom earned the honor by Kenzensho's family. Their eternal life was payment for honor in the Jade Army.

Those that longed for honor paid the cost at the first sign of failure. As the Kenzensho stood to his feet, he ordered that the guard's body be taken to the battle chamber. There, the body is dressed in full samurai armor and infused with the Jade Elixir. Created by an ancient evil wizard, the mixture of Jade and blood of the Kenzensho family gave the entire family evil powers of the shadow realm. When poured on the body of his victims, they became the undead warriors that followed General Taka on his secret quest.

For centuries he chased the desire of his empty heart… the world and control of everything in it. The craving for power led to his discovery of the Jade Elixir and Soul Devouring power. Ordering the room to be cleared, he proceeded to sit on his throne. His influence got him power, but the Elixir got him near immortality and great power. However, the price of his throne was more than great. He was forever damned to eternity as a mortal, but he was destined to ascend. Sitting upon his throne, his mind began to fade back to his life before becoming the Grandmaster of Jade Samurai.

Reliving is childhood in Japan, he remembered the old times. When Shoguns and the Samurai warriors ruled the many provinces of Japan. When he and his father were finally about to assume all of Japan, the Night Dragon first appeared and stopped their plans. It took many battles, but they were finally robbed of their honor and power.

Forced to the shadows, they became mercenaries for crime lords. At each chance for profit, the Night Dragon was there. Vowing on his father's deathbed at the hands of Night Dragon, Kenzensho promised to bring back the days of Honor and rule the world as his Father groomed him to rule...with complete control and power. Looking out the window, he could see the setting of the sun. The rising moon held a hint of green. The Jade moon would be rising soon. The time to ascend was finally near.

As she stood there, the hot, soothing water began to melt away stress and pain. Mya could hear her phone going off again. Ignoring the call once again, she just wanted to relax and rest. Working nonstop was finally taking a toll on her mind. Today was not her best work day. Most of her students forgot about the paper that was due. Her assistant principal lost all over her lesson plans that were not due until tomorrow, and she lost her backup files due to her computer crashing.

When she finally got home after three hours of traffic, she found a notice on the door that her apartment had been sprayed for bugs. She opened the door to find bugs and footprints all over the floors. Mya tip-toed past her bed room and placed everything into her closet. Her bedroom was the only room that was not touched. There she simply removed her clothes and began to run a hot shower. Her day was over but her long weekend was just beginning. As she could finally get her mind together, Mya finally walked over to the closet and pulled her briefcase out of the closet. Putting it on the bed, she walked over to her vanity and sat down.

For the first time in months she finally had a night to herself. Tomorrow would be the opposite. She had several appointments to make, starting in the morning. Especially since she had agreed to the last-minute side job. The payoff, in the end, was well worth it. The idea of seeing him again would be worth it as well. Mya knew that she was crazy for even thinking the thoughts in her mind. As she turned off the shower and began the diligent task of getting ready for the night, Mya began to think back there their first encounter. She watched as Night Dragon took on Hollywood Jones and his men.

The nightclub was packed and there was no room to maneuver. She was in her favorite red dress that celebrated her curves and breast all while demonstrating the power and silky grace of her legs with the matching red heels. She was only there to study her prey. At any moment her next target would walk in the door and she was under orders to make it look like an accident. However, Night Dragon's entrance into the club was big, loud and major. The way he took out the heavily armed man without a gun or his sword spoke wonders of his skill and power.

She would have completed the mission if the target didn't get away in the chaos. As she pulled and stretched into her skin tight one piece, she began to fantasize about another encounter with him just like the roof top. He would be a perfect mate if her bitter revenge allowed the sweet taste his arms and kiss just before she ended his life. Just a kiss is all she needed.

Mya continued to get dress while she began to fade away in her mind. The more she dressed in her battle armor, the more the mind of Mya Wells disappeared. Once her boots and chest armor were on, she began to stock her arsenal. She stared into the mirror and looked deeply into her own image. Wearing all black with white trim, Mya became the most dangerous assassin in New Peak City and the world. Her only equal was the so-called "King of Shadows". She finally got a chance to measure his abilities last night. His skills and swagger were on her mind all day.

Mya had to snap herself back to reality. She made sure to grab plenty of daggers and throwing stars. She then grabbed her .9mm and plenty of ammo. Placing her katana into the sheath, she reached for her mask and walked toward her closet. There she retrieved her phone and pulled the hidden leaver on a coat hook. The back wall of the closet split open to reveal her passage way to her secret loft lair. There she kept her files, weapons, and endless toys she has collected over the years since she was twelve years old. She grabbed her phone to lock it into her computer system.

With her successful kill count, she knew that any evidence of her identity would be a disaster. Connecting it to the system, it would seal her alibi. Walking over to her secret elevator she climbed inside to descend to her awaiting car. Unknown to the entire building, Mya was she secret owner that took over three years ago. The major renovation that took place at that time was to create her fortress.

To everyone in the building, she was the single middle school teacher that was too busy to date or for the gossip of the building. It was the perfect cover. She climbed into her blacked-out Dodge Hell Cat and became the White Rose. Her target would be in the perfect location to collect her 40 million bounty. She was surprised by the order she received at her lunch break. He was already on her list, but the money sweetened the deal. As she began to pull out of a hidden garage, she began to relish in the fact that her silent war was almost over.

Once she was on the street, she turned on her police scanner and made sure to ignore any potential police issues. She was surprised when she found out that most of the force was at headquarters due to a major bombing. She was totally clueless to the day's events due to her desire to protect her cover. She could understand why her target was ordered to die now.

With great hast, she pushed the pedal down and raced to her position. She was outside the Marque Hotel when she finally spotted him pull up. He was supposed to arrive over an hour ago. She waited until his men took their guard positions. She was parked in an alley across from the front door. She made sure to park in the shadows to avoid anyone seeing her.

White Rose climbed out of the car and quickly began to move to the back of the building in front of the hotel. Using the fire escape, she crept up to the top of the building. Thirty stories up in the air, she had no fear or worry in the world. She moved with great speed and precision. Every movement was timed down to the very second. With her bow and arrow already stashed at the top of the building she took aim. Waiting for the right moment, she held the arrow and bow perfectly still. Her cue was right on time as the midnight run garbage truck began to roll down the street.

Firing the arrow into the air, White Rose struck her target with perfect aim as usual. She attached a harness and slide across the line she created. When she reached the balcony of her target, she leaped over the railing and quickly moved against the wall. The door was cracked already which was often not a good sign to White Rose. She knew that meant the target was still up or someone was in already inside the hotel suite.

Just before she made her way through the air, she noticed that the target had turned off the lights. She could smell trap. Instead of calling off the hit, she wanted to find out who was behind this trap. Pulling out her climbing claws, she began to climb up to the roof of the building. There was another way in and she was going to collect her ten million bounty. Just as she began to ascend to the roof, the clouds opened and unleashed a viscous rain storm. Now she could use the weather to her advantage as she reached the roof.

As she opened a ventilation shaft, she questioned if she should spring the trap or sit back and watch. White Rose climbed into the shaft and made her way to the vent in the hall way outside the suite. Using a mini spy scope, she looked and watched the movements of the guards outside the suite doors. She needed to get inside that room. She noticed the broom closet across from the guards and decided that would be her key inside.

While she made her way to the lien closet, White Rose made sure not to make any noise or even breathe. She reached the vent and slowly began to remove the screws with a miniature drill, which she always carried with her. To be the best, she knew she had to always be prepared.

White Rose climbed out of the vent and was about to pounce. Then she noticed the service elevator within the closet. Her mind a massive idea. She wanted to keep the kill count down and no attention at all to herself.

Seeing the maid's uniform, she got an idea to get past the guards. Removing her gear and placing everything inside the supply cart, White Rose began to get into character. She knew from his habits that the target had worked out an arrangement with the hotel to conceal his midnight entertainment guests. A clean maid's uniform was always there every night for his paid entertainers in case the news cameras were nearby.

Her target was a public servant in New Peak City. That meant he was corrupt and had secrets all over town. And those secrets are what made White Rose's job easy at times. This target had an addiction to heroine and Viagra. She had a syringe full of a lethal dose of the cocktail. Stuffing her curves into the tight dress, she made sure to stuff a couple of throwing stars into her bra and collapsible club in her apron. The rest of her weapons were then stuffed inside the cart with her gear and mask. She kept her head down as she emerged from the closet in full disguise.

The guards automatically knew what to do. Standing up and keying her into the room, they simply looked away not to see her face on purpose. Once the maid went by them, the guards shared in a nod of approval at her perfect shape and curves. She closed the door behind herself and made her way into the suite.

Walking around, White Rose searched the suite softly calling out "Housekeeping" in a seductive tone. When she finally made her way upstairs to the master bedroom, she called out again, but this time received a reply. She walked into the room with her head down as she seductively unbuttoned the top of her disguise. She tried to keep her face from sight due to the dim lighting.

"I didn't order 'Housekeeping' tonight," the target said, as his face was hidden in the shadows as well.

"Yes, sir," White Rose replied, "It is compliments of the Marque Hotel, sir."

"Well, thank you," the voice said from the shadows, "But I am dead tired. Go ahead and take the money on the table by that door. I need to have the night off. Have a good evening."

"I am sorry, but I am not able to do that sir," White Rose said as she tried to move closer to the bed while preparing to inject the venomous cocktail. "I must turn down the bed sir. It is a complimentary service of the hotel Commissioner Thorton."

"Well, I see that ten million pay day is all you care about White Rose," the voice said as the lights were flipped on to reveal Night Dragon lying in the bed.

"You!" White Rose said as she threw the syringe at the heart of Night Dragon.

"Nice aim," Night Dragon said as he caught the syringe perfectly and held it with ease. "You are really good. I will give you that. I am not trying to fight you. I just need to speak to you."

"I'm going to take your head now," White Rose said as she reached for a throwing star and threw it straight at his head.

"Wait!" Night Dragon said as he fired a dart from his gauntlet straight into her thigh and nearly missed the star as it hit the headboard.

As the dart injected his special potion, White Rose lost all control of her limbs. She collapsed right there on the spot. Night Dragon got out of the bed, and he made sure to quickly get her off the floor. He gently placed her on the bed. He placed a pillow underneath her head and quickly tied her hands and feet together.

Once she was down, he made sure to that they were not interrupted. He grabbed her gear out of the cart and placed it upon her feet. The whole time he did this, she was wake but could not move. His potion worked well every time. He looked at the time and counted the time until the effects wore off. He put her things into a bag and prepared for a quick exit.

Looking at her he didn't want her to be any further involved than she already was. The fight on the roof was their first one on one meeting. He knew of her agenda and kill list. If he wasn't busy looking for the Dragon Heart, Night Dragon would have stepped in to stop the path White Rose was heading down.

He knew of her identity and unknown to her, he made sure to keep her identity a complete secret next to his own. When he learned of the hit of the Commissioner by Kenzensho, he knew that White Rose would be the target of a massive manhunt. He realized that Kenzensho was trying to force White Rose to permanently serve him as a slave in return for his protection or die. What she did not know was that General Taka was in the parking garage waiting to invite her or ambush her. Rushing in to provide aid, Night Dragon put his plans on hold to rush to her aid. He found his way into the hotel and quickly learned of the Commissioner's movements through the hotel each night. Posing as one of his guards, he set up the scenes of the evening.

Making sure everything was in place for White Rose's arrival. He knew that she was the best because of her attention to detail and keen intelligence. He learned her habits and preferred methods. Since she was only taking out the evil bosses and crime lords of the world, he knew that White Rose was trying to find her own way on the path of the ninja warrior. It cannot be forced. The path of the warrior must grow and mature like a young child. That was the same thing his master instilled in him.

In fact, it was the very last lesson he learned before becoming the Night Dragon. As he looked into her eyes, he wanted to tell her so much and be honest for the first time in his life. If he couldn't tell her everything, he at least wanted her to know he was his friend not an enemy. He wanted her to know that he did not murder her master. Placing his hand on her shoulder, he kneeled to speak with her before the epic fight that was about erupt. He had to let her know something that would let her know he was on her side.

"White Rose," he said plainly, "I am here to help you. You were tricked into killing the Commissioner tonight with that bounty. Kenzensho is trying to force you to join him and the Jade Samurai. You are to be greeted in the garage by the Demon Beast… General Taka. You are not meant to be the hired killer of that monster. And you do not have any chance of beating that other monster. Grab your things and get out of town for a while. You must lay low because a war is coming. You will not believe me, but you will be the last thing standing before good and evil. Now Thorton is tied up in the shower. You won't collect that bounty tonight. And to make sure of it, I will make sure to invite the babysitters outside."

Taking out Thorton's gun, Night Dragon fired three shots at the window. Throwing the gun to the ground, he ran outside the master bedroom. Looking over the railing he spotted the guards with guns drawn coming towards him. The tricked worked, but now he had to buy White Rose some time. They spotted him and began to fire. Night Dragon dodged the bullets and leaped over the railing. He landed perfectly on the floor and made a run to the door.

While one chased Night Dragon, the other ran into the bedroom. Finding an empty bed, the guard went into the bathroom to find his boss beaten up and tied to the shower. While he tended to his boss, his partner was going hand to hand with Night Dragon and losing. After knocking the guard out with a powerful kick, he then turned to leave only to find five more guards joining in on all the fun. Night Dragon took on all comers to allow White Rose a chance to get away. The longer the guards focused on him, the more of a chance she had to flee. After taking those guards out with ease, Night Dragon made his way to the stairs. He made his way to the roof only to find that General Taka was already waiting for him.

With an evil grin on his monstrous face, General Taka invited Night Dragon to finish where they left off. Although the idea was tempting, Night Dragon was in a hurry. His only concern was White Rose. He only hoped that he bought her enough time. However, when he held an unconscious White Rose up off the ground, rage took over the mindset of Night Dragon. Taka tossed White Rose to the ground and charged Night Dragon. Quickly forming a plan, he charged Taka with all his might. Ducking down to avoid the massive and powerful swing of his war axe, Night Dragon slid underneath the monster and popped right back up. With Taka turned around, he delivered a crippling thrust kick to Taka's knee.

Forcing him to kneel, Night Dragon leaped up to serve a power combination blow of his knee and elbow to Taka's head. The attack was enough to send the undead general to the ground. Once he was down, Night Dragon turned his attention to the unconscious White Rose. He rushed over to get her out of danger. She was coming to her senses when he kneeled to help her up. However, he was not greeted with a thank you.

Without warning he received a powerful left cross that knocked him onto his back. Standing over her latest victim, she removed her mask. To his surprise, the betrayal was not even expected after his guaranteed promise. As she stood over Night Dragon, an evil smile filled Lopez's face.

"Surprised," Lopez smirked, "Bet the King of Mystery didn't see this plot twist."

"No, I honestly didn't," Night Dragon said as he simply sat up. "I take that you were truly trying to kill your partner."

"Damn right!" Lopez admitted, "That self-righteous son of a bitch was about to ruin everything. Once Kenzensho gets what he wants, I get everything I want and more." Then you had to go and save his ass. Now I must find him and finish the job before he can get to the feds. So, are you going to make easy for me or do I have to let my boyfriend finish you off?"

"Boyfriend?" Night Dragon sounded confused, "Who decided to throw their life away on you?"

"Taka, have fun, my love" Lopez ordered as she stood aside.

"What the Hell!" Night Dragon exclaimed in shock.

With her orders heard, Taka devilishly obeyed. Picking Night Dragon by his neck and shoulders, he threw the deceived warrior across the roof top into a wall. Pain took over and Night Dragon was stuck in a serious trap. It appeared that his own methods were used against him. However, he was not about to let them stop him. Finding the strength, Night Dragon stood up slowly but kept his composure. Getting into a fighting stance, he welcomed a full-on attack from them both. With a simple nod, Lopez gave the order to attack. Taka thrusted his axe into the ground and rushed in to attack.

Ducking and dodging powerful blows, Night Dragon delivered his own furious fury of counter attacks. He grabbed a direct punch and used Taka's own momentum to flip Taka into the same wall he was thrown into. When Taka hit the wall, the wall collapsed on top of him. Before Taka could rise, Night Dragon unleashed his anger out with a viscous ground and pound attack. Lopez jumped in with a direct shot to Night Dragon' chest her Glock 20. Once again, he was on his back, but he was alive. Standing over him, she took aim straight at his head. Before she could pull the trigger, a shuriken came flying from nowhere and cut the gun in half.

"Wrong move!" White Rose yelled as she revealed herself in the shadows. "Nobody kills the Night Dragon but me, you-two-dollar tramp."

"Tramp!" Lopez replied, "No, it is time to whip out all ninja,"

"Time to die!" White Rose declared as she leaped to attack Lopez head on.

Night Dragon watched as he tried to get himself together. He wore armor but the bullets she was using were powerful enough to knock the wind out of him. He watched as the two different fighting styles clashed. Lopez was a well-known boxer, while White Rose seemed to be well trained in Jeet Kune Do and Jiu Jitsu.

Taking the time to rest, he could not remain a spectator for long. Night Dragon spotted Taka reaching for his Battle Axe to attack from behind. Leaping to his feet, he drew his sword and sliced the axe in half with one powerful slash. That look in his eye was more than present. It radiated throughout his entire being.

"You and I have unfinished business General," Night Dragon declared. "Last man, or in your case corpse standing."

"By all means," General Taka replied as he threw the pieces of his axe to the ground.

General Taka pulled out a sword of his own and exchange a deadly stare into Night Dragon's eyes. Reading each other's eyes, they rushed into each other with weapons drawn. Each slash and swing of their swords met the other's blade in a vicious dance of destruction. Neither warrior wanted nor thought of giving up. It was determined then and there that only one would leave that rooftop.

Fighting him one on one, Night Dragon knew that Taka and Lopez were a major combination. If he and White Rose did not stop them now, neither one of them would make it off that roof. As the two warriors fought the viscous pair of Lopez and Taka, Night Dragon and White Rose began to assist one another when their respective opponent began to overwhelm the other. Catching on to their own amazing teamwork, Night Dragon and White Rose began to combine all their attacks.

As the fight grew, Lopez and Taka began to combine their attacks as well. When he noticed that the fight could not be won that night, Night Dragon decided they had to get out of there. Throwing a smoke pellet, he grabbed White Rose and leaped off the roof. Just as the smoke cleared, Lopez and Taka were already there to try and find out their direction and trail. Without warning Lopez heard a beeping sound that began to pick up in speed. Realizing what it was, she ordered Taka to move, but she was interrupted by the huge explosion that blew them both back across the roof.

Just as they were coming to their senses, Lopez and Taka were soon surrounded by Jade Samurai. Ordering then to fan out and find the two, Lopez was closer to Night Dragon than Thorton had ever gotten. It was clear that her role was more than it was thought to be. As Night Dragon and White Rose watched as the loyal henchmen began to search for them, they made sure not to move or make a sound. While the Samurai began to move out and away from the hotel, they both continued to wait until Taka and Lopez finally were whisked away in a helicopter towards the Kenzensho's Penthouse.

He planned a perfect escape, but his plan was ruined by the trap set for the two shadow warriors. Night Dragon now planned to walk right out of the front door. When the smoke pellet exploded, he simply ran to the ledge with White Rose and hid in underneath them. Using the explosion to mask their escape into the hotel, they climbed inside the window blown open due to the explosion. Climbing inside the quickly, they made their way to the hallway. Night Dragon took out a key and quickly opened a room door and ushered White Rose inside behind him.

Once inside, Night Dragon lead the way to the master bedroom where he tossed White Rose a new disguise to get out of the building. When the authorities arrived within five minutes, the entire building was then overwhelmed by police and firefighters. As everyone in the hotel was evacuated and questioned, the Commissioner reappeared as if he were never there. He made a statement to the press and pretended to be heading up the investigation of what happen. He made sure that attempt on his life and the intervention of Night Dragon never happened.

As soon as the cameras were not watching, he called Kenzensho to report the attempt on his life. Kenzensho acted as though he did not know of the attempt, even though he gave the permission to use the Commissioner as bait to kill both masked warriors. While he continued to play the foolish act, White Rose and Night Dragon dumped their firefighter disguises.

Hopping into White Rose's car, they drove away from that side of town. They rode around until they made sure that they were not followed. Realizing they were clear of the Jade Army, the two knew they were now moving targets. Together, they had to join forces to end their mutual enemy. They also knew that the moment they stepped out of the car on the street, they could be spotted and have an entire city on them within minutes. White Rose knew the only option was to take Night Dragon to her place. In her mind it was already too late to hide her identity. He had already seen her face and the tracking dot was not found until she was already inside her home. Her location was already compromised. To be safe regardless, she took the long way to her apartment building.

Entering her secret garage, they finally climbed out of the car. It was there that she began to remove her mask. Revealing her true self, White Rose disappeared, and Mya was standing before him. She removed the rubber band that held her hair in a tight ponytail under her mask. Unleashing her natural curly hair, she began to loosen her gear and remove it bit by bit. She stood in a one-piece armor suit and her utility belt. She grabbed a towel off a nearby rack and began to wipe away the sweat. Maya made her way to the elevator and pressed the call button. Night Dragon stood in awe of her garage. He was jealous of her vehicles and motorcycle. As he admired her bike, Mya called him over to the elevator. Just as he was about to enter, Mya stopped him.

"Look, you are a free to visit, but you need to check your gear," she ordered.

"I just saved your life," Night Dragon began to question, "Why the lack of trust? I can assure you I am not your enemy."

"You and I are not friends, we aint' partners," she reminded him. "We have a shared problem. I only brought you here to keep an eye on you."

"The gear comes off, but the sword stays with me," Night Dragon declared.

Mya could tell by his voice, that he was serious. In a way, she respected him. She complied to his demand and vice versa. He placed all his weapons and gear on her work bench, but he kept his sword. He entered the elevator and they ascended to her hidden loft. Riding in the elevator, they stood on opposite sides and didn't say a word. They made sure not to make eye contact, but Night Dragon could not keep his eyes off her. Just before reaching the top, Mya finally broke the silence.

"Why were we in that hotel tonight?" she asked. "Why am I wanted dead by the Samurai?"

"I don't think you want to the answer to that question?" Night Dragon replied. "Besides, you are dealing with demons you are not ready for."

"Listen, I know about the Heart, the Eye and the Soul. When all three are brought together, the ultimate warrior is created. The Dragon King is the myth that has passed down through bedtime fairy tales," she said as they exited the elevator and she walked behind a folding screen to remove her clothes.

"Look, I am was just there to help you as our clans have done for each other for centuries," he admitted. "You don't know what war you are getting into. It is bigger than any personal vendetta you have."

"Actually, you are not my master nor my man," Mya said as her inner city girl attitude began to show, "Last time I checked I allowed you to live the other night and for the last few years since you are the one that destroyed my master." Unknown to his eyes, she had a dagger ready to slit his throat.

"Okay, I did not destroy your master," he admitted. "She was murdered by a fool who thought he was worthy of being Night Dragon. He was foolish to think that the mask and armor creates the Night Dragon. He is the one that murdered your teacher, my mother, and my father. The very same one behind everything."

"Kenzensho is already on my list," she told him, "Right under your name. If you think I am going to fall for your magic tricks and lies, then you need to leave. I was their when she died. I watched as she died by your arms. I made a vow to avenge her for her son," Mya told him. "And I dated her son for five years, and I just watched him die on live T.V. because of you and Kenzensho. Rick Steele was an honorable man that didn't deserve to die that way."

"Mya, I really wish you would open your eyes for once," Night Dragon said as he finally removed his mask and head gear."

A look of shock covered her face as the secret that everyone in New Peak searched for was revealed to only her. She walked over to the familiar face of the man she once called friend, then brother, and finally lover. Placing her hands on his face, tears began to fall as she touched the living ghost before her. She leaned in to give him a small but passionate kiss on the lips. Then, with all her might she slapped his face as hard as she could. Rick Steele took the blow and tried to shake it off. She was the only person to know his secret. A fact that he was now proud of.

The idea of continuing to lie to her was tearing him apart on the inside. Not even his loyal assistant, Adonai, knew his identity. However, Mya was full of fury. She began to throw punches and kicks to release her anger. Rick dodged and blocked each blow with precision. As her fists flew, her vision was blinded by her frustration. She attempted to throw a Superman Punch which Rick side stepped and cause her to stumble.

Falling into his arms, Mya pulled Rick into another kiss but this time she unleashed her true passion. Kissing her back, he wanted her love to be equally received. Removing clothing and placing his sword on the desk, Rick picked Mya up and carried her off to her bedroom. Mya was surprised that he knew the entrance into her apartment. It appeared that he knew the layout of her place as if he built it himself. Placing her in her bed, Rick kissed her forehead and began to tell her the truth. Mya did the same without hesitation. They opened their hearts to love until there was no secrets, no lies, no anger, no Night Dragon, no White Rose… only Rick and Mya. The talked and talked that night until the sun rose. They fell asleep in each other's arms. The two were finally on the same level.

RISE OF THE JADE ARMY

The helicopter landed on the rooftop of the large high-rise building in the middle of Downtown New Peak City. Kenzensho watched from his observation deck as a defeated General emerged from the massive machine. Layla followed, and her simple head gesture told of their defeat. Kenzensho was upset, but he knew that Layla's trap was the closest attempt to destroy Night Dragon. Her actions the night prior proved to be the motivation his men needed to fight against their unbeatable foe.

The Thornton's' failures were adding up and soon his ascension would be upon him. It was time to reach into his powers and release his full capabilities. However, with his status, he was not in proper position. Tonight's plan was not only to get rid of his enemies, but to also push his public face into the proper place of power to completely take over the New Peak Police Department. He took his seat at his throne and awaited the arrival of his two warriors. When they emerged before him, they dropped to their knees to show honor and respect in the light of their failure. Kenzensho knew that the trap was a failure, but he never showed his anger.

Kenzensho now regretted the fact that the top assassin was now focused on him. He knew that his actions were declarations of war.

Ordering Layla and Taka out of his sight, he dismissed himself from his throne room. Closing the door to his private chamber, fear finally appeared in his eyes as he looked at the mirror. The ascension was close at hand, and he was still without the pieces he needed to gain the ultimate power. Once he had the power, he could completely run the Jade Samurai and no longer be just a figure head.

The true Grandmaster left him in charge a century ago after the defeat dealt by Night Dragon. Over the years he has fought his sworn enemy through the years. They have never drawn swords upon one another, but the thirst for each other's blood was always there. The two warriors only saw each other in passing. Many times, Kenzensho saw his hated enemy as he escaped his many traps and failed plots.

Last night was the closest he has ever gotten to Night Dragon. Years ago, he realized that it could not be the same man behind the mask, but the fact that he himself was immortal always created doubt. Once the Jade Emperor awakens from his slumber at the rise of the Dragon Moon, Kenzensho wanted to be the one that defeats him and takes over his army of Samurai. It was his destiny to rule the Jade Samurai and the world.

Appearing from the shadows, a mysterious figure laughed at the look of worry on Kenzensho's face. The figure emerged dressed in traditional Samurai armor with just a Jade mask covering his face. He was in amazement at the failure before him. He was the only one to truly understand the power of the Dragon Heart and Dragon's Eye.

Being the student of the Night Dragon, himself, the Samurai Armored figure was well learned in the legend of the King of Shadows. He walked up to his so-called partner and refused to hide his disapproval. He knew that the only two people who could destroy the Jade Samurai were now forced to join forces. He looked at the disgraced Grandmaster and continued to laugh as he pulled a secret cord by the throne. The cord activated the pulleys that raised the throne and revealed a secret room.

Kenzensho followed reluctantly behind his former student now equal. His eyes flashed green with rage as he tried to hold back the urge to attack. It was time to report to their master. As the both fell to their knees, they channeled their energy. Both of their bodies produced a bright green glow. Extending their hands towards a huge mirror, they unleashed two powerful beams that merged into one. The combined beam shot straight to the mirror and caused the mirror to bend and ripple like water.

As the beam intensified, the mirror turned green and whirled around like a hurricane. As the mirror's shape continued to change, a shadowy figure began to form in the distance. The form of a huge head appeared in the mirror. The two wayward partners put their heads to ground to show respect. Bowing before their master, they were preparing for his orders. The time for one of them to ascend was approaching. Kenzensho prayed that his master still saw favor in him.

"You two have served me with loyalty," the floating head known as the Jade Emperor said in a deep voice, "However the Jade Moon will be upon us soon. The Jade Army will once again rule this world once more. Kenzensho you have built an empire under the eyes of the world. But you have also failed to destroy old enemies who can ruin The Jade Samurai. Night Dragon and White Rose still live. I sense they are combined as one once more. You know once they are one warrior the power of three will fall to their feet."

"Master I have disgraced you, but my men are on the verge of gaining the Dragon Armor. Combined with the Dragon's Eye, I can bring you out of your prison in the Spirit Realm. You will be reborn and unstoppable," Kenzensho told his master.

"You have served me as Grandmaster of my Klan since the old days," he told Kenzensho. "Now it is time to reward you. I have noticed you that you have been needing more souls,"

"Yes Master," Kenzensho admitted. "The Dragon's Eye drains the lifeforce from the barer. With Dragon Armor in the light of the Jade Moon, the Eye can merge and bring you back to the Mortal Realm."

"Kenzensho, you honor me," the Master said with an evil grin. "Here is your reward."

A bright green light shot out of the floating heads eyes. Then a bright white beam of light shot out of the glowing green eyes and struck Kenzensho. Letting out a blood curling scream, he could feel his life being ripped from his body. Kenzensho began to morph painfully into his true form. His skin began to turn pale and his nails grew long. His body began to show his true age of over 500 years old. Pain filled his body as he fell from his knees to his back. The Jade Dragon's Eye was stripped away from Kenzensho. In a bright flash of light, the Eye was floating in mid-air and Kenzensho on the ground turning into dust.

"Take the Eye and become the Jade Samurai. Fulfill your destiny." The Jade Emperor said.

With great pride he reached out for the Eye. Taking it into his hands, his armor began to fade away piece by piece. The last to fade was his mask thus revealing his identity. As he bowed his head, he showed respect to his master. His master smiled as he disappeared back to the Spirit Realm. He stood proud as his armor was replaced with a Jade Silk Robe. As he left the mediation room, he found his generals already ready to receive him. They were standing her with a green glow in their eyes as if they were in a trance. He smiled a huge smile as his Generals kneed before him. He knew the evil in the hearts of those before him. His powers feed off that energy. As he took his place on the throne, he rewarded his loyal followers.

"You all did well," the new Jade Samurai said. "Our plan has worked to perfection. Our enemies have eliminated Kenzensho from holding our army from Destiny. I am your leader, but I am your brother as well. From now on, you are my counsel. When I raise to Destiny, you all will raise with me."

"Master, what is your bidding?" Taka asked.

"Taka prepare your troops for war," he told his undead general, "You are the detraction. You men will be the opening the Commissioner needs to launch his new Police force. Lopez you will be the new head of the special force."

"What is my mission Master," the junior Thorton asked, "I am ready to prove my loyalty."

"You are?" the Master asked with a grin. "Prove to me you are ready to take your place next to me."

"Yes, Master," Thorton said with an evil smile. He pulled out his twin daggers and presented them to his new master, proudly. Without warning he plunged the daggers into his father's heart and neck.

Falling to the floor and bleeding out. The Commissioner stared into the eyes of his son as life left his body. His head hit the ground at the feet of the new master. Kneeling to the body, the Master took the Commissioner's Badge from the fresh corpse. He stood up and placed it in the hand of the Thorton. This dark ceremonial promotion put a smile on all their faces. Taka was never respected by Kenzensho and Thornton Sr. He was only seen as the gruesome monster to call in when the they were too afraid to get their hand dirty.

However, he was respected by the New Master and other younger generals. They learned from his past battle stories and training them in growth to their evil dreams. Thorton respected him because of his kills and ability to enjoy dishing out pain. Lopez started to stay around him to gain his knowledge of the afterlife and being immortal. However, she began to fall for him because of his barbaric practices. He trained her from a lowly street thug with a badge to a world class assassin. The Master saw an equal in the undead warrior. He was just as stronger and faster, but he respected the animal instinct in the samurai general. It was then the new Master decided to give the loyal monster his reward. He pressed a button next to the throne and a jar of Jade Elixir appeared from the floor. He grabbed the jar and walked over to Taka.

"General Taka," he began to explain, "I promised you that you would be healed. No more will you be a hideous monster. Scarred with the wounds of death. Drink this elixir."

"Yes Master," Taka said as he took the jar into his hands.

Drinking the elixir completely, he swallowed every drop. It was then, he felt sharp pains all over his body. A green glow covered his entire body. Dropping the jar to floor, he grabbed his face as a burning sensation took hold of his face and his skin. He let out pain screams as he fell to his knees. Smoke and the green glow continued to flow from his body. Suddenly, he burst in to huge green flames all over his body, but he did not burn. As the flames grew into one, Taka cried out in pain as his body went throw a metamorphosis. His new master and brother walked over and joined him in the flames.

Grabbing his oversize hands, he assisted Taka to his feet. He looked deep into Taka's eyes and exchanged a beam of Jade light between them. After a couple of minutes, Taka covered his face as the power continued to change him. As the flames died down, the Master and Taka stood eye to eye. However, Taka was not the undead monster. Keeping the same 7'4" height and bullish build, Taka stood before his fellow generals and new Master a new creature. His skin was no-longer pale-greyish. His skin tone yellow and his eyes were brown with life. His Asia decent could be seen rather than the undead being. Immediately he looked at Lopez who humble bowed before her unholy lover.

"I promised that I would reward you for being loyal and teaching me the way of the Samurai," the new Master said. "You are not a dog. You are a Samurai and must carry yourself as a Samurai. Taka you will not be treated like a dog. You are the Beast of the Undead. We will once again rule the world. You have the powers of the undead, but the Jade elixir is now your life force. No more decaying blood or muscles for you. Layla, take this vial and give it to your mother. Allow the elixir to take over her as she sleeps. It will heal her. Together my brothers and sister, we will bring the code of the Samurai back to New Peak. Within a year, we will take over major cities all over the world. The Jade Army will raise again."

"Hail to the Grandmaster!" Thorton shouted out.

"Hail to The Master! Hail to the Master!" the three cried out in unison.

"Now go prepare for the phase one," the Master ordered. "I must prepare my speech for the press. Tomorrow, our useful enemies will be placed on city's Most Wanted List for the murders of Detective Steel, Captain Kenzensho, and Commissioner Thorton. I will also announce your promotions in the morning. We will control crime and the law like the Samurai of the old country. You three are the only ones to see my face. I always want the Mayor to be a third party. Besides, I will use New Peak City as my perfect example law and order."

"Yes, Master," Thorton said, "But what are we going to do about the Night Dragon and White Rose?"

"I know that those two will never join forces," he admitted. "I want to turn them against each other. For now, I want them running from the guns on both sides. Taka put a ten million bounty on them both. You are now the figure head of Jade Army. Layla, you will lead your new team in Samurai training and conditioning. Thorton, you will join the ranks of the politicians and when the influence of the power and money in our favor. As Mayor, I will agree to the creation of the new Police force while also caving in to the demands of the people to structure the New Peak City government.

While they try to obtain the tools to ascend, they will have to fight an army of the law and the entire underworld. While they search, we will take control of the entire city. Then this country will follow without delay. Before long, my generals, we will each lead the Jade Army across the four corners of the globe."

"We made a great decision in following you," Lopez said.

"It's good to be there Mayor. Now go and get everything ready. Thorton have my car brought around. I must be in the Mayor's Mansion before the press show up."

"Master, what if they find the Soul Stone?" Taka asked.

"He won't"," he assured his generals. Opening his robe, he revealed a black jewel around his neck. I have it and Jade Eye. I can ascend without the Dragon Armor. Besides, Jade Armor always had a beautiful glow in the moonlight."

Letting out a huge victorious laugh, the Master relished in his successful plan and the excellent work of his loyal generals. Joining him in laughter, they all celebrated the victory and the spoils of war. They knew their only stepping stone was capable of any and everything. He was formidable. Night Dragon was able to break apart every plan that was put together. They never expected his actions this week, but when they spotted the opportunity, they used it to their advantage. They all could not stand the true goal of Kenzensho, to be immortal. Believing in a legend, the combination of the armor and stones turned the barer into a walking immortal, unstoppable force.

As the general, left to begin their task, the Master took his seat on the throne. He knew his plan was fair fetch, and the odds just tipped in his favor. Being the son of adopted son of Richard Steele Sr., he knew his brother would be a deadly and the best. He knew the whole story of the Night Dragon. He failed to reveal his connection to his generals for fear of betrayal. He rushed to have the Commissioner killed because of his knowledge of his real identity. Not even Rick Steele knew of his brother becoming the Mayor of New Peak.

Due to plastic surgery to cover his tracks, Hero Steele faked his death when he joined the Jade Army. Wanting to become the Night Dragon, he refused to be the assistant to his older brother. He finally gained control over his former master and partner, when he revealed that he was his son. Gaining his powers and defeating his father in a match before the Jade Emperor, he was appointed a key position within the Jade Samurai. At the same time of his rise through the ranks, he earned his position by setting up Kenzensho and Night Dragon.

Finding a similar Night Dragon gear, he posed as Kenzensho as Night Dragon. He later found out that it was the Night Dragon costume Kenzensho wore to murder Steele's wife. However, Hero made another copy of the Night Dragon costume. Unknown to his brother, it was he that slue their father. Their father figured out his betrayal and tried to talk him out. But Hero wanted the power. He took up the mantle of a Samurai because they controlled good and the evil. They were judge, jury, executioner, and the Lord of their territory.

That night he wanted to kill his brother but could not do it because of the life debt he owed from childhood. He chose his adopted father because he refused to show him the respect as warrior. He always felt the Ninja were inferior and cowards. As he sat on his throne, he thought out the rest of his plan and his words for tomorrow. Maybe it was time to share the identity on Night Dragon. However, the life debt had to be repaid first. It was a part of the Samurai code. A code his predecessor forgot for selfish reasons. He and his generals lived by that code.

As the sun began to raise, he wondered if he could turn his remaining enemies on each other. His brother was all about the people, right versus wrong. He had no true understanding there is just Justice and rules following the hierarchy of the Samurai code. He knew that White Rose was all about the money. She knew her place as a trained dog of the Samurai. It was then he realized that his plan to put out a street bounty would speak to her greed. White Rose would bring his brother down for him. He held an evil smile as continued to plan his destiny after ascending.

THE JOURNEY TO ASCEND BEGINS

As the sun began to bathe the cozy bedroom in light, two lovers continued to hold on tight to one another. They had not touched in what felt like eternity. Since their breakup neither wanted another lover. The fact of life was that they were created to love one another only. They both knew this fact at a very young age. Growing up in his mother's greenhouse and undercover dojo, they both learned the power of love, the strength of the heart, and the endless possibilities of the mind.

Derren's parents split up when he was twelve years old due to his father's absence due to work. He did not learn the truth until after his mother was murdered. It was then and there he began his own training to ascend and destroy the Jade Emperor. It was a task that his father hated and tried to deny him. However, his mother had already began his training ever since he could walk. Mya was the girl next door. They met her first day in New Peak City when her parents moved into town. Both families were military families. Mya father and both of Rick's parents served in the Marines.

Rick found out during training the true reason for his parents' separation. His father was given a role as a Military Contractor / mercenary as the Night Dragon due to his skills. New Peak City was a major factor in government testing and secrets. His father saved the life of several key people during many attempts to steal government secrets. Because of this, he donated the Night Dragon skills to the U.S. Government. His identity was never revealed nor his mothers'. However, like his forefathers, he took on the mantle of be the personal protector of the people. No one in the government knew his identity, but they knew that he only trusted Marine Sergeant Richard Steele. Using his cover as the Night Dragon liaison, he was able to protect the family secret. Traveling the world, Night Dragon served as the country's and even the President's personal one-man army.

Unknown to him, White Rose was moonlighting when she was not on missions or with little Rick. His mother being half Black and half Asian, saw the struggles of the people. Being the White Rose, she began to follow the original role of the White Rose Order, professional assassin. Personally, working to be a radical force to spark change and force a stop to injustices of the time. When she was captured by the Yakuza on an assignment, Night Dragon rescued her and gave her the ultimatum that created the split in the marriage. It was then they agreed to end the marriage and distance the partnership. That created the true split that past generations falsified to protect the family identity.

As Rick laid next to Mya, he opened his eyes to see her sleeping face gently on his chest. He promised his parents he would make everything right. The day she was murdered by the Jade Samurai was the darkest day of his life. She had retired from the role of White Rose to focus solely on raising the next Night Dragon and another beautiful, positive black leader.

Rick Jr. was her whole world. He was fourteen when his mother was murdered by a false Night Dragon. He knew it wasn't his father, whom appeared almost in the nick of time to save him and Mya from an attempt of all their lives. However, he was too late as his only love gave her life defending two innocent children. In the process of escaping, his mask came off as his father threw an exploding pellet at her murder.

While Mya held on to her teacher, Rick saw his face as his father went after him. He put his head on his dying mother's chest as he watched his father go after Kenzensho. When Rick and his father found out he was a police officer, his father left the Marines and his duties to get closer to the man that rob his son, his heart and the world of a great woman. When his father finally understood what his mother saw in him, he finally trained his son for the role created just for their son. Teaching him allow to tap into his powers, Rick gradually learned his true calling.

Now as she laid on the chest of the love of her life, Mya realized what his mother saw in her and Rick. After his mother's death, Mya began to seek the training and knowledge she felt she needed to be like her hero. Mrs. Steele told her secrets at the age of twelve that Mya later confirmed when she sought the White Rose Order. Amazingly, the order was aware of Mya before she was aware of them. Rick's mother already informed them of her training and decision to make Mya her successor. She already knew that Mya and Rick were meant to be together. Rick Sr. would beg her not to put the task on the two to avoid the path of Night Dragon and White Rose. He wanted his son to have a life away from the family legacy.

However, both parents knew there was something special about their son. Mya knew at first sight that Rick was special. She would often dream about him. She became a teacher because of his mother being the first teacher to ever reach her heart and spark her soul. As she held onto him, she was afraid to open her eyes. Mya was scared that this was a dream. She could feel his touch against her skin and in her natural hair. She remembered how he loved running his fingers through her hair. It was their inside joke that they were never the stereotypical black couple. After their arrival to her apartment this morning, that was a true and an amazing fact they loved.

For Rick and Mya, the world was too hard and demanding on their love before truth came out. He hid his training as they grew up from her and she did the same. After his mother's death, Rick's father adopted a classmate that always hung around them. Rick Sr. found out that the boy was orphaned and living on the street. The fact that he was being bullied and forced to commit crimes further advanced the desire to save him.

Mya, on the other hand, always had a bad feeling about him. Hero Steele was accepted by the father and son, but never fully accepted by her. She always kept an eye on him when he was around. As they grew older, she would constantly ask to be alone or find ways to stay away from Hero. At his death, she made sure to keep her feelings hidden and focus on loving her hurt lover. She supported Rick in his mourning. Rick was the only thing that mattered in the world.

After college, her father and mother died in car crash. She sold their old home and moved into her apartment. By that time, she was already in the business and making a name for herself. She made sure to keep her work secret from Rick to protect him. He was set to be a police officer like his father and even served in the Marines like him as well. She would often worry about him finding out or being the one cop that came after her. As Mya laid next to him, all her fears came back to life. She could feel her anxiety building and her heart race. Like that out of nowhere, Rick pulled her in tighter in his arms and kissed her forehead. It was like a heavenly medicine that could cure all her ailments.

Looking at his beautiful black queen, Rick began to feel the connection they once shared as children. It grew to the point of almost being telepathy between the two. He could read her mind and know what to do to protect and heal from her pain. He felt her heart beat race out of sync with his own and quick moved in to fix it. She loved his kiss upon her brow.

The two would often exchange kisses that way as their own way of apologizing or to simply say hello. He missed receiving and giving those kisses. Many times, while he was on patrol, that kiss was all he had to get him through the nights of fighting crime or serving as a police officer. In a way, he allowed her to function in his city because he loved her too much to stop her.

Last night was his only time to intervened in her business. He knew her secrets and without her knowledge protected her from investigation. When he found evidence that lead back to her, he made it disappear just like the evidence that lead to him. He made it his life mission to not only protect the innocent, but most importantly Mya. She was worth it.

In his eyes, she just needed to find her way back home. Something he always heard his parents say, "You will always find your way home no matter what". He knew he was only the best with her. She was the one being that could keep him in check. It was at that moment he thought back to the dreams and visions that robbed him of sleep for the last five years.

"In order to ascend, the rose must bind the heart of the dragon," he said to himself.

As the words from his parents played over and over in his head, Rick finally began to piece together everything. The training and the studying had a deeper meaning that finally just clicked. This was the moment they trained him for. Thinking about everything realized what the ascension was truly about. Rick realized he had to get back to the lair.

While Mya continued to sleep in peace, he gently moved her off his chest and laid her head on top a pillow. He reached for the Night Dragon suit and was about pull it up on him when a throwing star came whizzing past his head. He knew she did not miss. Rick lifted his head and saw his love hold the grin she loved to shoot at her prey.

"I know you are not walking out on me," she told her as he stood frozen in his place. "If you think you are going to hit this and run out on me again."

"In my defense, I was just getting back to work," Rick told her as he stayed in the same position. "I am heading back to work on a hunch."

"Then we can head over to your place together," Mya told Rick as she climbed out of bed. Revealing her nude, well-toned and ample curved body, Rick started to lose his mind and the blood in his head.

"I wish I can let you come with me, but I am not going to my apartment," Rick tried to give her a hint.

"Oh, I finally get to see your lair," Mya said as she grabbed a bag and some clothes out of her dresser. "I always wanted to see where you always went to hide out."

"Listen, I love you. I am crazy in love with you. I will move mountains and seas for you, but there is no way you are coming to the lair," Rick said as he tried to put his foot down.

"Richard Earl Steele, Jr.," Mya said as she pulled up her jeans and stood in front of him with a bra and hands on her hips. "If you every want to kiss these lips and touch my body, then you may want to rethink that statement. You might not want to live in fear of a hollow point drilling through your brain from five hundred yards, I suggest you get dressed so I can get my morning tea."

"Mya, we have to be careful right now," Rick tried to reason with her. "I have to get back to the lair and pack. I must prepare for the war that is happening. You don't know about the storm that is about to hit this city."

"Well, you are going to need help," Mya said as she pulled a tank top over her head. "You almost lost that fight last night. I hate to tell you this, but you are slipping."

"I am not slipping," Rick corrected her as he finished getting dressed, "I am losing my powers. At the time of ascension, my agility, speed and power disappear. It is part of becoming the Night Dragon. If I don't prove myself worthy, the powers can be permanently stripped away. And if what I think is going on is true, the Jade Samurai with raise an unstoppable Jade Army."

Before he could say another would, his gauntlet computer went off and her phone began to send the emergency notification. Both pulled up their respective notifications then looked at each other. Mya asked for the remote next to the end table next to Rick. He turned on the tv to see the breaking news report. Looking at the screen, they sat on the bed next to each other. They sat in shock at the breaking news.

Mayor Lee Heto was issuing a multi-million-dollar reward for the masked personas. It appears that their fight was put on video. There were both wanted for the murders of Detective Steele, Captain Kenzensho, and Police Commissioner Thorton. Conveniently, Taka and Lopez were left out of the video. It was all staged… too staged. The more he thought about it, the more he began to continue to merge the pieces of the puzzle.

"I need you to meet me at the cemetery, I need to go change in to street clothes," Rick told her.

"Here," Mya said as she opened her closet to reveal Rick's clothes. "I am glad I didn't throw them out."

"We need to get out of here right now," Rick told her, "We need to check on something that will put everything in prospective. We need to hurry."

"Why are we going to the cemetery?" Mya asked. "We need to get your powers back."

"It's just a hunch I am willing to bet will end all this mess and stop the Jade Army," he told her as he finished dressing quickly. Rick opened the door to go out the front door.

"Wait, don't go into the living room. It is a … mess," Mya said as she followed behind to warn him but was puzzle by the sight. He apartment was spotless. All the dead bugs and spray residue were gone.

"Oh, I am sorry. I left more than clothes in your place," Rick said as he opened a cabinet to reveal a small vacuum cleaner robot. I had it set to clean every morning at 5:30 in the morning."

Rick was lying through his teeth. He hoped that Mya was not still able to read him. She was the only person he could never lie to. Keeping a secret was one thing, but telling a lie was totally out of his abilities. Rick asked her to finish packing her gear and prepare for a long flight. Mya watched as he looked around her clean apartment. As he searched through some books, he found and took the atlas off the Mya's bookshelf. He made his way back to her closet and hit the lever to reopen the passage to her hidden workspace. He grabbed his gear and made his way to her car. He opened the trunk and began to pack up her weapons.

Mya watched as he packed up her gear as if she were being force out of her apartment. She continued packing somethings as well, but her girlfriend sense was tingling. She knew he was lying about her apartment being cleaned by the automated vacuum. She personally knew that vacuum didn't work because it accidentally vacuumed up an important flash drive. She stopped it the best way she knew how… she fired an arrow into it one evening she was having a bad day. That was the day Rick left her the message that they couldn't be together anymore. She couldn't find him, so the vacuum was the next best thing. When she saw Rick unhook her computers, Mya protested and demanded answers.

"What are you doing?" Mya said. "Put my shit back! What the hell got into you?"

"We need to get out of here right now," Rick told her. "We need to get away from the city right now it is not safe."

"What do you mean it is not safe?" she asked. "Just because you see a bounty on your head, you are ready to run."

"I ain't running!" Rick declared. "I am keeping you safe. I can't lose you. That bastard has taken everything away from me…my job, my city and my parents. If this bastard he takes you, then I will rain down Hell on this Earth. I almost lost you once. I am not losing you again."

"I can handle myself!" Mya replied. "I don't need you to save me. At least I am not afraid to get my hands dirty and spill blood."

"Oh, because I refuse to take a life, I must be weak!" Rick fired back. "Don't confuse my mercy for weakness. Because I can control myself, I can see things your bullets don't see. Now get your things in the car, so we can get the Hell on with this. And if you throw another throwing star at me again, we will have a problem."

"Is that a threat Richard Steele Jr.?" Mya asked sarcastically.

"No, that is a guarantee, Mya Olivia Wollert," he said back.

"You and I were a mistake," she told him boldly.

"The only mistake I have ever made was walking over to the new neighbors' house to ask a rude, overbearing preteen diva to come over to play basketball," he told her.

"The same preteen diva that kissed you two days later, when you begged her to be your girlfriend," she said.

"I was twelve and Tamika King from up the street turned me down," Rick fired back. "Now get your butt in the car and get out of here. Hurry up because they will be here shortly."

"I count ten," Mya said as she striped out of her street clothes and put her White Rose suit.

"Twelve," Rick corrected her as he put his gear back on. "There are two on the fire escape."

"Who sent them?" she asked.

"Doesn't matter," he told her, "you're just going to kill most of them anymore."

"At least I won't have to worry about them constantly coming back," she told him.

"Obviously, you don't know who I am," Rick told her as he put on his mask and powered on his suit. "Time for a quick game of Take Down."

Mya smiled as she put her mask on and drew her favorite weapons, twin daggers with the white rose as the handle. Rick knew what was going on but also knew if he gave Mya the truth, she would go after the man who betrayed them. Mya walked over to her security system and watch on her notebook as the attackers got into position. It was not the Jade Army.

Recognizing the men by the tattoos, Night Dragon realized it was the Yakuza and he Triads. Night Dragon tossed White Rose a special earpiece from his utility belt. He simply pointed to the ear, and she removed her mask to put it in her ear. She could hear him as he walked towards the security server. He opened a communication link on his gauntlet to Adonai.

"Adonai come in," Night Dragon called his aid with his distorted voice, "I need you to lock onto my signal."

"Yes, Boss I am here," Adonai responded. "I am happy to hear you are okay. I heard everything on the news. Did you get the package?"

"Package secure but we have uninvited guest appearing all over security feeds." Night Dragon said.

"Did your sense find them before the camera, Boss?" Adonai asked.

"You know it, Scan me and surrounding area for tracers or any type of bug. Then I want you to own her security." Night Dragon ordered.

"I was already on the scan the moment you called in, Boss. I just need you to hardwire the PGC to the hard drive," Adonai said as the sound of typing rang out in the background.

"What are you two talking about?" White Rose interjected, "There is no way you can get into my security System."

"Already in Boss," Adonai said as he continued to type away, "I have control of the entire security, and I have also tapped into every phone in the building. They are searching for Mya Wollert. It appears the Jade Army has a reward for her. They keep saying the Dragon's Woman."

"What is this Dragon's Girl bullshit?" White Rose asked. "And how did he get into my security system."

"White Rose, act like an assassin instead of a crazy ex-girlfriend," Night Dragon said as he cut her off. He focused back onto his assistant. "Adonai, do they have any idea what apartment she lives in?" Why the floor to floor search?"

"When she acquired the building, she never released that she lived there as well. The management team didn't know that she was the owner. She is not even listed as the renter's list. It looks like someone was following her." Adonai said as he continued to work on his computer. "They keep referring to The Jade Master wants her."

"That means the bastard is trying to get to me," Night Dragon said. "I think I have one more trick up my sleeve. I need you to put a tracer on her car. Then I need the package ready at the airport."

"Yes, sir," Adonai said. "I figured you would. I placed a trace on her car the moment you took the ride before you turned me off. I also prepared the private jet for your trip to the Dragon Temple."

"Why can't I go to the Dragon Temple?" White Rose asked as she revealed herself back in her street clothes. "I already know what you are going to ask. And you know I want nothing to happen to my residents. But my question is why you won't let me help you get them out of my building and help you with the Dragon Armor. You know you need me."

"You are the reason why I do this," Night Dragon admitted as he opened his face plate and looked her eye to eye. "You and everyone in this building are my reasons to fight. I owe this city and you my life. I promise you will get the man that ruined our families. But you must trust me. Keep the earpiece and place all your gear in the car. I mean load everything that you need in the car. Fill up the front and back seats, including the driver. Then send it down to the ground leave and get back into your apartment. Let them take you. Resist the urge to fight back. Hold everything in. Just be Mya Wollert, middle school teacher. When I give you the sign, unleash the fury of the Rose."

"I will," Mya said as she got lost in his eyes. Her dream man was right in front of her. The man that held her heart since they met as children and grew into adulthood together. "Whatever you desire of my King." She leaned in to kiss him with passion, but Mya was stopped when he pulled her into him. Kissing her with every bit of love, he wanted Mya to know the truth.

"Get started," Night Dragon ordered as he put his face plate back on, "I am going to buy you some time. Oh, and make sure you grab that white number I like."

She smiled as Night Dragon turned to head out of the secret door. Once he stepped out of the closet, he closed the door and started to plan his next move. He knew they must have found her apartment in the management office. He moved to the bedroom windows and place a small glass sensor attached to a small charge. He then set a small charge at the door to blow up once the door was opened. He walked into the living room and could hear the attackers outside her door. The apartment was now a kill box, and he was ready to spring into action.

Night Dragon took out his sword and braced for battle. He knew how many men were at the door and the fire escape. With the curtains drawn, the could not see in. He loved how his beloved turned a would be kill box into a perfect executioner's home. Night Dragon check his gauntlet readings. Adonai found a way to monitor Night Dragon's abilities and health. They could tell when Dragon powers were fading. Looking at his current levels, this was one fight he should avoid.

With his military and educational background, he and Adonai were able to create a new suit that could substitute his stripped away abilities. He also knew that with the fading of his powers meant the fading of his life. The Night Dragon came with a curse the family hid well. The purpose of ascending was to remove the curse for once and for all. He needed to ascend, or it would be the end of the world.

The sound of a squeaky floorboard brought his mind back into focus. He remembered that floorboard from his time living with Mya. Turning his suit into war mode on the gauntlet, his entire suit began to change colors. Normally blue with black trim, his gear turned all black with his eyes and insignia turning bright royal blue.

His visual display took over, and his suit was able to map out attackers and civilians. Spotting the two coming down from the roof. He sheathed his sword took aim at both the windows and front door. His equipment was able to pick up their radio signal, so he listened in.

Just as they were about to rush in, some kids were coming out of an apartment. He heard a scream from the children, and everything changed. He fired to shuriken out of his gauntlets to take out the two coming through the wall. He turned around in time to greet the door crew. Using just his sword, he disarmed all of them with ease. As they looked up from the floor, they were all screaming in pain.

Night Dragon heard the other two on the fire escape about to breached. Taking out two throwing stars, he hurled them through the windows. He missed the sensors he set perfectly. As he heard his targets scream in pain, he walked out to the hallway and saw the children dead. Some of their throats were slit, while others were shot. He walked over to the children to at least see if they were alive.

Tears began to fall as he kneeled at their bodies. Sadly, he found only one child still barely holding on. Night Dragon grabbed the little girl and carried her back into Mya's apartment. He walked over to closet and opened the door. There he found Mya playing the role he requested. She immediately recognized the girl and reached her hands out. The girl reached out to her and held Mya tight. He looked at the pair of them and could not erase the image of the innocent children.

Night Dragon knew who was responsible for this. His plan and control faded from his mind. Filled with vengeance, he turned off his gauntlet and tapped into his abilities. It was time to unleash the Midnight Monster. He closed the door but looked at Mya for the last time. He knew they would come after her and take them both. Before they did, he was going to kill most of them before they took her.

"Adonai make sure you keep an eye on her," Night Dragon said as he left the bedroom. "I am heading to the temple. As soon as I get the in the air, operate the garden."

"Yes, Sir," Adonai told him, "Your package is a block away. Shall I also be ready to pick you up from the temple?"

"No," Night Dragon ordered, "this is the last time you and I will speak. You have served me well. Now serve my queen."

"I understand, Boss," Adonai replied. "I am already getting everything together."

"Adonai, I do not want you and White Rose coming for me," he told his assistant, "There is no way either can leave this city unprotected. I want them out tonight. Goodbye my friend."

With that said, he shut off his headset and drew his sword. He walked back into the living room to find more men but dressed in Samurai Armor. Without delayed, Night Dragon unleashed his anger and rage. Each slice of his sword took a piece of his life energy. He continued to fight sending them through walls and out of windows. He could since his enemy nearby. However, he was not his normal self. As he took on each man, he did not hold back.

When he was done, the samurai were now well-dressed corpses. He could feel his life on the verge of fading. The samurai never once touched him, but his curse was taking a hold on him. Falling to his knees, Night Dragon began to gasp for air. It was then, the enemy he was truly waiting for appeared.

As he struggled to breathe and focus, his brother, the murderer, appeared. No matter the role or story given, Rick Steele always knew the truth. This was all part of the plan. Everything was planned down to this every moment. He left a bread trail that his so-called brother would pick up and plan against him. Standing in his full Jade Samurai Armor and a bright green shining glow, Hero Steele stood before Rick Steele. Now he was known as Mayor Lee Heto to the world, except Rick Steele and The Night Dragon. Taking out his sword, he welcomed Night Dragon in for the fight. Clearing the room, he stood before Night Dragon alone.

"I take it that you no longer want to be the Night Dragon Brother Hero," Night Dragon said, "Or should I say Mayor Heto."

"How did you know, Brother?" The Jade Samurai said as he removed his helmet.

"Does it matter?" Night Dragon said. "I am going to stop you!"

Jumping into action, Night Dragon showcased his master level skills with his sword. The Jade Samurai was no novice. Trained by their father, Richard Steele, the Jade Samurai was also a master swordsman. However, he was also a master of the dark arts. When Night Dragon had him on his knees, the Jade Samurai tossed an energy blast to knock Night Dragon back against the wall. He was slow to rise and fighting to stand up. The Jade Samurai charged his energy for one powerful blow. Night Dragon was dizzy and had blurred vision, but he could see what was coming.

Picking up his sword, he stood to his feet and prepared for the energy bolt. Hurling the energy with all his might, the Jade Samurai laughed as he released the full thrust of his power. Night Dragon had one shot. In one powerful slice, he cut the energy bolt in two. His action sent a shock wave that sent both to the ground. Night Dragon watched as his sword began to melt away into nothing. He knew he had to keep trying as he dropped to one knee. Night Dragon fought to breathe as he could feel not only his powers but his entire life energy fade away.

Night Dragon stood to his feet and at the same time as the Jade Samurai. Exchanging blows back and forth, they each showed the mastery of all martial arts. Moving in closer, Night Dragon took hold of his brother. He hoped that he would not have to kill him, but he knew his brother.

"You are your father's son," Night Dragon said, "You both have taken everything from me. But you are my brother. I will spare you if you turn over the Eye."

"Sorry brother," Jade Samurai said as he grabbed his brother's wrist and flipped him. "You and your family think your peasant way of life is just. I am a Samurai, a Lord of the people. It has always been the destiny of my family to rule this world." Extending his hand, he created a Jade color energy that formed a dagger. "Unlike our fathers, I studied and mastered the powers. Time for you to learn your place and realize we were never brothers!"

Jamming the dagger into Night Dragon's chest, he laughed as he watched him wretch in pain. Picking Night Dragon up off the ground, he showed how powerful he had become. Walking over to the window, he laughed as Night Dragon still had fight in him. Night Dragon throw punches directly to his face, but the proud Samurai warrior laughed at each blow. He lifted Night Dragon above his head and tossed him out of the busted-up window frame. He watched as Night Dragon fell ten stories into the car parked in front of the building.

Looking at his enemy laying there, the Jade Samurai laughed at the ease of killing his enemy. He did not have the armor, but the Soul Stone was enough to obtain all the power he and his generals needed. He reached for remains of Night Dragon's sword. He knew that the sword was made from the same armor. He put his helmet back on and ordered his men back into the room. Telling them to retrieve Mya Wollert, he made his exit to his awaiting car in the garage.

Driving by the car where Night Dragon laid dead, he smiled as he ordered the car to be burned. His men tossed explosives onto the car and all watched in amazement as the car and body burst into flames. Ordering his limo out of there, The Jade Samurai was taken back to the Mayor's Mansion. He laughed and enjoyed his victory. He didn't need anything else but to make Mya his bride. His only concern was the White Rose. However, with his new powers, she was not a problem. With the Dragon burning in his rearview mirror, the Jade Samurai and his army would rule New Peak City by the end of the week. He took one final look at his dead brother. Before he left the scene, he watched as his men whisked Mya and a little girl away to an awaiting helicopter on the roof.

"Finally, the Samurai will bring order to this city," he said to himself out loud.

His limo drove off as his police force made their way to the scene. He was finally in charge and his obstacles were eliminated. It was time to remove the mask he wore for years. He was beloved as Mayor Lee Heto. However, it was time for the world to be formally introduce to Leo Kenzensho Jr, The Grandmaster of the Jade Samurai Army.

THE TREASURES WITHIN

As Night Dragon drifted in and out of consciousness, he hoped that Mya was alright. Everything was planned down to the letter. That all changed when he rushed to her aid last night. Then the fact that his so-called brother took the lives of innocent children further destroyed his mental state. He was now fighting to life, but all his reasons were out of reach. Just before the Samurai and his army made their way to his body, Hollywood and his men saved him. They replaced his body with a corpse in his spare suit. Hollywood's men moved quickly and got him out of there in one smooth move.

Carrying him into the building next door, they quickly got him into an awaiting van. Hollywood was their beside him talking and trying his best to keep him awake. When Night Dragon's pulse started to fade, he ordered his men to pull over and get out. He ordered them to finish up with phase two. Following his ordered they jumped into the SUV that trailed them. Just as they pulled off, Hollywood took off the face plate, so he could give Night Dragon oxygen.

Hollywood was not surprised at the face of the hero. He was too proud of his godson. He promised his partner he would always look after his son. However, it was his godson that was always looking after him and saved him from evil. Putting the oxygen mask around on his face, Hollywood continued to talk to him. He got into the driver's seat and made their way to the awaiting jet.

When they arrived at the airfield, Hollywood was surprised at the size and futuristic of the awaiting plane. With what few words he could put together, he told Hollywood to drive onto the plane. He followed Night Dragon's orders. Once they were inside, the door closed. Hollywood got out and walked over to the back of the van. He grabbed the wounded hero and quickly helped him to his feet. As he carried Night Dragon around, he called out for help but no response. It then that Night Dragon told him that there was nobody else.

Telling Hollywood to take him to the cockpit, Night Dragon said he was the only one that could fly the jet. Placing him in the pilot's chair, Hollywood stood back as Night Dragon began to take off. Once he was in the chair, he hooked up a cord from the control board to his gauntlet. He had already programed the coordinates to the Temple. Now the only concern was if he would make it there in time. Hollywood began searching for some type of first aid medical kit. Once it was found, he rushed over to Night Dragon. He bandaged the wound and tried to keep him awake.

As the autopilot took over, he told Hollywood to take his seat. As the jet began to take off, Night Dragon looked at his city out the side of the window. Taking off into the air, his only worry was the hell he just unleashed. His beloved was fair and just, but she had no more mercy. Her parents were gone, her teacher murdered, and the love of her life could not be with her. He knew she would not have any type of mercy towards Hero and his samurai army. He loved Mya with all his heart, but just like him, when that mask comes on, White Rose is a different creature.

Rick knew he made a mistake all those years ago. He should have told her that he and his father were the Night Dragon. He should have told her about the curse of the Dragon Blue Heart Stone. Since he was born with power of the Heart Stone, he fulfilled the vision of the first Night Dragon centuries ago. Thanks to his and Adonai's work, he was able to extend his life. However, with the energy of the Eye coursing through his bloodstream, his life was in danger. He knew the risks, but he knew it would be the only way to get the power of three.

As he could feel the two powers fighting for the life energy with in him, pain shot out throughout his body. The fact that his plan worked with only one hitch still bothered him. He never thought Mya still loved him. She would serve as the perfect protector of New Peak City. However, he was more determined to ascend for her. For once in his family history, love was the motivation of the Night Dragon. Looking at the horizon, Rick Steele didn't know what was ahead of him. His only concern was to get back home to Mya Wollert.

Once the jet was set on his flight plan, Rick asked Hollywood to grab the IV solution in the Med-Kit he found. He complied to the request, but Hollywood was more concerned about Rick. He passed the solution to Rick and took a deep look at his godson. Looking into his eyes, Hollywood saw the man his father was always trying to be. He let go of the kit and gave Rick a gentle pat on the back. He took his seat and strapped in. Rick smiled as his godfather took his seat. His father would have love to have been there to see his old friend join the team. As he inserted the special medication into his arm, Rick was too familiar with the process as it took no time at all. Secretly he needed the treatment since he was twelve, when his powers started to fully develop.

The Blue Stone was known as the Dragon Heart because it increased the strength, agility, senses of the beholder. It increased the heart of a person to superhuman levels. However, it also took pieces of the life energy of the barer. The Night Dragon had to be mental, physical, and emotional grounded to wear the stone which is embedded within the Dragon insignia. However, with Rick, it is totally different. With the powers within his body due to his family history with the stone, it was only natural that he would be born a hybrid among the bloodline. After major battles the stone and the barer need to recharge. The stone in normally charged by the light of the moon. The barer with the stone will feel a sudden rush of energy in the moonlight. Like a battery, constant recharging will also wear down on the stone.

Rick Steele was the stone made human. He, too, would wear down after major feats of strength and agility. His mother and father began his training early due to his powers appearing after he could walk. At the age of twelve just before his mother was murdered, Rick trained with her when his father called for help while on a mission. She could not leave Rick with anyone, so she took him along.

Arriving on the scene, she had to rescue him from a caved in building. Hovering over the collapsing building in the Dragon Jet, White Rose began to help her husband. In the process of helping him, she had to continue rescuing the hostages Night Dragon was trying to save. While she struggled to hold on to the hostages, his dad's line snapped, and he fell back into the building. Rick was young, but in his heart was the same little boy who began the Night Dragon Legacy.

Dressed in a black Gi from head to toe to protect his identity, Rick took his first step as a hero. He grabbed a rope and leaped into the building. Leading perfectly as if he were wearing the stone himself, he made his way to his injured father. Just as he reached him, the floor caved in once more. Rick was wearing a radio headset, so he kept his mother informed.

Telling her to release the rope from the wench, he took the rope and tied it to a pillar. Tying the other around his waist, he ran towards the hole and dove in. He found his father under a heap of rubble. He untied himself and rushed to his father. His dad was unconscious and not responding. He was buried under concrete and steel. Tapping into his power, the Blue Stone in his blood filled his eyes with blue light. Rick took his father's sword and slice the beam on top of his father with ease. He lifted a huge steel beam off his father's legs and a wall of his chest. He grabbed his father and tossed him over his shoulders. He then took off running at the sight of the building caving into the ground.

As he was running for daylight, his father woke up. When he saw his son rescuing him, he was proud and in awe of his son's true powers.

Young Rick saw a window and told his mother to meet him outside. Picking up speed, his body began to glow the bright blue glow of the Heart Stone. With all his strength, he leaped with his father through the glass into the air. They soared through the air over the Dragon Jet. Landing on the next building, his mother watched in amazement of her son. His father was in pain, but he thanked his son and told Rick how proud he was of him.

Just as he helped his father into the jet, Rick passed out from being drained from his powers. His parents developed the medicine to wake him from the fifteen-day coma he was left in. From that day on, his mother intensified his training until the day she was murdered. When his father took over Rick's training, he unveiled all the secrets to his son. His parents wanted to make sure that his powers were not his demise.

The medicine was a special cocktail that his parents developed, and Adonai was able to improve. After each mission or nightly patrol, he had to take an IV bag treatment to function normally. It had been a week since his last IV treatment. He had been pushing himself to see if he could finally learn to live without it. Once the IV cocktail was in his system, he could feel the battle within him subside. Taking the controls into his hands, Rick Steele could finally feel his first bit of peace as he climbed higher into the clouds. He reached into his utility belt pocket and pulled out the Black Soul Stone. Grinning his sly smile, he was glad he still had the light fingers of his mother. Reliving his fight, he took the risk to get close not only for the Eye energy, but also the Black Soul. He put the stone back into his pocket and turned the plane towards his homeland…Africa.

As he watched the plane fly out of sight, he made sure that his boss was safe and secure. Adonai was just like his father before him. Humble servants of the Night Dragon who owed a life debt. For years, passing down from father to son, they serve the Night Dragon. Promising to devote their lives to help him protect the innocent, the entire family served the Night Dragon and White Rose. Keeping their secrets while refusing to know their real names. In a way, it was the only way to truly protect the only fair justice in an unfair world.

Focusing on his next mission, he pulled up the security cameras in the building. He hated to break the rule, but his boss ordered him too. For the last few years, he helped to keep an eye on Mya Wollert and the White Rose. For a while, he thought they were two different people. However, Night Dragon decided that Adonai had deserved and earned the right to know everything.

Night Dragon revealed the identity of White Rose to Adonai with the mission to protect and assist her without her knowledge. When the time came, it would be Adonai's job to assist her in becoming the protector of New Peak City. Just as he was about to open a link to speak with her a message came in. Before leaving for his mission, Night Dragon set up a previously recorded message for Adonai.

"Adonai," Night Dragon called out through his distorted voice machine, "You and your family have served my family for far too long. For every Dragon before me, we thank you. I have revealed more to you because I don't see you as my assistant. You are my partner and friend. Night Dragon his only as strong as the team he has behind him. The power of three has always worked. It is the real secret power of the Night Dragon. I now have the power of all three stones with me now. Once I ascend, I may not return. Your mission is to not only help White Rose, but to also bring justice and protect New Peak City, yourself. You must protect White Rose from consuming Mya Wollert. You will find the new armor and weapons specks attached to the file. They were a gift from my dad to my mom. She will be able to use them. Also remember to unlock the Greenhouse. She will need access to the White Rose files and archives. You will also find weapons and weapons designed just for you. You and your family will be taken care of. Lastly, you deserved the full truth."

Removing his helmet, the Night Dragon persona was finally removed before Adonai. Pulling off an additional mask, Night Dragon revealed his true self. Adonai watched as Rick Steele Jr. presented himself to his lifelong friend. He watched as his mysterious friend finally let him in. Adonai continue to watch as the plans and desires of his boss were revealed. After watching the video and looking at the plans from his boss and previous Dragons. He began to process the data and quickly began to build the tools for the new protector of New Peak City. Just as he began to work, a call came in on the lair. It was coming from Mya's earpiece.

"Hello," Mya called out, "Is there anyone there? Hello? Can you her me?"

"Yes, ma'am. This is Keyz. I will be assisting from this point on. Are you ready to escape ma'am?" he asked. As he began programing the varies weapons and tools for her usage, Adonai pinpointed her location with the built-in GPS. He was ready to do whatever she needed to get the job done.

"Yes, Keyz," Mya said as she spoke softly, "How soon can you send an extraction?"

"I can have you out of there in no time, but I can have White Rose there to pick you up in exactly thirty minutes. Wait…am I reading your location correctly?" Have you…"

"Yes, I am at the Mayor's Mansion," Mya cut him off. "Send her as soon as you can. It is time for her to introduce herself to the world."

"Yes, Boss," Adonai told her proudly, "I am sending the Fair Lady now."

HAIL TO THE QUEEN

As she sat in the Mayor's Mansion, she questioned the mayor's motives for the assault on her building. According to the media and other sources, she was the target of retribution against the former police detective Rick Steele. Apparently, the Night Dragon and his ninjas carried a huge vendetta for the local hero. They would not rest until his memory and family were wiped off the face of the Earth. It was for that reason the Mayor launched his new special unit of police called the Samurai Guard. Lead by Detective Lopez, they were the special unit set up to handle and maintain marshal law the Mayor issued on the city. The Samurai Guard was a mix of the Swat Unit, Military soldiers, and the old Samurai of Feudal Japan. Mya knew exactly what that meant. Within a month, she knew that every cop in New Peak City would be replaced.

After Night Dragon left the child with her, Mya forced herself to stay in that closet. She knew that he could handle the fight, but she wanted to unleash her rage. Mya was a teacher simply because of her love of children. When she wore that White Rose mask, her love intensified. She protected children with her very own life. Mya would move many children and their families into her building off the streets.

Most of her students were tenants in her building. It was getting to the point where she had them living there rent free.

Creating a program that helped those parents get training, education, and work experience, Mya created a village that her parents and Rick's parents always spoke of. In Mya's mind, every corrupt, evil being White Rose vanquished, created that village.

When that door opened, she hoped to see Night Dragon. Mya tried to hide her rage when Lopez appeared. She put on the front that she was happy to see Lopez and her Samurai Guard. As she was ushered out of her apartment and out of the building, she could feel eyes following her out. She knew who it was and could not wait to break his neck. She saw what his men did to the children and fought back the urged to kill.

As she continued to play the role of damsel in distress, she almost snapped when she saw Night Dragon stretched out on top of the crushed car. Mya fought back tears as she watched the Mayor in his Jade Samurai armor set his body on fire. There was a long shot, but there was a chance that Night Dragon survived the fall due to his powers and armor. Everything changed when she saw his body set on fire and burned. The little girl was taken to the hospital for treatment. While she was whisked away to be treated and united with family, Mya was taken to the Mayor's Mansion at the Mayor's urgent request.

When she arrived, she was taken to a bedroom and locked inside. Once she realized what was going on, she quickly began to check the room for bugs. It was a habit she formed due to her business. Hidden in her watch was a special scanner for listening devices and tracking dots. As she checked the room, she made it look like she was pacing back and forth staring at her watch. Mya also searched for cameras and any two-way mirrors. She was anxious to get to work. She was going to end her successful assassin business and focus solely on revenge.

For as long as she could remember, Night Dragon served this city. Even when she thought he murdered her teacher, Mya thought it was because of her assassinations of crime bosses and murderers. He was the masked lawman that was serving justice. She now had to make sure that someone was there to take his place. To Mya, it was time for White Rose to make a real stand.

Once the room was clear and safe, she used the earpiece still in her ear. Thanks to her long natural hair, she was able to have it without being noticed. Turning the earpiece on, she immediately tried to reach out to the voice she heard earlier. Once the man was on the other end, she knew she was about to have fun.

After she gave the okay to Keyz, Mya began to plan her escape. She looked outside the windows and spotted that the Samurai Guard covered the front of the house heavily. Since she was locked in that room, Mya could not see anything else. She hated to improvise. She really hated the situation when she saw the news crews parking in front of the mansion.

It was at that moment she decided to follow in the footsteps of Night Dragon. It was time to make a statement to the Mayor and the Jade Army. She knew that Mayor Lee Heto would show up soon and make his intensions known. She never trusted him anyway. Mya always had feeling that he was involved with Kenzensho. As White Rose, she tried to collect as much evidence as possible to have a plan ready. On one occasion she almost caught him in the throne room with Kenzensho plotting. It wasn't until she saw him in the samurai armor at her apartment, that she gained her evidence. Even if it were for a split second through a keyhole, it was all she needed to see.

Remembering that a true ninja works in the shadows, she knew that she could do more damage that way and reveal all of truth. In her eyes, he was guilty and deserved to be punished. However, death was too good, too simple and too quick of a punishment for him.

Hearing footsteps, she put her watch's special feature away and started her next acting role. Mya was not surprised that it was the Mayor himself. Dressed in one of his custom three-piece suits, he moved with the swagger of a conquering King. She could already see the next play coming from the would-be Casanova. If she wanted to make the next move the best move, Mya had to keep her cool and reframe from splitting his face open with her bare hands. In her mind she tried to keep her cool, but her strong black woman card would not let her. She wanted to light into him, but thanks to Keyz in her ear keeping her calm, she kept her rage in check.

"What the hell is going on?" she screamed at the Mayor. "What am I doing here? Why are you keeping me here? I promise you, I will have my attorney and the NAACP here on you like that! You have no right to hold you hostage!"

"Ms. Wollert, I apologize for the delay," the Mayor began to plead for forgiveness. "It was brought to my attention that you were the target in an ungodly war between the criminals of this city and law enforcement. It appears that you past associations have made you a target to a very deadly man."

"What are you talking about? I am a middle school English and Math teacher at Thomas Junior High. I have no past or present associations to justify my students being killed and my home being destroyed," Mya said to put him in his place.

"Yes, Ms. Wollert, I am sorry for the loss of your students today. I will be speaking to the families very shortly. I just wanted to explain what happened today," he expressed.

"I am still waiting on why my students were killed and why my home was destroyed?" Mya demanded.

"Your former fiancé, Richard Steele, was recently murdered in that vicious car bomb. I am sorry for your loss. However, due to the nature of his work and his success rate, he made a lot of enemies with the city's underworld. One of them being the masked assassin called Night Dragon. Detective Steele was on the verge of capturing him and his compatriots," the Mayor explained.

"What does the work of my ex-boyfriend have to do with me?" Mya asked reluctantly, "He chose to fight crime than to fight for me. He loved this city more than he ever could love me. Now why are you keeping me hostage?"

"Well, I do apologize," he began to explain, "I made a promise to my old friend that I would always take care of his family. You probably don't remember me. I was always a little shy around you and my big brother, Rick."

"Hero, is that you? Mya asked puzzled, "I thought you died in a plane crash?"

"In a way, I did," he told her. "I survived the plane crash, barely. I was originally pronounced dead at the scene like everyone else. Locally, a paramedic didn't give up on me. I was badly burned and in a coma. I was overseas and alone when everything happened. When I was older, I legally changed my name. I separated from the family because of a fight with Steele. I had to have plastic surgery to repair my face. I was never the same again. I just feel guilty that never let them know I was alive and back in town. I made a promise a long time ago to take care of the family. I missed out with Dad and Rick. I don't want to miss out with you."

"Well thank you for your concern, but no thank you," Mya declared. "I will miss Rick, but he and I severed ties years ago. I shed my tears for him already. I just want to live in peace. Now if you don't mind, I have to go to the families of my students."

"I understand your feelings," the Mayor added. "However, you are now the target of vicious killers. My new Samurai Guard eliminated Night Dragon, but his followers are going to look for blood. I have ordered that you be placed in protective custody. If you would like to, you can stay here in the Mayor's Mansion. It is a fortress. You will be safe here, with me."

"Look, you can't keep me here and I refuse your protection," Mya told him straight, "Besides after tonight, I have had it with New Peak City." Just as she was about to make it to the door, she heard the music to her ears.

"Boss, the Lady has arrived," Adonai whispered into her earpiece. "Brace yourself."

"I want to go home," Mya demanded as she focused on the lying Mayor. "You brought me here, you can take me to a hotel."

Before the mayor could say a word, there was a furious knock at the door. The Mayor answered the door to find it was Lopez. She whispered in his ear and his facial expression changed drastically. He tried to remain quiet, but his anger was unable to be hidden. Sending her out with orders, he slammed the door.

"Mya, you have to stay here," he declared, "The other killer is attacking now. You will be safe here. Once my men have her in custody, you will be free to go. I promise."

Just as those words, were spoken, the lights went out. Mya let out a blood curling scream. The Mayor called out her name and reached out for her only to be flipped onto his back. Receiving a mean punched to the face, he was knocked unconscious for a couple of minutes. Within no time, Lopez and her men broke down the door to find the Mayor laying on his back. Rushing over to help him, Lopez tried to figure out how White Rose got pass them. Ordering his Samurai Guard to find Mya and kill White Rose, the Mayor's eyes began to glow jade green due to his building rage.

Mya was grinning from ear to ear at the sight of egg on the Mayor's face. She was hiding inside the laundry basket. She watched and waited for them to clear the room. Once the close was clear, she made her way to the door. She waited until the hallway was clear. Mya made her way to the dumbwaiter she spotted as she was escorted into the mansion. Once she was inside, she climbed down to the basement.

As soon as she reached the basement, Mya found her care package waiting. While she was dealing with the Mayor, her new assistant found a way to crash a car through the front gate. While guards responded to the crash, he managed to use his computer skills to hack into the mansion computer system. Causing some equipment and tools to go haywire, he created the perfect distraction. Just when the guards approached the crash car, machine guns appeared from panels of the car and opened fire.

When the action started, Adonai found his way into the house and quietly hid in wait for Mya. Presenting himself to Mya, he proudly introduced himself as Keyz, but Mya already knew his real name. Adonai was not surprised. Night Dragon told him that Mya was always ahead of the game. Without delay, he provided Mya with her gear and quickly went to guard the door. While he watched the door, he made sure to keep his eye on all the surveillance cameras through his tablet. He was already plotting their escape while Mya made sure to leave no trace of her presence.

Within no time, White Rose was ready to wreak havoc. Adonai had a mask that hid his entire face. Giving the him permission, White Rose ordered all the camera feeds to be killed. Moving out of the basement, she wanted to get them out of their before they could be spotted. It was then that she realized she needed a hostage. Grabbing a sheet, she smiled through her eyes at her idea. It wasn't a perfect idea, but Night Dragon would have love it.

The Mayor and Lopez were standing in the middle of the foyer. They were barking orders as the Samurai Guard searched for Mya and White Rose. As negative reports continued to come in, the Mayor was beginning to lose control of his anger. White Rose wore a huge smile under her mask. While she watched from the shadows of the air vent, she sent a text message to Adonai to begin their perfect escape. She began to laugh out loud proudly. Her laughter echoed throughout the entire mansion.

Anger and frustration filled the room at the sound of White Rose toying with them. Suddenly there were loud pops ringing out. It was light bulbs exploding thanks to Adonai. Then all the other electrically devices began to explode. When the televisions and monitors began to explode, everyone pulled out their guns and took aim in any direction they heard her laughter echo.

"You honestly think you will get away with murder," White Rose said between the laughter. "Amateur fool! You dare to murder a man then try to sleep with his woman! I will personally send you to your special place in Hell!"

"Show yourself you peasant bitch!" the Mayor ordered. You will learn your place in my world. You breathe because I allowed you to for this long." Just as he spoke those words, the lights all went completely dead. The Mayor and his henchmen were standing in the darkness.

"Who are you calling a bitch!" White Rose said as she appeared as the light turned back on. She stood in the middle of the foyer with a dagger against the Mayor's throat. "I see why both Steele and Night Dragon were ready to kill you. You mouth writes a check your ass can't cash."

"Look, you fake wanna be," Lopez said as she took one step towards White Rose. "Know your place when you are in the presence of the Mayor. I will personally cut your tongue out and feed it to my dog."

"Oh, so that is the way you landed Taka," White Rose said laughing. Lopez and her men were about to open fire when White Rose stopped them in their tracks. "Stop or the Mayor dies. Check your pocket Mayor. You will find a nice compact explosive that looks like your pen. It is amazing what one can do in the dark. Especially for someone with a glass jaw."

Ordering his Samurai to lower their weapons, he held himself in check. The Mayor knew that he was not strong enough to handle such a threat yet. He was still learning and mastering his powers. Backing out of the room, White Rose held the remote where everyone could see it. Just as she was about to leave the room, she let out a sinister laugh while pressing the button. The guards and Lopez hit the ground to brace for the explosion. Instead of a bomb, White Rose triggered a super charged stun gun. As electricity surged through his body, the Mayor feel to the ground in agonizing pain. Exiting the room, White Rose took off at top speed. Seeing her master on the ground, Lopez leaped at the chance for revenge. Ordering her men to help the Mayor, she chased after White Rose.

Running to the back-patio doors, White Rose was reaching for the handle when she was tackled from behind by Lopez. They both crashed through the glass and wood framed doors. White Rose hopped up on her feet and tried to run. However, Lopez was not going to allow her. She charged White Rose with a knife only to be blocked by quick hands. She slapped away the thrusts from Lopez's blade like each was just an annoying fly. In one move, White Rose simply grabbed Lopez's wrist, kicked her in the face, and finally flipped her back into the house via a window.

White Rose had no time to enjoy the embarrassing scene. Adonai already was in the escape vehicle behind the mansion. Out of nowhere, guns were firing at her. Running towards the back fence, White Rose leaped the high barrier like it was just a small puddle. She knew something had to be different about her gear, but she didn't have the time to ask. Hopping into Night Dragon's favorite car nickname the Slayer, she jumped into the passenger seat and allowed Adonai to take them to safety.

"So, Adonai?" White Rose began to ask, "Do you have somewhere to hide? I seem to be homeless for right now."

"Yes boss," he told as he began to correct her. "The Night Dragon has left you his Lair in his absence for tonight. Tomorrow, we head to the Greenhouse. He wanted you to have it since his mother left it for you ma'am. I had all your equipment and your car moved there. Also, ma'am Keyz is just a call sign when you are in unfriendly territory. Whenever you are in need, I will take care of it, boss."

"I know you will Adonai," she told him. "It is nice to meet you. How far are we from the lair? We need to make sure we are not followed before we get there."

"Already taken care of, Boss," he told her as he cruised at top speed. I took out all their vehicles and destroyed all communications around the mansion. If fact, I forgot the special present Night Dragon left for the Mayor."

Pressing a button, he told White Rose to look back towards the mansion. In a blink of an eye, a huge explosion flashed, and a fireball went flying in the air. The crashing sound of the metal frame falling back to the ground could be heard for miles. White Rose turned around and just gave Adonai a pat on the back.

"Great work!" she told him. "Remind me to let you handle all my getaways."

After he drove around to make sure they were not followed, he turned down a sewer access road. White Rose was surprise by the location, but she began to recognize the neighborhood as her own. The sewer access road lead into river canal. As they drove through the canal, she spotted her building. They continued into the darkness, but as they moved, they began to go deeper into the river. It reached a point when they were driving in the river. Adonai pushed a button and a secret wall opened.

As water rushed into the opening, the car pushed through and the door closed behind them. Following the lights directing the path, they moved up a long ramp. At the top of the ramp was a circular parking slot. Once they parked, the slot began to raise. Moving up a hundred feet, it finally stopped. Lights began to turn on revealing a garage full of toys. Adonai got out of the car, and White Rose quickly followed behind him. They entered an elevator that immediately took them up to the Dragon's Lair.

The door opened to reveal the office and inner sanctum of Night Dragon. She removed her mask and walked around. She began to see him working away at his massive computer and work desk. As she continued to walk around, White Rose paused in front of the case the held and envelope with her name type on the door. Inside the case was a new uniform that looked better than his own uniform.

White Rose disappeared as she read the handwritten letter from Rick Steele. Confessing his deepest feelings, desires, and plans, he told her everything. When she was done, tears were falling. Adonai knew she needed to be alone. He led her to Night Dragon's chair at his desk and turned on the video. He left room to allow her to have one last private moment. Adonai knew that his friend was in love with her. As he closed the door, he took on more look at the Queen of the Dragon's heart. It was time for her to assume the throne. He left her to enter the apartment through the hidden door.

The entire wall closed as Adonai walked into Steele's apartment. He went into the kitchen and prepared a simple meal. It was a habit of his to prepare a week's worth of meals for his boss. Steele would work and not eat. Sometimes he went without sleep, so Adonai made sure to be there to keep him healthy.

Remembering what Steele told him what Mya's favorite meal was, Adonai always had that meal prepared every week. In a way, it was Rick's way of remembering his love for Mya. Adonai prepared the meal and took it to her as soon as it was done. Knocking before he entered, he waited for her to invite him in.

Walking into the room, he found Mya at the desk reading the journals and papers from the small library. Placing the warm food next to her, he proceeded to tell her where she could change clothes and sleep. He left her alone to finish his duties. However, Mya didn't want to be alone. Inviting him to stay, she asked questions and had Adonai explain all he knew.

They worked into the morning hours only to fall asleep respectively at the work bench and desk. Adonai woke up when his arms and legs started to hurt from the awkward position. Mya was still sleep and holding Rick's last family photo in her arms. Adonai picked her up in his arms and carried her to the bedroom. He tucked her in while she continued to hold on to the picture.

Once in the bed, she turned to the side and began to smile in her sleep. Adonai knew she was thinking about Rick because of the way she held his pillow tightly. Adonai smiled because he knew his friend would be home soon and his home would be complete when he returned. He closed the bedroom door and made sure the apartment was locked down. He went into his apartment across the hall and laid down. He knew that when he got up later, his training would begin. He needed to rest so that he could take on the mantle given to him by Night Dragon…the Phantom Wolf.

As Adonai and Mya finally gained rest and peace of mind, across town, the Mayor and Lopez were being treated by the Mayor's private physicians. The special gift Night Dragon left for White Rose created a major health issue. He tried to use his powers to end the grueling torture. However, tapping into his new powers intensified the electric shock and caused an aneurism. He was now in a coma like sleep. Lopez suffered from a concussion. She came to after being thrown through the glass window.

When Lopez rushed back to see about her Master, finding him suffering from a seizure then passing out before her eyes, her rage took over. She rushed out the front door to give chase, but Lopez was halted by the explosion. It sent her flying back through the mahogany French doors. Lopez's head and neck took most of the force when she landed. She now laid in the room next to the Mayor with an angry, vengeful monster watching over her.

General Taka had never felt this way about anyone before. He lived many lifetimes over in the name of the Jade Army. Both alive and dead, he has served his Jade Master and rained chaos down on the world. In all that time, he had never felt that way about another soul. His loyalty was always to the Jade Samurai and the Jade Army. All that changed when he first met Layla Lopez.

When he was alive, women were his toys. He was known for celebrating his victories with the women of his conquered enemies. After each conquest, he would violently rape and murder the women of his enemies. When he was not taking lives, he was creating Hell on Earth for the innocent and weak. While alive women feared him but still would throw themselves at him. When he gave his life willingly to become the undead monster, his destruction and mayhem grew to no limit.

As Kenzensho grew with power without aging, the monster became more monstrous and uglier. Unlike his former master, he could not go out in public. He was not as feared until he showed his true destructive power. Then it all changed when he was handpicked by the Mayor to be Lopez's teacher in the Jade Army. He was ordered to teach and guide her in the ways of the Samurai.

Kenzensho hated the idea until his master agreed in the Mayor's choice. Taka was hesitant at first, but he could feel the Samurai heart within her. Teaching her that she was more than some badge toting street thug. She honored her sensei with each mission. He knew she was more than capable of taking out Night Dragon and White Rose. He was proud when she was promoted to the Mayor's Head Samurai Guard. As he watched her sleep, he worried that his knew form would keep him from his mission. For General Taka, it was always the next mission. He only wanted to please his master and gain his honor. Now everything changed the night she kissed him.

Taka and Lopez completed her training and were on a mission. A major crime family decided to move onto the master's territory. They were given the kill orders. In one night, they executed and destroyed an entire crime family without malice. Just as they took out the boss, his loyal lieutenant tried to avenge him. Layla knew that Taka was undead, but she put her heart into her sensei and his teachings. He fired a shot while Taka's back was turned. Lopez leaped in front of Taka and took the bullet to the gut. Taka turned in time to see her take the bullet and fall into his arms.

Holding her as she fell to the ground, he looked into her eyes as he could feel the life ooze out of her. He eyes glowed Jade green as he stared into her eyes just before they rolled into the back of her head. Leaping to his feet, General Taka grabbed his war axe and hurled it at full strength. The blade went cleanly through the lieutenant's chest. Pinning him to the wall, he was still alive somehow. Taka slowly walked to his prey growling out his rage. When he was face to face to the pinned man, he grabbed the injured man's head and began to squeeze. With both hands wrapped around his head, Taka applied all his strength in his hands. He squeezed and squeezed as blood began to pour from his eyes, ears and mouth. Taka laughed as he squeezed. In a blink of the eye, the man's head exploded like a melon.

Blood and brain matter covered his face and chest. He walked over to Lopez and held her in his arms. He could feel her slipping away. Tapping into his powers, Taka beamed his powers out of him eyes and mouth. Layla's body began to glow green as Taka's powers began entering her body. The bullet was pushed out of her body and the wound began to rapidly heal as if it never happened. As she came back to life, she opened her eyes to see Taka passing his Jade energy to her. The action intensified her feelings she developed for her undead sensei.

Without warning she pulled him in for a passionate kiss. Taka kissed her back, and the hint of love finally entered his deceased soul. He helped her to stand on her feet. They looked into each other's eyes with a desire that neither of them had ever experienced. They grabbed their weapons and walked out of the small private bar in the Little Italy part of New Peak City. Just as they climbed into their waiting getaway van, Lopez pulled out a remote.

With a simple nod from Taka, she pressed the button that activated explosives attached to the gas line. The flames and the debris began to fall from the sky. They pulled away from the scene and not a word was spoken. Both rode in silence due to the boundary that was broken. Taka and Lopez made their way to the hideaway the Master set up for them to get rid of evidence. The location was a cabin in the woods. It was where they would continue the last of her training before gaining her elite status. Pulling up to the cabin, Taka got out of the van and made his way to the cliff just above the cabin overlooking the entire forest. A few minutes later, Lopez joined him in silence.

"We cannot go any further," Taka told him. "Our duty is to the Master. We are to serve the Jade Army."

"Sensei, I will serve the Master and the Jade Army with honor," Lopez told him, "But my body belongs to only you, Taka."

Kissing him with all the new life he just gave her, Lopez made it clear that she belonged to him. Taking Lopez in his arms, bit by bit, he ripped away her armor and clothes. Having his way with his student, he allowed life to enter his heart for the first time in centuries. Right there in the light of the moon, he took her body, and she humbly submitted to him.

From that point on, they were only separated by her day job on the police force. She kept that secret from all her so-called friends and family. Only the Jade Army and her Master knew of her promise and life oath to Taka. Becoming Taka's right hand, Lopez helped to educate him on the current century, while he taught her the sins and torturous act of the Samurai History.

Now as he sat at her bedside, his rage continued to build. Instead of the hospital, the Mayor and Lopez were transported the skyscraper the Samurai called their base. Kenzensho's building had its own medical unit the Jade Army used constantly. He could not take it anymore. Taka jumped up from her bedside and rushed into the Mayor's room. He could now move freely through the mansion due to the Samurai Guard surrounding the building. The Samurai sealed off the entire block as a precaution.

Walking into the room, he saw Thorton speaking to the doctor. He walked over to Thorton and just looked him dead in the eye. Exchanging glances, Thorton looked him back in his monstrous eyes and simply nodded approval. Taka turned, rushed out, and made his way to his dungeon in the bottom of the building. There he trained his undead warriors. He trained them to show no mercy and death before dishonor. In his dungeon, he walked into his private war room. Taking his War Staff of the mantle, he ordered for it to be sharpen and his warrior to be ready for war. After the destruction of his War Axe, he knew the battle would not be easy. With Layla lying in that bed, Taka needed to release his anger.

Pulling out a picture of White Rose, he ordered that she be captured and left alive. Her head belonged to the Master and Lopez. Any warrior that killed her would be brought back to life just for Taka to destroy slowly. He returned to his war room and began to plan the destruction of White Rose and New Peak City. His master and woman were laying in hospital beds clinging to life. That meant that he had to kill an entire city in their honor.

Upstairs in the penthouse, the doctors were pleased with the improvements in Lopez's health. She was still asleep due to the heavy medication. The bruises on her brain finally stopped swelling. However, the only concern they all shared was her memories. The part of the brain where memoires are stored took most of the damage. Only time would tell if she would ever be the same again.

The main concern of everyone was the status of the Mayor. The cameras caught the attack just before the entire area lost electricity, radio, phone and any other signals. The entire area was sent back to the dark ages as White Rose released her fury on the Mayor and his Samurai Guard. Unknown to his men and the doctors, The Mayor was in the room. His powers backfired on him however he was still awake and in control.

Astro projection was his only way to save his brain and powers from the trap White Rose used. It appeared that Night Dragon was still getting the last laugh. He recognized the pen from the fight with Night Dragon in the evidence vault. It was one of the many weapons that were booby trapped. However, he altered it, so that it would only affect the powers of the Jade Eye. The Mayor's body was now fighting to save itself from self-destruction. As he watched his men protect him and plan the Jade Army's revenge, he felt true pride. Under his father, they still would be fighting for control from the other organizations in New Peak City.

The Mayor continued to watch over his men as he tried to tap into the spiritual world. Heto needed to know how to save his own life. As he continued to summon his master, another spirit began to respond to his call. However, to his surprise, it was not the Jade Emperor. It was his recently disgraced father. Laughing at his son's current state. He enjoyed to seeing him suffer. To him it helped to build the case to become the Jade Samurai. Due to the shared connection between the Jade Eye. The Emperor and Kenzensho can only see what the Mayor could see. To their knowledge Heto's only positive accomplishment was the complete destruction of their only formidable foe, the Night Dragon.

As his spirit stood before the spirit of his father, he could feel the anger building. The years of disrespect and hatred between them has lasted since the day the Mayor could walk. Finding out that he was born of the Jade Eye, gave him abilities just as Night Dragon. Ever since he found the truth about his father, Mayor Heto plotted his revenge. Tricking his father's enemy into taking him in, he initially wanted to kill the Steeles'. However, the way Richard Sr. and his son took him in to help him be his own man, Heto was partially ready to leave his path of revenge. Everything changed when his adopted brother was still chosen to be the Night Dragon. He allowed the revenge within him to take over. Heto knew that his destiny was in total world domination.

Learning his heritage, he went ahead with his plan. The night he killed Richard Sr. was the first and only time his father worked together with him. Bringing his son into the Jade Army, Kenzensho showed that he was a father by giving his son instant high status. That was only thing he did for his son. Now as he stood spirit to spirit, essence to essence, there was no love or family connection between the two. With everything in him, the Mayor had to focus on healing his body. He had to get back to his body soon or be stuck in the spirit plain.

"Your disrespect and dishonor are my fuel, father," the Mayor told his father. His Jade Essence began to glow and shine brighter. He saw the look in his father's eyes. It was not a look of fear, but a look of pride. Extending hand out, Kenzensho reached for his son's hand. The Mayor took his hand and a surge of power was released into him.

"You have honored me," Kenzensho said as he released his remaining powers to his son. "Now fulfil the legacy of our family."

Absorbing his father's energy, the secrets of his father were finally revealed. Their mind meld into one. The Mayor gained the answers for what he desired for many years. As his father gave away his remaining power, he began to fade away. His father completely dissolved away into nothing and left the Mayor all alone. The Jade Eye was still with him and began to emit green electrical sparks. The Eye was completely taking over him now. He could feel the Eye connecting him back to his body and changing him completely. In a brilliant flash, he was out of the spirit realm. Opening his eyes, he found himself surrounded by Thorton and the Samurai Guard.

"Everyone out, I must speak with the Commissioner?" the Mayor said. "Now!"

"Everyone out and I want all of the Doctors to be sworn to secrecy," Thorton ordered as he forced everyone out of the room. Pulling one of the guards aside, he whispered his true orders. "Keep the head doctor and one of the nurses here. The men can have fun with the rest of them." He turned his attention back to the Mayor and rushed by his side. "Yes, Master."

"Where is Taka and Lopez?" he asked Thorton. "And where is Mya Wollert?"

"Lopez is hurt, sir" he admitted. She attempted to chase after White Rose, but a car bomb injured her. She is in the next room. We don't know if she will be any good to you. Taka is preparing his men to avenge you and Lopez. Just say the world and he will draw out the White Rose."

'What about Mya Wollert," he asked again. "Where is she?"

"We do not know. She could not be found when we searched the house or the neighborhood. I have men stationed outside her place to retrieve her as soon as she returns. Also, sir, I have news…"

"Night Dragon is still alive," he cut him off, "That peasant is like a street magician. He must have help. I want him. Put guards within a ten-mile radius of this building. He will be coming for the Soul Stone. Put it inside the vault and get me Taka."

Just as he retrieved the stone from his chain around his neck, he found the true reason his powers back fired on him. The Mayor held in his hand a replica of the Soul Stone. It was badly burned from the electric shock from the pen. Closer inspection revealed that it was a power amplifier. His rage was now at his boiling point.

"Tell Taka to burn this city to the ground," the Mayor ordered. "Let him ascend, when he returns, he will find his bitch and his partner strung up. Night Dragon and White Rose will be executed. And his woman, Mya, will watch everything from our marriage bed. Then I will take her head. He will meet the Jade Samurai at full strength. I will bring my Emperor the head of the Night Dragon even if I must burn this entire planet. Go and do my bidding."

Leaving out of the room, Thorton was more than pleased with the orders given to him. He passed by Lopez room and stopped in. Looking at her, he never truly respected her. He may have been an outsider to the culture, but he was also a student of the old Samurai Code. No woman was meant to be a noble or warrior. They were property. When she became the property of Taka in his eyes, she only earned the place of being Taka's personal lap dog.

With his new master, he never voiced his option. He remained in his place. However, he never missed an opportunity to rain down his form of justice and order. Now as he looked at the motivation of Taka's true power, he began to plan his next move. Walking over, he looked at her sleeping face.

Thorton was pleased that she respected her role and place in the Jade Army. He placed his hand on her exposed leg and ran up to her thighs. He still felt the scar from the night she stepped out of line. He was drunk, and she was a rookie on the force. Raping her right there in the police department, he asserted his dominance. It was a secret she was forced to keep due to his name, status, and vicious nature. He smiled as he turned to give Taka the news.

As he made his way towards the underground war room, Thorton planed his own rise to the throne. What was unknown to him, Layla Lopez was reliving her vicious rape over and over in her unconscious state. Even though Lopez was unconscious, her senses still worked. Smelling his unforgettable stench sparked her memory of that night. Over and over, it played in his mind. No matter what she did to fight, it was useless. She was now trapped in her mind, reliving the night she died again and again.

THE HEART, EYE, AND SOUL

The jet was finally approaching their destination. Hollywood slept the entire way as Rick remained awake to fly and receive his treatment. With the battle of the Heart and Eye within his body, he was constantly swapping out the IV cocktail to deal with the pain. He has never experienced pain like that before nor had his body reacted to his medicine the way it was now. It appeared to ease the pain away, but it was only temporary.

As soon as one IV was complete, he needed another immediately. The pain continued to get worse as they flew nonstop from America to Africa. Thanks to his advance tech, Rick was able to travel without refueling or depending on anyone else. Just as he was checking his current flight path, an incoming video call came in. He normally welcomed the call, but his current situation was not favorable.

Three masked figures greeted Rick with the traditional greeting. Forming fists across their chest and giving a simple nod. Rick simply nodded and welcomed the call from his brothers and sisters. Raised on different continents and dealt different roles in life, they all shared the proud profession as protectors in their native lands. Finding out about each other during Rick's heritage quest. While he served in the Marines, he used his worldwide traveling to complete this rite of passage for the Night Dragon.

Following the writings of his father and grandfathers all the way to the first Night Dragon Warrior. Meeting while he was stationed in Africa, Japan, and the Middle East, he met his fellow students of the Shadow Guard while tracing the roots of the original orphaned Night Dragon. Finding the creation of the Shadow Guard in his travels, he learned that they were all students of his great, great grandfather and his first team of heroes. Little did he know that he would need them to protect the world against the greatest weapon ever.

The Shadow Guard consisted of White Rose, Phantom Wolf, Iron Bear, Sandstorm, Sand Cat and led by Night Dragon. Each member was trained and fought beside the Foreign Warrior. Each took his teachings and silently taught their knowledge to their bloodline. Learning from the truth from their collected stories, Rick understood why his family was always drawn to serve all people. He informed the masked figures that he would return at the proper time.

Amazingly, they all were more informed than Rick thought. Explaining that their respective ancestors kept journal explaining the link to between them all. It was then that Rick explained that his heritage journey was also a mission to save his life. They all kept in touch, and when they each were on missions in the States, Night Dragon was always the first to call.

Night Dragon served as their partner when they were Stateside. For their American brother, they proudly protected his secrets and the secret temple deep in the heart of the African Jungle. The Night Dragon Clan had respective safehouses in each of their respective cities as well. However, the Dragon Temple served as the base of operations for the former Shadow Guard. It served as the ultimate library and training center for shinobi warriors. It was also there where the secrets of the stones were protected.

The stones were created from the mythical creatures that ruled during that time. The stones were the remains of the Great Dragons that ruled the Earth. While their domain was mostly found in Japan the land of Foreign Warrior that visited centuries ago, the stones were split at the destruction of the three dragons by Kenzensho in his efforts to become the Jade Emperor.

When the stones were scattered from the heavens, the Heart stone fell to Africa. The Eye was created by Kenzensho to tap into an evil dark power. The Emperor of Japan sent his favorite advisor and secret ninja warrior to study the meteorites his star gazers spotted. They were dealing with rise of an evil shogun that terrorized his Emperor's empire. Unknown to the Emperor, it was his own general Kenzensho preparing to steal his throne.

It was because of those actions, that the Night Dragon was created. Passing the duty on to through the bloodline was the perfect method to keep a very priceless mineral safe. That blood combined with the Heart Stone created a new being in Rick. Not only did it give him superhuman strength, agility, and intelligence, it also allowed him to tap into deeper and stronger powers he was afraid to even learn about. While Rick and the masked figures continued to catch up, he could feel some peace finally take hold of his body.

Hollywood on the other hand was in shock at the world he was thrusted into. He had heard of the masked warriors in his circle as one to be feared. He watched as the four carried on a conversation as if they were old friends. They referred to each other as cousin due to the closeness of their families. Rick introduced Hollywood to his friends.

Just as Rick was in mid-sentence, and a sharp pain shot throughout his chest. Releasing the yoke, he grabbed his chest with both hands. Falling back into his seat, Rick cried out in pain. Hollywood moved quickly to grab the controls. Pulling the jet back into the air, he leveled off and turned on the autopilot.

"Cousin! What is wrong?" Iron Bear screamed out "I will scramble the Dragon Temple to assist you."

"No!" Rick stopped him. "I have all three. I need you to make sure nobody comes near the temple. And if I don't ascend, please make sure

Hollywood and my people receive all my assets out of the vault. And please make sure my father is taken care of."

"I promise in the name of our ancestors," he told Rick, "I will make sure they are taken care of even if I have to bring them to my home."

"That won't be necessary, cousin." Rick assured Iron Bear as he sat up fighting through the pain. "Mya won't leave the states unless she is on a mission or vacation. Please be ready at her call. I know that some may object at her past, but she is more than worthy to lead in my absence. She is going to need you all. Please keep your oath to the Shadow Guard. And know that all the weapons my family had developed, I am giving to White Rose and you, Desert Twins."

"Even in the face of possible death you stand tall. Be brave my cousin, you will make it," Sandstorm wished for his family.

"In case I don't make it," Rick began to add, "that twenty million I owe you Bear for the World Cup bet is in the vault as well."

Signing off, Rick disconnected the call and took over the controls. As soon as he had the yoke, Hollywood immediately rushed to the Med-Kit and grabbed another IV cocktail. He remembered the steps and immediately swapped out the empty bag. When the IV was exchanged, he grabbed a second IV kit and hooked it up into his other arm. Before the police force, Hollywood was an army medic as well as paramedic once he was out of the service. In emergencies he would patch up himself and his men after shootouts and vicious fights for territory. Hollywood stood back and questioned the injured pilot.

"What do you mean your father?" Hollywood asked.

"Well Uncle H," he began to explain. "The night my father was killed, I was battling an imposter dressed in the same old Dragon armor. The same armor worn by the imposter that murdered my mom. When he drove, the sword through his heart. I found a pulse. I used the same cocktail that keeps me alive to help him. However, it put him in a coma while it healed him. The man you thought was me in that apartment building was him."

"But why would you have me wearing the mask of your face?"

"One, to have enough time to get him out of there. And two, you needed to find out the monster you created with Layla." Rick told him, "I can't give up hope on family. Mom and Dad raised me to never give up hope. Besides, I promised Dad before he went into the coma that I would save you from yourself."

"Richard was always trying to save my butt," Hollywood said.

"I just hope this plan works," Rick added. "Any other questions before we make our final approach?"

"Yes, what money?" Hollywood asked.

"My family is worth billions. Much was given to us for saving countries, members of royal families, and our family company, Blue Steele Technology." Rick admitted.

"Why do you live like a bum as a cop? And are you crazy? Hollywood asked with a bewildered look.

"The Steeles serve the people not Executive Boards. Besides, it is hard to be free when you are in the spotlight," Rick said as he continued on his flight path. "Besides, you think a black man worth a hundred billion dollars can walk without the spotlight."

Hollywood was blown away by the truth given. Part of him wanted to kill his best friend for hiding the truth from him. The other part wanted to hurry up and land, so he can see about his long-lost friend. The idea that Richard Sr. was still alive began to fill the emptiness in his heart. He was already excited that he was made to be an agent of the Night Dragon. It was his way to get back onto the side of good.

Converting some of his enterprises into charities, Hollywood finally felt like a human being. He lost some of his men due to their refusal to live the honest life. However, that did not matter, for as long as he served the people. Hollywood took his seat as Rick made the final approach. As they hovered over the beautiful landscape where jungle met mountains and the desert in one fixed point, there was a small temple like structure. Rick hovered for a minute before vertically landing the jet just in front of the temple.

Sitting back in his chair, Rick paused for the moment. The last time he was here, it was for his research into ascending. Learning the prophecy at an early age, he never wanted to be the Night Dragon his great, great grandfather envisioned years ago. It was on his travels to Africa that he learned of the temple from his cousins whose entire families used their warriors to protect it over the centuries.

Looking on the temple, he was not surprised when the hooded elders appeared from the temple doors. He could barely move without pain, but nothing was going to stop him. Pressing a button, a door next to the cockpit opened and a ramp retracted from the jet. He made the walk out to greet the elders. Hollywood was beside him. Just as he stood before the elders, Rick passed out from the strain of the pain. Hollywood caught him, and one of the elders removed his hood to assist his grandson.

"Ricky! Ricky!" his grandfather called out.

"Grandpa, I have it. Dad is in the jet. I have the three," Rick muttered before a medic rushed over with a breathing mask.

"What does he mean Harry?" his grandfather asked as he recognized his son's former partner. "What is going on?"

"He has the energy from the Jade Eye in his system. Here is the Soul Stone." Hollywood told him as he gave him the black stone.

"I told him that plan was too dangerous," his grandfather scolded.

"He was able to stabilize himself with that special IV cocktail," Hollywood told him.

"He made it worst," his grandfather said. "Quickly, get him to the infirmary and begin a blood transfusion immediately."

"What is going on?" Hollywood asked.

"He has poisoned his life energy and his blood. Unless we get the blood out and replaced with fresh clean blood, he will be dead within hours." His grandfather said.

"No!" Rick said as he opened his eyes and grabbed his grandfather. "You must take the stones and grind it to powder. It must be put into my system. I have to have the three inside of me to…" Rick said before passing out completely.

"He was talking about saving his dad's life," Hollywood said, "Did you know Richard was still alive?"

"Yes, I know Richard is alive," grandfather said, "But he was supposed to be with you two. I thought he was aboard with you two. We have been monitoring his status the entire flight. Quickly, you three check the inside for a medical pod."

Springing into action, the three hooded figures rushed inside the jet. Within a few moments, the cargo bay door opened. Emerging from behind the plane, the three were hovering over a floating bed. They proceeded to rush the bed past the crowd to the infirmary. While they rushed the comatose Richard Sr. inside, another crew arrived to get Rick. As they placed him onto the hover gurney, Hollywood stood by as the elder Steele began triage on his grandson. Removing the armor from Rick, he discovered that the stone that powered his armor and gear was broken, and Rick was stabbed in the chest. It did not reach his heart, but it did enough damage. His body began to ooze blood and a mixture of a Jade fluid.

Normally, he could heal rapidly, especially when he had his special IV treatment. He should have died during the flight, but somehow, he survived. The two energies inside his body were a volatile combination fighting for supremacy. The worst of the mixture was the fact it was destroying Rick from within. As his grandfather rushed Rick to the infirmary, Hollywood remained close by and refused to leave his godson's side.

As he stood outside the surgery room, Hollywood was on pins and needles. Suddenly, someone came rushing past Hollywood with a tablet. Entering the tablet into the operating room, they held it up for Rick's grandfather that was leading the operation. When Hollywood investigated the room through the observation window, he noticed that it was not Rick on the table. Seeing his friend laid out on the table, tears began to swell in his eyes. As the Senior father began to work on the injury to his son, he watched as a he continued to watch the tablet. Hollywood could not wait. He spotted a pair of scrubs and surgery clothes. Washing his hand after putting on the scrubs, he grabbed a mask and proceeded into the operating room.

He stood in the background as he watched father work on son with a deep focus. Pulling out a piece of a Jade colored shard, he placed it into a jar that was whisked away. Within seconds of removal, he began to work furiously on his son. Sealing the wound with liquid stitches, he then poured a blue solution like the special cocktail that Rick used to stabilize himself. As he continued to watch, he heard Rick's voice. He rushed over to find the tablet contained a recorded message from Rick himself. Just as he finished instructing his grandfather, Rick had a message for Hollywood.

"I know that Hollywood is there," Rick spoke to the camera, "You are there to help my grandfather bring my dad back and up to speed. New Peak City needs a team to protect it from the war that is coming. By the time you are watching his, the shard taken out of my father is being grinded down and place inside of me. Once all the stones are me, I am to be locked away in the vault. I must surrender to the stones and walk in the spirit realm. I must ascend to gain understanding of the three stones. Tell Mya I am sorry I won't be able to spend forever. I just hope she finds the one worthy of her love. Goodbye."

Watching his grandfather and Hollywood react to the video, they were unaware that he was assisting the entire time. He hid the fact that he was in pain that reached unbelieve measures. As soon as the shard was removed from his father's spine, Rick watched the vitals improve as he walked out of the room. Walking past Hollywood, he made sure to avoid eye contact. To everyone in the temple, he was still unconscious and in the other medical trauma unit. Nobody was aware that he rigged his monitors and systems to give false readings. The only way to ascend was a mystery that only one man knew. Despite the stories and legends told of his death, Rick knew that he had to find the him.

Risking his life and the hope placed on him, he had to find one person in the world who could train, teach, and help him ascend into the powers of Night Dragon. Armed with only his sword, he took off in the Dragon Jet. Taking off into the night, Rick Steele disappeared into the sky. He made sure to disconnect all the tracking systems and hide his flight path. He knew his ancestor would not welcome the outside world. He kept the truth from his entire family since the day he found him in his travels.

As the very first Night Dragon continued to live and train in secret over the centuries, he kept a close eye on his descendants. Upon the discovery of Rick's powers, he broke his rule and made contact. Finding out the truth of the family bloodline. The two kept in contact until Rick began his plot to ascend.

As he began to open a link to his great, great, great grandfather, he began to feel the pain take hold of his body. Looking at his reflection in the windshield, he saw his eyes glows a bright blue light. His chest had a green glow from the wound. He reached for the Soul Stone and was not shocked to find a white glow around the black stone. Looking at the night sky, he was in awe of the Dragon Moon. He placed the smart jet on autopilot and made his way to the medical bay. He continued to fight the pain as it took over his ability to function.

Struggling to walk, he could feel the Jade Stone corrupting and destroying every cell in his body. Rick reached the Medical Bay and sat down on a special bed. He placed all the stones and pieces together inside a special compartment. Locking them away, he then laid out on the bed after attaching another IV treatment. The moment his head hit the pillow, a glass and steel door dropped down on top of the bed. The door locked and sealed him into the special medical pod. Oxygen began to be pumped into the pod as Rick began to pass out due to the pain. As he fell into a deep sleep, Rick hoped that his final signal was received. The only way that his jet would land safety was through his isolated relative responding to the signal in time.

While Rick slipped away into a deep sleep, the Dragon Jet continued to cruise at top speed to coordinates he imputed just before takeoff. The more he drifted from reality, the more he was unaware of what was around him. He was warned of the effects of the stones and his powers at the Ascension of the Dragon Moon.

Rick made it to the special medical pod within perfect timing. His life force was being drained away. Normally, the Dragon Moon strips away the powers of the stones during Ascension. However, Rick was not like his predecessors. The Blue Heart Stone was in his DNA, his blood… his entire life source. While he was unconscious, he was unaware that his grandfather was already on his way to him.

As Kuroi Hagane followed closely behind his great, great, great grandson, his heart and mind were filled with worry. He had been following Rick since the first sign of his powers as a boy. He remained in the shadows and kept a far distance to allow him to grow as his own man. It was a rule he followed since his son took over the mantle of Night Dragon. When he retired from the role, he never informed his descendants that he was still alive. His son took his immortality to his own grave to help to protect the family from the corruption of the stones.

For decades, that has helped to keep the family grounded. However, the deception kept the truth that would have better prepared the family for Rick. Being the prophecy that could end the Jade Army and the Jade Samurai, he could finally end the family mission. Just as his jet began to catch up to the Dragon Jet, he began to receive the signal Rick sent out to him. Using a code and frequency that only they knew, Kuroi was able to learn the distress his young descendant was in. He was happy that his grandson trained him on the computer and how to master the new technology.

However, he could not get the jet to respond to an emergency landing procedure. He decided to rescue his grandson the old fashion way. He flew the jet over the Dragon Jet and opened the cargo bay door. He grabbed a line and attached it to his belt. Grabbing his sword, he leaped down to the Dragon Jet. Kuroi whipped out his sword and swiped his blade across the roof of the doomed jet. With a kick, the metal fell inside the Dragon jet. Kuroi dropped in to find Rick inside the medical pod. Moving quickly, he pushed the emergency escape button. Within seconds, the medical was dropped out of the jet. Kuroi quickly leaped out the Dragon Jet with perfect timing. When his grandson entered the coordinates, Rick set the jet on a flight path through mountains.

Kuroi pulled on the line and was pulled up to his jet. He closed the door and rushed to the controls. Pulling away from the jet, he turned towards the falling pod. Within moments, the Dragon Jet crashed into the side of a mountain. He watched as the chutes opened for the medical pod as it fell to the ground. Kuroi followed his grandson to the ground, landing close to the crash site.

Kuroi rushed from the jet to find the pod in one piece. He opened the lid and checked for a pulse. He was relieved when Rick began to come around. Rick pointed to a drawer just before closing his eyes again. Kuroi opened to the draw and smiled. His grandson pulled off his plan. He feared for Rick's safety, but he trusted in his abilities. Kuroi gathered the stones inside a pouch and used his super strength to carry unconscious hero his awaiting super jet. He had to hurry and get his grandson back to his home. His poor grandson was the key to saving lives. Looking at him, he prayed for his strength to endure the pending trial. They had one week left until the end of the Dragon Moon. The very last night is the night for the ascension or destruction of Night Dragon.

First Day of a New Protector

As the sun began to set over New Peak City, White Rose stood over the city. She could sense a feeling of belonging come over her. The city was still reeling from her attack on the mayor's mansion. Sleeping all day in Rick's apartment, she felt cooped up in the spacious loft apartment. Adonai made sure to continue his day to day work.

Maintaining the weapons, computers, and vehicles, he worked to keep the mission going strong. Building from the blueprints and digital files left behind by Rick, Adonai knew that he had to finish the latest weapons. He worked with all his might to complete the plans his boss had. He was hesitant while working, but it was not because White Rose. It was because of himself. He was worried about being the Phantom Wolf. Remembering the history of the warrior, he worried of stepping into the shoes of a great ninja master.

When Mya finally rose from bed, she found a new uniform with armor waiting for her. She waited until sunset to begin her patrol. Dressing in the new gear, she felt her master smiling at her. She moved in silence across the roofs of New Peak City. Seeing the bell tower of Old

City Hall, she wanted to see the view of the city Night Dragon defended with his life. As she scaled the building freehanded, she moved with a new purpose and power. White Rose could tell something was different about herself. She had a feeling of what the change within her could be. When she reached the top of the tower, she checked her surroundings before removing her mask.

Exposing her identity to the empty surroundings, Maya looked at her Power Gauntlet. Being White Rose was who she truly was. Taking on this new role as a protector was a major difference. She began to read over her new system and armor. When she opened the system data file, a special video message popped up. It was a message from Rick. Tears began to fall as she heard his voice again. Deep down, she missed him more because she knew the truth. The entire time they were apart was due to the secrets they feared to share. Now there was no secrets, and the distance hurt worse than a bullet. Sadly, she knew the pain of being shoot, but still preferred it over being away from Rick.

"White Rose, I wanted to personally explain your present," he began to tell her. "Your armor and new weapons are made from the Heart Stone. The suit is powered by the Mystic White Rose and the Heart Stone weaved into every stitch of your gear. Your years of training and mastery of combat have enhanced your natural abilities. Normally, you could lift two to three times your weight. Now multiple your abilities by ten. You armor is bullet proof and virtually indestructible. It only has one weakness. It is the same weakness as me…Jade. I am on my way to Ascend and end this war. Protect the people and be careful. I love you"

As the video ended, Maya was in tears. She knew that he had limited supply of Heart Stones. She also knew that the armor was a dream of her master's. Rick's mom designed the armor for herself. Maya was honored to be in the armor and wear the White Rose mask. It felt as if he was holding her one more time. Placing mask back on her face, she became White Rose proudly for her lover. She climbed up to the edge of the tower and climbed up to the very top. White Rose stood strong and confident as she looked over the city.

Lights began to turn on as the sun disappeared from the night sky and the moon rose high. As she began to lose herself at the sight, Adonai warned her of a major street fight downtown. Innocent people were trapped in the crossfire of a gang war. Without hesitation, she leaped of the tower. Firing a grappling line from her gauntlet, she swung to next building and made her way to the fight. It was seven blocks over from the bell tower. As she moved closer, White Rose could hear the explosions of gunfire continuously ringing out. When she reached the fight, she saw a bus full of people trapped in the center of a fight between the Triads and Yakuza. It was time for a field test in her mind.

Leaping off the building, she pulled her new twin plasma blasters. White Rose opened fire as she glided down off the building. Drawing the fire from the bus, she landed superhero style on one knee. She allowed them opened fire as her armor absorbed the bullets. Standing there boldly, she laughed out loud, mocking the would-be gangsters.

The two enemies combined forces to attack her. Pullin out swords, axes, and machetes, they both charged her with everything they had. With an evil smile hidden from her attackers, she whipped out her twin tanto daggers and welcomed the attack. Grace, speed, and new-found power helped White Rose to defeat each man with ease and precision. Normally, each man would lose a limb or life for attacking her. Within four minutes, ten men found themselves on their backs and in great pain. White Rose kept her promise not to take life from her enemies.

Hearing the sirens, she quickly got out of there. White Rose ducked into an alley and watched as the police arrived. They arrested the injured gangsters while the paramedics arrive to assist the innocent bystanders. Before she could truly observe the aftermath, Adonai called her to a robbery in progress. Rushing to the roof, she made her way to the bank six blocks over. She was really feeling the powers of the armor coursing through her veins. Her muscles and reflexes felt brand new. She felt superhuman and wanted to test her abilities more.

White Rose arrived at the bank to find a major shootout with the robbers and police. Unfortunately, the police were losing badly. She had to do something but had to avoid the risk of being seen by the police. The officers were outnumbered five to one. There were only three officers on scene and not idea of help on the way. Using her stealth, she took out her shuriken and razor discs. White Rose used the shadows to take out the bank robbers who took to safety behind the cars on the street. Taking out ten shooters, she had to worry of the remaining shooters inside the bank.

Spotting an injured officer, she used her grappling line to swoop down and threw him over her shoulders. Running at top speed, she avoided the oncoming bullets from the inside shooters. She risked being seen due to the serious of his wounds. Here new masked contained a super computer and multiple scanning capabilities. Plus, with Adonai in her ear, she had the right tools to make the best decision. The thought of Rick also influenced her decision. He would never leave a man down. She took him to his fellow officers.

"Call an ambulance," White Rose said with a distorted voice, "He needs immediate attention and blood. Go ahead and call in the fire department. I am going to take care of this."

"Wait, we have orders to arrest you on site," one of the officers tried to stop her.

Turning around at the touch of his arm on her shoulder, White Rose shot a look of shock. Her face was hidden, but her body posture told her story. The injured officer's partner waived the zealous officer off and allowed White Rose to do her job. Focusing on the mission before her, she took out her twin plasma blasters. As she approached the bank, the number of shooters increased. White Rose opened fire to push them back into the bank. Taking her knowledge of crimes into mind, she knew that the assault on the front of the bank was to clear a way for the escape. Their escape car had to be in route or they were using another way to escape.

Ordering Adonai to scan the layout of the bank for additional parking or loading structures, White Rose wanted to make sure there was no escape. When the answer came back an underground loading dock, she knew what the next step was. Firing into two parked cars outside the bank, White Rose triggered two huge explosions. When the flames died down, she was gone. The shooters rushed outside with the thought that she was dead. They informed the others the street was clear. Within one minute, an armored van appeared, and they all piled inside. Pulling off just as fast as it appeared, the remaining police fired at the vehicle. Unknown to them all, White Rose used the explosions to hide her entrance into the sewer grate. Adonai provided her with a schematic of the sewer which lead to a maintenance access door. Picking the lock, she crept into the underground garage.

Creeping into position, she quickly and silently took out each man in the underground garage. She stealthily made her way towards the underground vault. However, she was not prepared for what she found. Entering the vault, she found no one. She moved towards the vault to investigate. When White Rose entered the empty vault, she found a pair of twin daggers in the center of the room.

As she moved closer to investigate, she could sense someone else in the room. While she searched with her eyes, her equipment and Adonai were in her ear giving negative reports. White Rose knew someone was there. As she walked up to the daggers, she recognized them as Lopez's Daggers. It was then when she realized that the scanners could not see through lead. The vault door is made of lead and could hide a body. With blasters drawn, she turned towards the vault door to see the door close and reveal an awaiting General Taka.

His eyes glowed an evil Jade hue with a hint of destruction and rage glimmering in his pupils. He was ready for war. With the thought of his beloved in a coma, Taka walked towards White Rose with his War Staff drawn and blades sharpened with a purpose. Tonight, he would leave with her head to place at the feet of Layla. Before he left on his revenge mission, Taka received word that there was no change in the Master nor his precious love. With the image of Layla laying in that hospital bed with IV's and tubes giving her oxygen and nourishment, his mind was now set for pure destruction. White Rose stood firm as he began to walk towards her. She put away her blasters and pulled out both her twin tanto daggers.

Before her stood the only creature on Earth that she feared. The journals and recordings of the White Rose Clan were filled with the tales of destruction and death at the hands of the monster in front of her. The only person able to stand up to him was now gone and left her to defend the people of New Peak City. Her confidence began to dwindle with each step he took. With weapons ready, she waved his attack in.

General Taka let out a blood curling yell as he swung his War Staff with great power. Blocking the blow with her blades, she absorbed a great deal of force. He continued his viscous attack. White Rose continued to block and fend off each swing. She continued to stop his attacks, and her confidence began to come back. The fact that her new armor increased her already superhuman abilities never occurred in her mind. Adonai was watching and monitoring everything. He reminded her of the enhancements and tried to encourage her. White Rose realized the truth and stepped back into herself. She snapped her mind back into focus. Taking a swing at Taka, she unleased a furious attack of her own.

As her blades danced through the air, sparks flew with each strike of her blades against his staff. Taka could not absorb all her fury. She whipped her blades through this staff and his skin. White Rose revealed his green Jade colored blood, but she could not take the fight out of him. At this point, the no kill rule was off the table for the undead general. In a single slash, she split his infamous War Staff into two pieces. However, that would not stop him.

Throwing his destroyed staff to the ground, he used his hands to unleash his rage. White Rose was not like Night Dragon. A fight was a fight, never give up the upper hand in a fight. She continued her assault with both weapons in hand, but the favor changed hands. Taka blocked and dodged her attacks with great ease. She knew he was going to kill her, so she had to step up her attacks. As she took a swipe with one of her daggers, Taka blocked with a simple clap of his hands. Taka smiled as he flaunted his martial arts skills holding the blade with his hands. His smile was wiped away as White Rose stabbed him with the other blade in his side.

The look that Taka shot White Rose was one that spoke of his disapproval. White Rose held on tight to the blade in Taka's hands, but she could feel herself losing grip. She released her hand from the dagger in Taka's ribs and grabbed her dagger fighting Taka's grip. With both hands, she tried to gain leverage on the undead monster. Even with both hands, she could still feel his power and strength. Her helmet displayed showed that she was already at max capacity with the strength enhancers of her new battle suit. However, she could feel that she was not in control any more.

With on smile on his face, Taka snapped her blade into pieces then delivered a devastating front kick to her chest and abdomen. Absorbing the entire power of his kick, White Rose went through the air and crashed into the shelves of the vault. Taka let out an evil laugh as he stood strong and unfazed. Throwing her shattered blade down, he began to slowly walk towards her, ready to finish her off. He yanked the dagger out of his ribs and snapped the blade in his bare hands.

White Rose was banged up but not ready to give up. She began to climb to her feet gingerly as he came towards her. Once on her feet, she knew that fight was more than she could stand. Adonai was watching the whole fight and already trying to find a tool to use. Spotting a new weapon in the armor specks, he quickly armed the weapons remotely. He told to pull out her blasters. Without delay, she retrieved her blasters, which transformed into twin plasma blades.

Feeling a little confident, White Rose stood her ground and welcomed Taka to attack. With an evil grin he paused and held out his hands. Channeling his energy, his hands glowed Jade green as he formed a Jade Battle Ax out of his powers. Neither one of the combatants would allow the other to gain the upper hand or leave that vault alive. Before they could leap into battle, they both heard footsteps coming towards the vault. Adonai warned her that the bank was now surrounded by the Jade Army. She had to get out of there, but Taka was in front of the vault door. It was more than apparent that he would not allow her to get through that door.

Adonai watched in horror as his new boss and master was in the worst situation possible on patrol. He didn't know what to do. He watched as the two warriors went after each other with high-tech and mystical weapons. He wished Night Dragon was there. He was the one soul that was more than capable. Receiving word via the automated system a mere hour ago that the Dragon Jet crashed, he only hoped that Night Dragon was still alive. Even if he were alive, he was on the other side of the world. Adonai had to do something and quickly.

As he watched the bank and street fill with Jade Samurai warriors, he knew that he had to get her out of there. The worst fear of the entire Night Dragon Klan was happening before his eyes. The Jade Army was finally rising to power. Looking over at the armory, Adonai knew what had to be done. He had to send the one weapon that he was truly afraid of. He set the computer on automatic as he went into the armory to prepare the special weapon.

As he stepped inside, his mind was full of fear and doubt. This was the one weapon he prayed that would never be used. He was trained on it and was surprised when his master told him it was mission ready. He needed more training from White Rose, but Night Dragon personally prepared him with the basics. It was now the only way to guarantee that White Rose would come out of it alive. It was time for the Electric Wolf to emerge from the shadows. Just before he headed out in White Rose's car, Adonai sent the destress beacon that he swore to only use as a last resort. It appeared that the first night without the Night Dragon was the fall of all justice in New Peak City. He only hoped that he reached White Rose before it was too late.

Back across town in the bank vault, the fight continued to rage on. Neither side back down. When she was finally cornered, White Rose knew this was not her style. She was holding herself back and to Night Dragon's standards. Deep in her heart, she knew he would not approve of it. Remembering their last night together, she heard his heart spoken words as they laid in each other's arms.

"You are the one I have searched for and loved my entire life. Just be yourself and I will be me. Because we will always love and come back to each other no matter what," he said as he kissed her lips gently but passionately.

With his words speaking to her mind and heart, White Rose took her stand. Throwing the plasma blades to the ground, she went back to what made her White Rose, the dangerous woman in the world. This was Night Dragon's style of fighting. He was the master of mind and body. She was the mistress of death and torture. Standing there, she was only armed with her twin Sai, throwing stars, and her bare hands.

White Rose threw up her fists and invited Taka in for one more round. Taka saw her and welcomed the fight. He made his Axe dissolve in the air. He put up his hands, which still glowed Jade green. General Taka took his stance as White Rose began to bounce on her feet. Moving into him, she wanted this face to face fight. It was time to prove her dominance.

Throwing a quick jab that was blocked by a powerful smack, White Rose wanted to gauge his speed. However, that test was quick and done. She made sure to double up her punches. As the punches and jabs flew between the two, her plan to escape was working. She also wanted to get into the monster's mind. Connecting with her fists and kicks, White Rose began push Taka away from the vault door. Just as she appeared to have the upper hand, White Rose ducked a viscous punch, but she was shocked by an upper cut to her stomach that sent her into the wall.

"No, my dear," Taka said with an evil laugh, "You are not going out of the door unless I drag you out."

Using his true power, General Taka picked the injured warrior up above his head and launched her into the air with great force. Hitting the wall, White Rose fell to the ground hard. He enjoyed the sight so much that Taka picked her up and through her through the vault door into another wall. This wall began to crump and fall into pieces on top of her. She tried to move away, but she was hurt badly. White Rose spotted that she was out of the vault.

Crawling towards the stairs, she had to get out of that bank. Taka was enjoying this. He walked behind her laugh and toying with her. When she felt him about to attack, she rolled in the nick of time to barely miss his boot crashing through the cement floor rather her body. Laying on her back, she quickly used her gauntlet to fire a line into the huge air vent. Her aim looked to be off, since she almost fired the line into his face.

"You missed my dear," he told her with a laugh.

"Actually, I didn't bitch!" White Rose said as she pulled the line.

A huge boom erupted in the air vent. The sound of metal scrapping across metal began to screech through the air. Looking up, General Taka spotted a huge object crash through the vent and ceiling. White Rose pulled the huge air condition unit and a huge industrial fan out of his resting place for the vault. Landing on top of Taka, it appeared that her current problem was solved for now. She knew he was not dead, but at least she had a chance to escape and regroup. She was badly injured and could barely move.

That last punch broke some ribs. The wall falling on her added to her problems. The rubble which hit her in the head might have given her a concussion. As she moved towards the door, her new-found peace was crushed with the sound of feet coming towards the vault. White Rose braced herself for the oncoming fight. Her only true concern was that General Taka remained knocked out in time for her to escape. Getting into her fight stance, she reached for her twin Sai.

Rushing through the door were Jade Samurai Soldiers with swords drawn. She held no fear as she stood before them. Racked with pain and fighting to breathe, White Rose stood there without a flinch. As they moved in slowly to attack, she analyzed their movements and stances. She could predict their attack patterns and threat levels from just watching them move.

Waiting for their attack, she only hoped that she could defend them in time. The truth that was on her mind was that she had to get out of there before Taka got up. One powerful blow to her ribs and she was a dead woman. Her ear piece had an annoying beep that began to grow in volume and frequency. Before she could make her own move, her gauntlet sync to her mask with a message. "Get Down"

A loud whistle came from the sky. Knowing that only one thing whistles from the sky, all the Jade soldiers ducked down to the ground to brace for impact. Inside the bank the whistle was heard, and everyone braced for impact. White Rose leaped under a desk in the hall way. With a blink of the eye, the ceiling came crashing down on the entire bank. As walls and the building exploded at the force of the impact, everyone was blown back across the street. On the inside of the bank, the building caved in on everyone. When the dust settled, a huge pod was in the center of the basement next to the vault. White Rose check to make sure she was okay. Before she could move, she received another message on her gauntlet. "Stand Clear".

The door to the pod opened slowly, unleashing a ton of smoke. Crashing from the heavens, the Jade Samurai worried if it were a bomb. It was pitch black inside the pod when a pair of red lights, more like eyes began to shine from within. The Samurai were back on their feet and ready to kill whatever was in side. However, they had no idea of the trouble they were in. Leaping out of the pod, a ninja in red trimmed in black appeared with red backpack.

Standing there before them, they didn't want to ask who he was. They attacked only to be stopped with just his bare hands. Taking them down with all his might, he was able to disarm them with ease. Before long more men appeared. Reaching for his hip, the new warrior pulled out a whip. Turning on a switch on the handle, the whip emitted an electric pulse.

Moving quickly into action he unleashed his electric fury on his attackers. Once they were on the ropes, he threw a pair of smoke bombs and blinded the would-be attackers. When the smoke cleared, he and White Rose was gone. Suddenly, a pile of rubble began to move. Leaping up with great rage, Taka came to in time to see his trap failed. His rage could be seen in his eyes and the Jade in his blood began to bleed glowing green. It was time to fully unleash the power of the Jade Samurai army. Ordering his men to retreat, he wanted to avoid the police sirens he heard in the background. He and his men made their way to the nearest sewer entrance. They had to return to prepare for war.

ASCENDING OF THREE TO ONE

Watching the Jade Army scatter, White Rose and her rescuer continued to keep a low profile while they waited for the area to clear. Just as he threw the smoke bombs, he made his way to White Rose and helped her out of sight into a nearby office. Once inside, he opened a window and helped her to climb to up to the street. Once they were on the street, he helped her into her awaiting car. He carefully put her on the back seat and climbed into the driver seated. He pulled off and used the alleys to avoid the police and Jade army. As they made their way to safety, White Rose removed her mask, so she could breathe.

"Thank you, Adonai," she said as she struggled to breathe. "I am glad you came in. And it was the perfect time to unleash the Phantom Wolf."

"I am not the Phantom Wolf. I only put this on to get you out of there," Adonai replied as he removed his mask. "This is the Electric Wolf Prototype. The boss created this as an emergency backup. You and the armor took a real beating. I was not going to let you die."

"And that is why you are the Phantom Wolf. Now where are we heading?" Mya asked as she continued to fight to breathe.

"I need to get you to the hospital," Adonai said as he raced to get her help. "And please stop calling me that."

"You have to get me back to the lair," she told him. "They will be looking for a woman with damage to her ribs and lungs. Trust me, the Grandmaster has people everywhere. Just take me to the lair and patch me up there."

"There is no more lair," he told her. "When I saw you in trouble, I activated a distress beacon as I activated the Electric Wolf armor. The entire lair began a self-destruct. That's why I came in that pod. I was launched to your position just before the lair exploded. I was glad I was still able to uplink the master system to my gauntlet, or you would not have received my warnings."

"Where is Ricky's safehouse?" she asked as she continued to struggle to breathe.

"The Lair was all the boss had other than storage sheds all over town. The sheds only hold weapons or transportation. If I don't get you to the hospital, you will die," he told her.

"Wait, if there was a distress beacon, then who was it sent to?" Mya asked before a smile appeared on her face. "He is coming back, Rick is coming back."

"Ma'am, I don't think so. I receive a message from the onboard computer of the Dragon Jet. It was an emergency signal. The jet crashed. We are all alone in this fight ma'am," Adonai told her.

"Well, we don't have time to mourn, we have company," Mya said as she spotted a car following them. "We have to lose them before we head to the Greenhouse."

She knew it was the Jade Army. Before she could react, they pulled out automatic weapons and opened fire. Ducking down in pain, she knew her car was not bulletproof, or so she thought. Reassuring her of their safety, Adonai admitted that he had her car fitted with some major upgrades while she rested. However, the upgrades were not useful to the innocent people out on the street.

Seeing the bystanders, Mya worried about their safety. Putting her mask on she pushed a button that flipped the backseat around and revealed her arsenal of weapons. Grabbing her bow and arrows, she had

Adonai open the sunroof. Becoming White Rose again, she moved the front passenger seat all the way up so that she could stand. Once she was set and ready, White Rose took aim at the car behind them. With just one arrow, she took out the main gunman firing a mounted fifty-caliber assault rifle. That was not the end of the chase.

As attackers continued to pull guns, she took them down with ease and no hesitation. Before long, the single car was joined by five more, and none of the occupants had mercy in their sights. With the image of innocent blood being spilt in her mind, White Rose went into the place in head where she locked away her rage, anger, and the monster within her. Remembering all her training and the words of her master, she closed her eyes for a brief second then exhaled.

Opening her eyes, she breathed in then released her pain on the exhale as well as an arrow. With great precision and power, every target became a corpse. Throwing away the standards of Night Dragon, she stepped back into her element, back into herself. She is and always will be an assassin that robbed life from those that devalued the life of the good, innocent, and peacefully people of this Earth. The White Rose is a dealer of death to the evil and wicked. It was time to be the woman she always was.

The battle of New Peak City raged on in the streets. While the two new protectors made their escape, at the same time an aircraft was flying overhead. He had been flying most of the day and was low on fuel. Rescuing his great, great grandson, the elder Kuroi was concerned about the current legacy holder. Rick was the strongest and the best warrior in the entire family. However, he shared the burden he passed down through his bloodline. The toll of being the Night Dragon drained life and years from the bearer. He hid the fact that he was still alive from the family to protect them from ascending. To move to the higher plane created a power that no man should have.

The power of Mind, Heart, and Soul gave one being the powers of a god. Being the man that he was, there is only one God, and He didn't need help. When he rescued Rick from crashing, he was barely able to use his sword. If it were not for the special medicine that Rick used and shared with him, he would not be about to control or maintain his abilities. After his last training session via video chat, Rick claimed to have stumble on the answer to ascending without the side effects.

After the call, he went into deep mediation and decided to move closer to Rick without him knowing. Studying his descendant from a safe distance, he noticed the changes in him. He also learned the devastating pain and problems the Heart Stone powers put on Rick. They fact the Rick was born with the powers was one issue, but the fact that it drained his life force faster and heavier than every man before him was heartbreaking.

Remembering his life centuries ago, he thought about the training of his king and adopted father. Teaching him that the heart of a man filled with good and justice was the greatest and most powerful weapon and tool. Kuroi knew that the Night Dragon was what the world needed. He never knew of any man more just and fair men than those two. Growing up in a foreign land was difficult, but his new mother and father loved him unconditionally. Upon his arrival in Japan, he learned to play the role of servant in public, but alone with his adoptive parents he was their beloved son.

Training him on their culture and way of life, he learned the power of the good. Now after following his descendant to the sacred temple, he was more than sure that Rick Steele was the one man that could end the war between the evil Samurai Army and the people of the world. Seeing the temple, he experienced pain since being in the site where his own son is buried along with both his biological and adopted parents. He built that temple to maintain and protect the Night Dragon legacy. His son and grandson turned it into the headquarters it is today for gathering information, weapons storage, and archive. It soon became a retirement village and cemetery.

Everyone except Rick Jr. saw it as a refuge. He saw it as a tool to use in the fight against evil. It served Rick well as he traveled the world to become his own Night Dragon. However, Rick was not yet at the level he was capable of. As he was flying this morning he intended to return to the temple and reveal the secret Rick kept from the family, but the distress signal was bittersweet reprieve.

After getting Rick out of that doomed plane, he knew that he could not help his descendant without the interloping of his family in that temple. Rick knew what to do but he was missing one key fact. His amazing descendant lack the trust and confidence in himself to succeed. In his own training and mediation, he learned that was the same issue that all the Steele Men… trust in their own heart. To ascend, the heart must trust in self to guide the path of the warrior to be a protector and keeper of fair and equal justice.

As he made his way back to New Peak City, he received the distress signal from the lair. Rick personally designed the signal to go to him instead of the temple. He knew that his dear descendant trusted the woman he loved and his assistant with New Peak City. From his observations, Kuroi was more than convinced that Rick was correct in his judgement. Seeing them for himself, he could see the good in their hearts. Despite their actions and quirks, they both were true Shadow Guardians. The White Rose and Phantom Wolf were his closest allies in the Shadow Guard. Their respective predecessors would be honored that they carried on the fight in their names.

If they were in trouble, it was serious. He knew that Rick had faith in them and that was more than enough for him. Relieved that he was already flying there, he climbed higher to catch a lift in a Jetstream, he pushed his custom, advance plane to maximum power. As he flew over the city, he picked up the action on his police scanner. He then heard the radio chatter between Adonai and Mya. He used the supercomputer in the jet to find them. Locating them as they raced through downtown, he tried to find a way to get them out of danger. Navigating around skyscrapers is difficult enough but trying to pull off a rescue made it even worse.

He was glad that Rick designed the jet with cameras to help better pilot their jets just like the cameras on modern cars. Spotting White

Rose fighting back and protecting the innocent bystanders, he was proud of her. Living up to the name his late wife created, he could see why Rick was in love. However, he heard the of the issue of her broke ribs. Suddenly, he was filled with worry as the Jade Army began to unleash their full fury. It was worse when General Taka appeared in the road ahead of them.

Thinking of the people, he watched as she climbed out of the car and leaped at Taka. In one move Taka swatted her with one hand into a newsstand. Wolf then turned the car towards Taka who summoned his Jade energy axe. Driving the car directly into Taka, he hoped to end the monster right there. He bailed out of the car just before Taka smiled as the car drove towards him at top speed. He used his powers to enlarge the axe to a monstrous size and sliced the car in half down the middle.

Calling out her name into the headset, Kuroi tried to find a way to get to her as he circled the downtown warzone. He placed the jet on auto pilot, so he could try to help somehow. However, he didn't need to. Without knowing, Rick was up. He was still bandage up and hooked up to an IV. Rick was not Rick nor Night Dragon, but something else. His glowed a bright blue and appeared to be in a determined trance. Even his voice was different when he spoke. Grabbing a sword and a utility vest, Rick was determined to join the fight.

"What are you doing son?" he asked in pure shock.

"Just drop down and keep the rest of the goons off my girl. I am going send him back to Hell!" Rick said with a deep monstrous voice.

Ripping his IV out of his arm, Rick became Night Dragon once more. He suited up and reached for his mask. He looked at it just before putting it on. Once he put it on, he held a look of focus and determination He grabbed the sword and prepared for one last fight. His great grandfather lowered the jet and hovered over the fight on the downtown streets. He opened the cargo bay door and after firing the jets guns at Taka's men. Once he cleared a path to White Rose, he waved the sign for the go ahead.

Night Dragon leaped out of the plane without grabbing line. He allowed gravity to pull him down with great force and speed. Coming down hard, Night Dragon performed a superhero landing with the power of a meteor hitting the Earth. After the dust settled, Night Dragon was standing with sword drawn and rage unleashed. Looking directly at General Taka, he began to move towards his enemy.

Walking with pure determination and controlled rage, Night Dragon was going to make Taka suffer. His determined walk turned into a quick stride, then into a full sprint. Before he knew it, Jade soldiers rushed in to attack Night Dragon. With his eyes locked in on Taka, he unsheathed his sword and took each down each attacker with a single slash. He kept his eye locked on his target while his master opened fire on would be attackers that turned their attention to White Rose. Wolf was back in the fight as he rushed to aid the injured White Rose. To everyone's surprise, she was still able to fight. Using her bow and arrows, White Rose continued to fight off Jade soldiers.

When he finally stood in front of Taka, the two locked eyes and braced for their battle. The look they shared spoke of this being the final meeting of the two. In unison, the two bowed to show respect but their eyes were still locked. The two stared one another down as if they were having a deep conversation. In a simple instant, the two both waved their respective people away. They both wanted this fight as traditional and even as possible.

Knowing what was in store, Kuroi briefly landed to allow Wolf a chance to help White Rose out of danger and into the plane. She was holding her ribs as she clutched her bow. Wolf allowed her to use his shoulder as a crutch as she struggled to get into the jet. Looking back at Night Dragon, she spotted him looking at her. Even through their mask, their eyes met. Looking at the love they shared in that glance, they each knew this was not the end of them. She nodded her head in appreciation and love. Night Dragon turned his head back to General Taka. It was time to teach the monster who was the true beast between the two of them.

Charging the undead monster with all his might, he began his attack without fear. The General whipped out a brand-new battle axe that was just as powerful as his previous weapon. The two exchanged blows back and forth with their weapons but neither gain the upper hand. It was like their first two battles, but this time Night Dragon grew stronger and stronger. The poisonous mixture of the three stones that was once killing him, was now giving him the true link to his untapped power. General Taka could feel the energy within Night Dragon grow. Summoning his own power, his eyes glowed that Jade green as he began to fight harder to gain an edge over the midnight hero.

"Enough of this Night Dragon," Taka yelled out, "It is time to show you the real General Taka." Once he said that, the undead Samurai let out a blood curling yell. A green flame began to cover the general's entire body. He transformed into a huge monster with a devilishly transformed battle axe.

"About time you stop playing games," Night Dragon said, "I am not in the mood for your games. Now are we going to fight, or do I have to wait for your master to give you permission to die.

"Die! Taka yelled as he swung his battle axe to chop the head of Night Dragon in half. Stopped with a powerful block of his sword, Night Dragon laughed in Taka's face. "One more laugh before you die. Wishing you had the honor of the Samurai before you die? What is so funny Dragon?"

"You really think you were on my level," Night Dragon laughed as he pushed Taka back. With three slashes of his sword, he sliced the axe blade to pieces and then handle. Standing there in shock, Taka fell to his knees in admission to his defeat.

"Finish me now Dragon warrior," Taka said. "For mercy is fuel to my revenge I will take on your beloved Rose."

"Nobody touches my White Rose," Night Dragon said as he past judgement and allowed his sword to fly.

Standing there covered in Taka's green blood, Night Dragon sheathed his sword and turned towards the awaiting jet. Taka's body fell to the ground oozing out his Jade glowing blood as his head rolled to the feet of his awaiting soldiers. With his eyes still open, the jade glow in them began to fade and reveal his natural eye color. His face morphed back to that of the human man it used to be centuries ago. The face then turned to dust as did the rest of the now destroyed body.

Nothing was left but the Samurai armor and the spilt Jade blood. The dust blew away into the wind leaving the soldier dazed and confused. Rage grew as they saw their leader's remains blow away in the wind. As they clinched their swords, daggers, or guns, they allowed the small Jade energy within them take over. Pausing in midstride, Night Dragon stopped and slightly turned his head. As his body emitted the energy of the Heart Stone, a light but strong blue glow surrounded his body and his eyes glowed blue light.

Five Jade Soldiers rushed Night Dragon with all their might. Night Dragon spun around to catch the first with punch straight to the chest that instantly stopped his heart. The second received a spinning back kick to the face and neck, killing him instantly. The third and fourth leaped into the air with swords drawn. Night Dragon caught both blades with his gauntlets. The soldiers were in shock of the feat as Night Dragon stood there strong.

Waving the blades away, he flipped into the air while executing a double kick and landing perfectly on his feet with his sword drawn. The two jumped to their feet and attacked again only to be stopped with one slash of Night Dragon's sword as he leaped over both. Just as he landed on his feet, their headless bodies fell to the ground. The fifth soldier stopped in mid stride as he watched their heads roll to his feet. Remembering his duty to The Jade Samurai, the solider rushed Night Dragon. He was stopped with Night Dragon's sword as it was slashed his own blade into pieces. Fear filled his and the onlooking Jade Soldiers' eyes. With one punch, Night Dragon knocked the fifth soldier at least three hundred feet into the air where he landed at the feet of the Jade Soldiers.

"Deliver a message to your master," Night Dragon ordered. "I will see him in one week. His head belongs to me."

With that said, Night Dragon pulled out his sword and stabbed it into the concrete street. He turned towards the White Rose and Wolf. Night Dragon began to walk away as the soldiers ran to the aid of their defeated comrade. They grabbed him and the remains of their dead.

Smoothly and calmly, Night Dragon moved towards the awaiting jet. He could hear the movement in the fingers and the trigger of a crossbow. In a brilliant flash of light, Night Dragon spun around and caught the arrow that was fired. With ease he twirled the arrow in his fingers and then flung it back into the would-be assassin. Struck in the heart through layers of thick Samurai armor, the failed archer fell to the ground dead. Seeing the actions of his abilities, they all released their weapons and allowed him to leave in peace.

Night Dragon bordered the jet proudly with the cargo bay door closing behind him. The jet hovered off the ground then took off into the night. The Samurai scattered at the sounds of police sirens. However, they were more afraid of Thorton and his wrath. He was unlike the traditional, General Taka. Taka was vicious and deadly, but he focused on honor and duty to his master. Failing him meant that your soul was your only way to gain honor. Thus, his undead army would never run out of troops.

With Thorton, failure meant death. He was too ambitious and determined to worry about honor. The Samurai rushed to their awaiting cars. While some made their way in the opposite direction of the police, the rest were rushing out of their Samurai gear into to police gear. Only a handful were on the Mayor's Samurai Guard, and those officers were not allowed on the street just yet. Especially with the Mayor confined to bed due to White Rose's attack on the Mayor's Mansion. The new Police unit was a failure in the public eye. The wide spread damage all over the city would bring the television news crews out. They also had to make sure that the scene and witnesses supported their stories.

As usual, they people were too afraid to speak against the crooked, corrupt police department of New Peak City. The death of Rick Steele proved to be the best motivation. He was the leader of the only honest lawmen in town. Without him, the bad cops won. The honest cops were too afraid of what could happen to them or worst, their families.

As the police vehicles arrived, the remaining soldiers quickly set up a perimeter. A blacked-out SUV pulled up to the scene, and Thorton, in his new Police Commissioner role, hopped out of the back. Surrounded by his entourage of lackies he began barking orders as the new crews arrived with cameras already rolling. He already knew his fellow Jade Samurai Master orchestrated the demise of White Rose. His true hope was that General Taka and White Rose took each other out.

However, a look of worry appeared in his eyes when his men surrounded him to protect him from the cameras. One man took the remaining armor of General Taka stained with Jade blood and kneeled to present it to Thorton. Flashes of Jade filled his eyes. He ordered the soldier to put the armor in an evidence box and take it directly to the Mayor. Before he could turn around and storm away, the same man informed him of the news. The loyal soldier stood and pointed to the sword stabbed into the street.

The crowd of officers parted and made a path towards the blade. Thorton walked up the path to the sword. Standing there, rage could be seen in his eyes and fists. He took hold of the blade and tried to pull it out. That feat alone was not happening. He tried his best to remove the sword but couldn't. Thorton ordered his men to close the street off and keep it closed until the sword is removed. He stormed off in a rage. He and his entourage got into his SUV an immediately left the scene with the remains of General Taka in tow. Arriving at the penthouse stronghold, Thorton feared the outcome of the news. Upon entering the master's room, he was surprised the Mayor was standing at the window looking out.

"I take it that General Taka failed," he said with a deep monstrous voice. Bring me his helmet. Finally, my plan is succeeding as planned."

Turning to reveal his face, Thorton was surprised to see his original Master, Kenzensho. "Prepare my armor, we have to prepare for my ascension." Laughing his evil laugh, he turned back towards the window. Gazing at his new empire, he knew that New Peak City was ripe for the taking.

As the door of the jet closed, Night Dragon made his way towards the cockpit. In midstride, he fell to his knees. Wolf was there to help him up. He knew what to do to help his friend. He immediately took him to the medical bay. There White Rose was already in a medical pod. Her injuries were more serious than originally thought.

Wolf put Night Dragon into the pod next to her. He connected the IV cocktail to Night Dragon's arm and sealed him in the medical pod. The medical pods were able to analyze the injuries of both warriors. As the pods began to work, Wolf removed his mask and became himself again. Adonai made his way to the cockpit and took a seat in the co-pilot's chair. When they were clear of New Peak City, they landed at Kuroi's hidden airfield. Once they were refueled and stocked, the jet took off once again.

Kuroi kept the jet on a straight course to the Dragon temple. It was a trip that he had been dreading for years. Now with the fate of the world resting on his great, great grandson, he swallowed his pride. The two barely spoke to each other. Adonai was in awe of the presence of the first Night Dragon. Kuroi could sense the questions and unwanted conversation building inside his co-pilot. Since he was dealing with his fears head on, he decided to begin the conversation himself.

"So, I hear you are the Phantom Wolf," Kuroi said to Adonai.

"I am no Phantom Wolf," Adonai said, "I just saw her in trouble. I took a vow to help the protector of the New Peak City. I promised my friend that I would be there when I was needed. She needed me."

"And like the shadow, you are always there. Like a wolf, you defended your family with unlimited vigor and determination," Kuroi told him.

"I have heard of the Phantom Wolf, but I never knew the truth until ND told me about it in his video. I don't know what he was thinking. I am just tech support for heroes," Adonai told him.

"If my great grandson believes in you, then you are more than what you are labeled," Kuroi told him as he continued to pilot the jet. "Besides, it is you're your blood. Just as your father when we get to the temple."

As they flew at great speeds across the sky, Adonai continued to make sure they were not followed or tracked on any radar. He and his family have been helping the Steele family since the man next to him first dawned the Dragon Mantle. His great ancestor made the ultimate sacrifice when cornered by Jade Samurai soldiers and General Taka. For that, the Steele family has made sure to always care and look after Adonai and his family. Most of Adonai's family migrated from Japan to the USA and finally to Africa. Side by side, the two families built a web of connections all over the world. The Night Dragon had agents everywhere that evil ruled. As knowledge and progress continued to grow, so did the role of Adonai's family.

To be honest, Adonai wasn't the first to stand in battle. His family served as the support team, but they were always seen as a partner. The very first Phantom Wolf was Adonai's great ancestor that was wounded in battle. He was too injured to fight, but he kept his vow to his friend. Assisting Night Dragon with all his plans, he became the major support Night Dragon needed. In building the support team, he kept the secret identity of Night Dragon with him. When General Taka arrived at their village one fate filled day, he refused to give Kuroi and the rest of the Shadow Guard up.

It was the ultimate sacrifice that split the Shadow Guard apart. Kuroi made the promise to protect his family forever along with his own. Not a soul has worn the Phantom Wolff mantle since. Adonai knew of the Phantom wolf and his legend, but until Night Dragon's video he never knew it was his ancestor. When Adonai began to take over from his father, the wildest dreams of both Rick and Adonai came true. Together, they found a true partnership.

To them, it was more than a partnership. It was a brotherhood. In the eyes of Rick Steele, he saw Adonai and his family as true family.

As Adonai sat back, he constantly continued to monitor both injured heroes. Looking towards the horizon, Adonai and Kuroi both held an uncertain look in search of hope. The keys to saving humanity were currently in medical pods, fighting for life. Kuroi continued to talk with Adonai about the Phantom Wolf. It was there that he spoke the full truth about the Shadow Guard and his beloved best friend.

Behind them, White Rose was lying in the medical pod, opening her eyes. She realized that she was in a jet, then looked over at the pod next to her. Seeing Night Dragon, tears began to all as she watched him lay unconscious to the world. She opened the pod from the inside. Once the pod opened, she removed the oxygen mask from over her face. Mya slowly began to sit up and gain her bearings. It was painful but she was able to turn towards Night Dragon.

Gingerly, she climbed to her feet and shuffled to his side. Opening his pod, she looked at him with serious concern. Removing his breathing mask, she wanted to look upon the face of the man she loved. Mya leaned in and gently kissed his forehead. Amazingly Rick opened his eyes to see the brown eyes he fell in love with as a small boy. He was too weak to speak nor move. However, he needed her in his arms. He slowly sat up in the pod and moved over. Making sure he didn't remove his IV by accident, he invited Maya to join him in the pod. She held a slight grin as she recognized the gesture. They used to watch as his parents would share a hug in the hammock that use to hang on the porch of Rick's childhood home. While they played in his tree fort, they would enjoy the view of his parents embracing during lazy afternoons.

Climbing inside the pod, Maya was in pain. However, the pain disappeared at the presence of Rick Steele. He was her medicine, protector, teacher, mentor and lover. They were two different personalities, but when they were one when together. Cuddling up together, they both ignored their pain and just held each other. Neither shared a word. They just held each other for as the pod closed. Neither cared about anything else but one simple fact...they were one.

3 INTO 1

Waking up in the infirmary, Rick was not surprised to be back at the Dragon Temple. He was amazed to be still lying next to Maya. Fluttering his eyes open, it was the touch of her hand in his that woke him. While he slept, his dreams were filled with images of her. The smell of her hair was the sweetest aroma. In a way, it was one of the connections that kept her in his dreams. Hearing her voice as she hummed, Rick would hear her voice in his dreams.

As his senses and awareness returned to him, he noticed that his beloved assassin still had bandaged ribs. Looking at her, he was in love with the sight of Maya asleep. He still was on an IV treatment and by the looks of the bag, his dosage was upped to an amount for an elephant. He blew that observation out of his mind and cured up next to Maya. At that very moment, his health didn't matter. His heart was just happy to see her one more time.

Cuddling up next to Mya, Rick tried not to move her. Like clockwork, she adjusted herself in her sleep to cuddle closer with Rick. Just as he was about to close his eyes, the door opened. Adonai stood in the door way silently to avoid waking Mya. He simply nodded at Adonai, who knew to leave. He held a smile as he watched them hold each other. Adonai loved to see Maya and Rick together. To him, they were the example of what true love is. Respecting his friends, he closed the door and ordered that they not be disturbed.

Adonai proceeded to the library where a meeting of the elders was in place. Richard Sr. and Kuroi were in deep discussion off in a private corner, while the others were debating over the Night Dragon. Adonai knew his place but everything in his being was telling him to demand they respect their leader. Hearing their claims that Rick must be replaced, angered Adonai. When they said the Night Dragon powers must be stripped to save his life, he was filled with rage. He knew that Richard Sr. and Kuroi did not agree, but they were ignored by the majority lead by Rick's and Adonai's uncles. At that point, he couldn't take it anymore.

"How dare you disrespect your leader?!" Adonai screamed at the top of his lungs. "We don't have a say in the matters of the Night Dragon. We are his followers, not his masters. He is not a weapon. He is our leader and protector of this Earth. Respect your Master. He has risked his life over and over to save us all and you seek to destroy him. You are no better than the Jade Samurai."

"Hush boy and know your place. You serve the Night Dragon. The Night Dragon is a weapon," one of the elders screamed back. "This counsel has determined the path of the Night Dragon Clan for centuries."

"You are dead wrong," Kuroi answered, "The Night Dragon is a single voice. One single man who takes the responsibility to defend the weak, the innocent and equal justice for all. I know because I created that oath. An oath I passed down through my bloodline. Rick Steele is the current Night Dragon. He has led this family proudly and gained the knowledge so many of you neglected. He knows more about the enemy than any of you. He risked his life to save his father and to get the piece of the Jade energy back to the Temple. He was the only one in the bloodline born of the Heart Stone powers. And before arriving at the temple three days ago, he personally destroyed General Taka."

"My son has personally saved my life and waged war with the Samurai all alone," Richard Sr. told the counsel. He has proven to be the only Steele capable of ending this war."

"This war is coming to an end!" Rick yelled into the library. Standing in the doorway, Maya was standing beside him holding him up. As they both depended on each other for support, the walked into the library, both using canes. "The Jade Samurai is on the verge of collapsing due to their own greed. Justice and equality will be defended by the heart of the Dragon. Those are the words that each of you swore by. You sit here in judgement because I do what is needed and not what you demand. If you dare, challenge me now!"

Standing in the middle of the vast library, Rick stood before the people he once called his family. The Night Dragon was passed from father to soon, but there was always an issue of jealousy from the sons not chosen. The amazing fact that the White Rose warriors withdrew from the clan because of this internal disease added to the fire. Forming their own clan, they kept the wishes of the two separated. It was Rick's mother that led the separation.

His uncles and cousins always felt as servants rather than a part of the family legacy. His father spent many years keeping the family together. The internal divided weighed so heavily on him that it was the reason his marriage failed. Losing his precious White Rose, he was never the same warrior.

On Rick's side stood his father, grand ancestor, Kuroi, and the Adonai's immediate family. They all respected the tradition that Kuroi and his adopted father started to defend the people. In keeping with tradition, the elders were respected and revered. Those on the Rick's side were the first on the field of battle or volunteered their lives for the people. Staying in the background, the others were keepers of the Night Dragon secrets.

However, being apart of the Night Dragon Clan didn't come without selfish desires of those within. It was always given to the first-born son due to the simple fact of responsibility. Just as the eldest son must learn to take care and lead the family, so must the Night Dragon lead the clan and protect the innocent from injustice. Standing before what he thought was family, Rick was still leaning on Maya for strength. He pulled away from her and stood on his own. Dropping his cane, Rick stood before his so-called family. He made a decision that defined him as a leader.

"The Blue Heart Stone is a part of my DNA. It makes me who I am with or without the mask. My powers flourish even without the light of the moon. I have dedicated my life to serve the people of New Peak City and the world. None of you have dared to risk your own life for others. You cowards bring shame upon the Steele name," Rick declared. "Your words mean nothing when innocent lives are taken at the hands of the Jade Samurai and other Evils of the world. I also know that one of you is the traitor that helped our enemy destroy my family. You are guilty of helping the men that murdered my mother and almost kill my father. That is why I have kept my plans from you all. I challenge the coward to stand now. You want Night Dragon. You want to lead this Clan...then take it from me!"

With that said, Adonai sealed and locked the door of the library. Standing in front of it, he refused to allow anyone to leave. Revealing his power gauntlet, he keyed in a code and locked down the entire Temple. Rick stood in the middle of the library with nothing but pajama pants and nothing else. Taking a fight stance, he was determined to finish his plan. Maya was blown away by the news, but her mind was ready for the fight. She stood back and watched her man take his role as head of the clan. Looking over at his father and Kuroi, she knew they believed in Rick and were ready to follow him without hesitation. She shot a nod to them as they revealed themselves in battle armor. Just like Rick would, they returned a devilish grin to her in agreement.

Rick stood in the center of the room and continued to welcome on the fight. Raising his hand in the air, he simply pointed to the traitor. Inviting him to step out for the challenge, everyone watched as Richard Sr.'s brother reacted to the allegation. Shaking his head, he tried to turn and walk away only to be stopped by Kuroi and his brother. Looking at his brother in the eye, Richard Sr. could see the truth to his son's discovery. Rage began to fill his hurt and destroyed father. He looked at his son who was ready to end the fury. Rick saw what was about to happen and gave a nod to Maya. She backed up the room as Richard Sr. pulled his sword out and tossed it to his son.

"For your wonderful mother and my beautiful wife," he told his son as Rick caught the blade by the handle.

"You honestly think you can stop me boy," his uncle replied. "You think you can handle a Master Warrior. All your training came through me and my counsel. I built this Temple to the level it now holds as a beacon of Honor and Justice."

"You speak like a Samurai," Rick said boldly as he pressed a button to reveal the truth on video. "That explains why I have this video of you giving the Night Dragon Gi's to the Grandmaster and the traitor, Hero Steele. You killed my mother and tried to kill my father. You were the one to betray this family!"

Rick presented the truth and caught the traitor red handed. All those that were with his uncle were now against him with weapons drawn. They surrounded the room along with Kuroi and the others. Moving quickly, the disgraced uncle tossed his cloak into Rick's face to distract him as he withdrew his sword. His cocky ego was going to be his downfall. Just as he was about to stab Rick, he found that Rick was ready and awaiting to block the attack. He held his signature grin as he locked eyes his uncle.

At that point, the fear could be seen on his uncle's face. The time for Ronald Steele was now. With a nod, Ronald, Rick's evil uncle, gave to sign for his followers to leap into action. High above the library was a skylight. Samurai soldiers burst through the glass ceiling and through the library doors. Before they could attack Rick, Maya and the others leaped into action to help. Richard Sr. and Kuroi pulled their blades. Adonai grabbed Sai off the wall after tossing a bow and arrows to Maya. The war was now inside the inner sanctum of the Night Dragon. Rick and his true family were determined to clean house of the Samurai infiltrators.

With the Night Dragon legacy was at stake, they had to rid the temple of the evil infection. The reason for the discourse and struggles of the entire family were finally revealed and being settled in that library. As a massive duel between Rick and his uncle took center stage, Kuroi lead the others against the remaining attacking Samurai. Of the twelve council members, four, including Rick's uncle were now traitors to the Steele family. Realizing that they were wrong and corrupted by lies, the remaining council members grabbed their respective weapons and took the side of Rick Steele, the true leader of the Night Dragon Clan.

It appeared that Rick and his true family were winning without having to harm a soul. However, that all changed when the door busted open with an army of one hundred Jade Samurai soldiers. It appears the entire temple was secretly taken over and infiltrated with the enemy. As their eyes glowed the dreaded Jade green, it was clear that his enemy had planned this very moment. As Rick continued to fight his uncle, he channeled his pain and rage that he kept hidden since the day his mother was stolen from him.

At this point, there was no more holding back. Each member loyal to Rick saw his rage unleased as his eyes began to glow a brilliant blue hue. Tapping into his powers, he was about to wipe the samurai from this Earth. His uncle saw this and tried to retreat. Aided by his men, he was able to run out the door. As Rick began fighting off his road blocks, Maya aided with perfectly placed arrows.

"Get that bastard for both of us!" Maya shouted as she picked up a katana and joined the others in battle. "So am I okay to kill people now!"

"Yes dear!" Rick said proudly as he went after the man behind his mother's murder.

Following behind his evil uncle, Rick found the innocent people that live and worked at the temple being attacked by Jade Samurai soldiers. Seeing the sight of the innocent being beaten and murdered created more rage than he has ever held. Releasing all his power, a bright blue glow covered his body and blade. He let out a war cry and took out his rage on every samurai he saw. He tried to keep an eye on his prey but the site of innocents being butchered was why he became Night Dragon. The innocent needed a defender.

Rick focused on saving lives rather than take his uncle's life. Shortly after, he was joined by Adonai and Maya. They saw the carnage themselves. They both followed their hearts and their leader. The three worked as one as they took on attackers as if it were nothing. While they fought the endless fight, the traitor made his way to the roof of the temple where Kuroi's jet was still sitting. He made sure it was there just for this occasion.

Ronald's great escape was his last gift to the Jade Army. He made plans with Kenzensho and his son decades ago. Waiting for his moment to complete his plan, he was happy when Lee Heto called him to with the orders to execute their final plan. It was also the night that his father transitioned to the Jade Stone Realm. His plan to turn on his father was perfect thanks to Ronald. Ronald secretly supplied weapons and technology from the family business and secrets of the Night Dragon in exchange for a seat with the Jade Samurai Army and power. Everyone that joined Lee's side received their rewards instantly. Now with the fall of the Night Dragon, he would be given the honor denied by his birth.

He was never meant to be second to anyone, not even his older brother, Richard Sr. He reached the roof to see the jet ready for takeoff. Rushing to get away, he opened the door to board only to be greeted with a viscous punch to the face. He was sent flying back into the air and crashed on the ground. Richard Sr. walked slowly up to his downed brother massaging his now sore hand.

"You only live because you are my brother by blood," Richard told him as he squatted down with a dagger to his throat, "You are alive because my son gave mercy to you. If he wanted, your head would be in his hands now. You betrayed our family for your so-called honor. You murdered the only woman I have ever loved and the mother of my precious son. Bastard, she was pregnant when you had her killed. You killed my child too."

"No, my son," Kuroi said, "You are better than this. You are a warrior not a murderer."

"Well, things change ancestor," Richard snapped back. "Because of him our family is now destroyed. He stolen everything that I have to live for."

"No, my child," Kuroi corrected him, "The evil of the Jade Samurai corrupted him. You must be better. The only true honor is that of love of family. He is your brother."

"I have no brother!" Richard shouted as he thrusted the dagger in the air.

"Dad, no!" Rick shouted as he walked onto the scene. "Dad, I didn't bring you here to lose you. I know he has wronged us, but we can't sink to their level. You raised me to believe that."

"He is not family," Richard said, "He is nothing to me."

"Dad, I will not allow you to become what I defend against," Rick said. He and the entire Jade Army will pay for every life they have destroyed."

"That is why you and your bastard offspring have led this Clan to shame," Ronald uttered to his brother, "You don't even have to courage to finish the mission. To shed the blood of our enemies. Hell, the Samurai realize that our enemies must be removed from the Earth, and people must know their place in the world.

"Enough!" Kuroi ordered. "You bring dishonor to me and my blood line."

"What honor!" he fired back, "You are immortal and turn your back on the Clan for these two to destroy everything. Keeping a tradition that put the wrong men in control. The wrong son was put into control."

"Speaking of knowing your place, shut your mouth boy!" Kuroi demanded as a black glow emitted from his eyes. "I left because there can be only one head. And I am not Immortal, I am cursed. Consumed with the power of Black Soul Stone. Half alive and half dead. Cursed to walk the Earth a phantom. You destroyed the only piece of my father that was left."

"Adonai, please put this trash in the holding cage in the jet," Rick ordered, "Dad, get everyone out of the temple and head to the hanger. Kuroi will come with us. We must end this. I have a special surprise waiting for you."

"Son, you will need help. I can help you," Richard Sr. offered. "The Samurai has too strong of a hold."

"Dad, you and mom trained me," Rick said proudly. "We three are one. We can stop them. You are needed to get our Clan to safety. I promise you and the Clan, Justice for the innocent. Let's roll, we have to keep moving."

Following his orders, Richard Sr. led his father and Adonai's father down to help the remaining Clan members. There were other past Night Dragon warriors who were denied a seat on the council. They held the same belief as Rick and therefore were treated like nothing in the eyes of his evil uncle, Ronald. Spending their retirement years training and resting, they longed for one more battle. The night that Rick transitioned to be the new Night Dragon, they were pleased and proud. He was just like both parents. They could see the path that Ronald was heading down, but they never would have thought he would betray the family.

Following the custom of the clan, they all married and loved women of the White Rose. However, with the infighting created by Ronald, the split from the Clan ruined all their marriages. With the White Rose Clan moving away to their own secret location, each of the remaining past Clan leaders lost the loves of their life. Many homes and families were broken up and the Temple became less of a home.

The Temple was now no longer a home but a massive grave. In total with Richard and his father, there were four former Clan leaders. Adding Adonai's father and his family members, there at least fifty people that had to be moved to safety. As Richard gathered his clan, he saw what his son saw. He had been awoken from a deep coma thanks to his son. The surgery was because of the endless planning and research of Rick. His son saved his life and now he wanted to be the man his son saw him as. He knew Rick knew what he was doing. Richard and the others lead the clan to the hanger. It appeared that the infiltrators destroyed all the jets. There was nothing left to escape in. Looking around he was lost. Then an alarm message came in on Richard's gauntlet. It was a message for Adonai.

Operation Dragon Flight Access Granted. Mind the floor. -Adonai.

Alarms began to sound, and the hanger floor started to move. Splitting open, the floor revealed a secret staircase that descended beneath the Dragon Temple. Not even Adonai's father knew of this staircase. They quickly began leading everyone away from the temple. Using his gauntlet, Richard closed the secret opening. He and the others lead everyone down a lighten path to an awaiting jumbo jet. Recognizing the designs of their sons', both fathers were proud. Upon walking up to the jet, the group were greeted with old friends. Mouths dropped open with shock as the White Rose Clan welcomed them aboard.

It appears in his travels, Rick mended the wedge between the White Rose Clan. Running to their respective spouses, the former leaders were lost as their lovers embraced them. One person was waiting for Richard. It was his own mother. She was the one that trained his wife and brought her into the White Rose Clan. When he and his wife split, his mother proudly went with her daughter-in-law because of the love they shared. She knew the pain of her son from the word of her grandson. She proudly wrapped her arms around him and invite him into the jet. Looking at her stubborn husband, she rolled her eyes at the sight of him. With everyone aboard, they were whisked away just before the temple began self-destruct.

Watching his father take off, Rick knew that his fight was not over. Adonai was inside the jet locking the traitor away. Just as he returned to the cargo bay of the jet, he found Rick and Maya fighting off Jade soldiers. Leaping into action, he refused to back away from a fight.

Grabbing two metal Tonfa clubs, he unleashed a whirling fury. Maya used her bow and arrows with great precision. She was a true archer, but she was a devil when she used her twin Sai. Rick welded a katana in each hand. His blades were in a perfectly choreographed dance of death. Bit by bit he took out each attacker with ease and viscous fury. He ordered Adonai to activate the escape plan. It was something they planned years ago as teenagers. They always feared this day. As a young man, Rick knew the importance of a good plan.

After his mother's murder, he reached out for his grandmother and the White Rose Clan. It was with her, he gained the knowledge of the many secrets never revealed to him by his father and elders. In secret, he moved the White Rose Clan into the valley next to the Dragon Temple. They secretly watched and reported back to him. They also kept him in alignment with Maya's training until she separated from the clan. He didn't want the truth leaked out due to the many infiltrators he found and personally imprisoned in a hidden location.

Maya was left her clan to make her own decisions. Rick respected her and the others that left the clan for personal growth. He wanted her and others to be their own person. Rick watched over Maya and protected her from a distance. Afraid to let her into his world because of the Hell that surrounded him, he always kept his distance from those he loved, especially Maya.

As he put his plan into action, he realized that he could not live without Maya nor keep secrets from her. The night that he found out about the set up to kill her, Rick personally threw his plans to the wind to save her. He knew she could not handle General Taka alone. When he knew it was time to let her in, he made sure that she had the weapons and help she needed to defeat him. However, that all changed when he heard Maya needed help. When they finally caught a breath and put the last of Jade soldiers down, Rick and the team boarded the jet which Kuroi was already aboard and starting the engine.

Once aboard, Adonai pulled up security footage and watched as the clan boarded their escape plane. Once they were aboard, he began the self-destruct sequence. Another wave was about to attack, Rick took over the controls and waited until they were in range. With guns loaded and ready, he opened fire and took them all on. He began to take off when he spotted an entire garrison entering the temple. Patiently, Rick waited until the White Rose Clan were clear to make his next move.

With an evil grin on his face he looked at Adonai and gave the order. The temple began to erupt in countless explosions. The temple fell apart brick by brick, imploding on the evil invaders. Taking off into the sky, Rick set a straight course to the next phase of his plan. It was clear now that he was the leader of the clan, and his family was now safe. Most importantly, he and his friends were one body working together in unison. With his elder along with them, he knew they all were ready to stand as the protectors the world needed against Jade Samurai. As they continued their course, Kuroi and Rick where the only two people who knew where they were going. They traveled a top speed in the supersonic jet that was still too advance for the modern world. Thanks to the many advancements that to the Blue Heart Stone, Rick Steele and his family were able to make technology that was centuries ahead everyone. The secret They had been flying for over twenty hours when the silence was finally broken.

"So, my son, are you ready to train?" Kuroi asked.

"Yes, Elder," Rick replied, "We are ready. No more tricks or secrets. This time, it is a straight fight."

"Excuse me," Maya interrupted, "I need to speak to you, now"

"Yes, dear" Rick said reluctantly.

As he climbed up from the controls, both Kuroi and Adonai avoided eye contact. Kuroi was almost five hundred years old and knew the tone of her voice meant trouble. He kept his eyes on the skies ahead while Adonai buried his head into his computer. Rick was terrified of what Maya had on her mind. He followed her to the cargo hold where he could see that she was upset and fuming. Before she began to even open her mouth, she began to pace back and forth. He was about to speak when he was stopped by a sharp stinging right cross from Maya.

"Ouch!" Rick said as he held his jaw. "What was that for?"

"If you scare me like that again, I will kill you myself. If you keep secrets from me again, I will kill you. And if you make one more plan without letting me know what the Hell is going on, I will personally shoot your body full of dull, poison tipped arrows," Maya cut him down just before wrapping her arms around him. "I love you, don't make me kill you."

"I am sorry. I was trying to protect you and respect you. I should have kept you in the loop. Does this mean you will be leaving the team?"

"You know I am old fashioned," Maya said with the same evil grin Rick always carried. "White Rose is heart of Night Dragon. And if you keep me in the dark again, I will personally give you a rose through the heart."

"Partners then?" Rick asked as he leaned in for a kiss.

"That depends," Maya answered, "Where is my ring?"

"Well…" Rick said frozen in his tracks. "What does a ring mean? We are partners…best friends…lovers. What does a ring say? Just a stupid status symbol."

"Before you open your mouth, remember who I am," Maya warned him.

"At excuse me, love birds?" Adonai interrupted, "While two of you talk about walking down the aisle with matching swords, I just want to know our next step"

"That is easy," he replied, "Home. It is time we learned to work as a team."

Extending his fist out, Rick welcomed the others to join him. Without hesitation, Maya put her fist out with a smile. She was in pain but enjoyed the thrill and ability to make the evil suffer. Adonai held back. He was afraid of the joy of battle he experienced. It was one thing to come to Maya's aid. Everything changed when he grabbed those Tonfa clubs off the wall and unleashed years of fury. He hesitated because his fear, but Rick believed in him. If Rick believed in him, then there was nothing to fear. He looked at the pair and realized that he was welcomed and loved. His work mattered to them. Even with the short amount of time together, Maya respected and admired Adonai. He extended his fist in agreement with the others. Just as he joined the others, Kuroi walked in on the newly formed team.

"Are we back at the Lair?" Rick asked, "We are arriving in good time."

"Actually, Rick," Adonai stopped him, "I launched the Electric Wolf Program. It set off the self-destruct sequence. Sorry, your loft is gone."

"Okay," Rick said with a small amount of shock. "Did you at least save my guitar."

"Of course," Adonai said with a smile.

"Great," Rick said. "But I was talking about the real Dragon's Lair. That is where we three must go to ascend. Am I right Master Kuroi?"

"Yes. Well, I am glad to see you three are on the page. And now you three must survive," Kuroi said as she hit a button that released the floor underneath the three warriors. The jet was hovering over a forest as the three crashed to the ground. Standing over them, Kuroi looked with sense of determination. He simply pointed towards a mountain that to be a hundred miles away. "Meet me there."

With the simple orders given, the door closed, and the jet took off towards the mountain range. Disappearing within the clouds, it was clear what had to be done. Looking at their surroundings, Rick saw what around them. Maya was already holding her ribs as she began to make her tools. Rick knew what was going on. It was time to ascend. Adonai was still thrown by the actions of the elder, but he also knew what was going on. The three began the hike towards the highest mountain peak. Maya found some bamboo and reeves. From them she made a crude, but more than efficient bow and arrow. Adonai found a tree limb and used a rock to whittle it down into two matching Tonfa clubs. Rick, on the other hand, began to build a fire. Maya and Adonai were shocked by his actions. He was normally the man with a plan.

Before long he had a fire going and disappeared. He reappeared with fish from a nearby stream. Telling them to rest, he made it clear they had to rest now to travel nonstop tomorrow at dawn. He kept the fire growing through the night. When the fire got hot enough, he pulled out a small metal brick. It was the same metal brick he removed from the fake chest. I spotted his elder toss the brick down as they fell from the jet. It was at that point he began the task of ascending.

Using wood, rocks, and the surrounding elements, Rick began making the perfect tool he would need at the end of their journey. It was a make shift forge, but following the training of his ancestors, he did the best he could. As the rays of the morning sun began to wake Adonai and Maya, they found Rick was already awake. He was sitting up looking at the sunrise. Maya walked over to him and asked if they were heading out. He nodded and then thought for a moment. He had been up throughout the night and was able to learn their location by the star constellations.

"We are in Jade Samurai territory. This is their training grounds and headquarters in the Nampo Islands. It is their home. To get to the mountain, we must go through their land. There is only one way we do this. We must rely on each other. Maya, you have the best aim and awareness. Adonai, you have the best inventive spirit. But we need our weaknesses to prevail. Maya, you don't trust and never show restraint. Adonai, you don't believe in yourself. Me, I depend on my weapons, powers, and shadow games to win."

"Why are you telling us this?" Maya asked, "What is this all about?"

"Because we are about to meet some Samurai guards soon." Rick admitted.

"I thought I smelled the awful stench of the bull crap," Maya said as she stood and leaned against a tree.

"How far away are they?" Adonai asked. "Why didn't we see them yesterday?"

"Because they were too busy preparing for the Dragon Moon Celebration," Rick replied. "I am willing to bet they are searching for what made a plane appear on their radar."

"We better get to moving," Adonai said, "We don't have armor nor weapons strong enough for them."

"Actually, we do," Rick corrected Adonai as Maya nodded in agreement.

In the blink of an eye, Rick picked up a rock and hurled it in to a tree. Knocking a man out of the tree, he was not surprised by the hidden attackers. Revealing themselves, the passing Samurai patrol showed their weapons and attacked. Maya moved with great speed as she unleashed her arrows with fury and precision.

With great ease, she took out hidden archers. Being a skilled archer, she knew the best places to sniper victims. Adonai picked up on their presence and sensed the would-be attackers behind him. He kept his batons at his feet and welded it with a kip-up. Whirling it around, he blocked arrows aimed at him. Rick moved with great speed to avoid the arrows shot at him. Using tree bark he spotted on the ground, he turned it into a shield.

Moving quickly, he ran towards two sword welding samurai without fear. He took leap into the air and took out both with a double drop kick. He fell to the ground with the kick, then leaped back to his feet with a flip. Rick unleashed his fury as he took out attackers with his bare hands. As Maya ran out of arrows, she then used her bow as a club. Adonai continued to show his skill with his make shift batons. As each of the warriors took on the patrol members, they began to pile the fallen samurai.

When the last man fell, only the three warriors were left. They gathered the unconscious samurai and tied them up. Rick and the others took their weapons and armor. Gathering everything together, they followed the practice of the ancient ninja. Taking what they could from their enemy and the elements, they formed what they needed to protect themselves. It was at that moment, Rick held a dazed over look on his face.

"This isn't real," he said out loud. "This is not real."

"What are you talking about?" Adonai asked as he continue to prepare.

"This is not real. I know our tech is the best but there is no way we flew to Japan in a matter of twenty hours. The Dragon Jet is supersonic. We would have been there in mere hours. And Adonai you are good, but there is no way you created time travel. Look at their armor and weapons. There is one way to provide it."

Taking a sword into his hand, he walked over to the tied-up bunch of defeated samurai. He paused as he looked the now waking soldiers in the eyes. In one powerful slash, he decapitated three of the men at once. Maya and Adonai were both in shock by his actions. They were more surprised by his discovery. The heads that fell were the heads of androids. Rick knew what was going on and quickly threw his sword towards the fire that immediately began to create sparks.

Watching Rick's actions, Mya began to fire arrows from the quivers of the samurai archers into the sky. She was not surprised to find that the arrow struck clouds and began to spark as well. Adonai followed both their leads and began the assault on the nearest tree. Again, proving their fake surroundings, he threw his weapons away and dove into the wiring. Within minutes, he created a short that revealed that they were still inside the Dragon Temple. Standing there in shock and awe, the three warriors looked up and saw that they were being observed by Kuroi and the other elders.

"Look, I am tired of these games," Rick declared. "We need to get back to New Peak City. I came here for help and you play these games."

Walking out of the simulation room, Rick was furious and upset. He passed a digital clock on the wall and began more furious with the date. It appeared that they had been at the Temple for three months. Maya followed behind and shared his rage. Apparently, her injuries were completely healed. Adonai was more confused than angry. He never knew that he too was in the simulator.

Adonai and Rick created the simulator for training purposes when the training grounds were overrun with the elements. He thought it was a good idea due to the secret weapons they developed. It was the proving grounds before taking a new weapon out into the world for real world testing. The last thing he could remember was getting Rick and Maya into the medical pods. Next thing he knew, he was in the library listening to the council demean his friend and partner. He gave a scolding look at his father and followed behind Rick and Maya. They were a team. And messing with one was a fight with all three.

Maya and Adonai followed Rick to his own personal room in the temple. Walking in, they were blown away by the space. It was as if it were his own loft apartment within the Dragon Temple. Adonai was simply blown away since for years growing up his best friend had to hide his face from him. Now he finds out that his best friend was told lies and kept in the dark just as he has done. The three knew something more was happening, and nobody was going to tell them. They had been away for months. It was more than apparent that the elders and Kuroi were up to something.

For years they preached that he must be ready to ascend. Then with the Dragon Moon upon them and the tools to ascend, they purposely keep him and his team away from the mission goal. He didn't agree with the methods nor the tricks being pulled. Rick was the one that normally pulled the wool over the eyes of many. He was a sore loser when it happened to him. The more he thought about it, the more he began to piece together the actions of the elders. His only concern was the many lives in danger in New Peak City.

Across the vast oceans and worlds apart from its heroes, New Peak City was being ravished and plundered by the Jade Samurai. Watching from his throne, Kenzensho enjoyed the terror his new Samurai Guard reigned over the citizens. Stealing his son's body, position, and ideas, he created his own paradise. Ever since he stepped back into the Realm of the Living, he enjoyed the chaos he created. Kenzensho planted a false story that he had to fake his own death to find those responsible for the attack on the Police and City Government. With his son's mind lost and the story of the Mayor in a coma, Kenzensho relished the throne that he gained back.

The fact that his great general was destroyed did ruin his victory, but he had already chosen a suitable replacement. He only waited for Lopez to wake up. Checking her status every day for three months, Kenzensho knew that he only needed her to pledge her allegiance to him. With that oath, he could completely control her and her dark powers. Thorton lead her Samurai Guard that was now gaining national attention in their three-month lifespan.

As he returned to life in public, he also pulled off an amazing impersonation of his son. With his renewed powers, he morphed his appearance into his son's form When the media needed proof of life. He mastered the ruse of a patient who was still recovering from his attack from White Rose. Listing both Night Dragon and White Rose as the most wanted criminals in the city, he even got the man hunt for both so-called criminals to spread out nationwide.

Now wanted by the federal government, there was no way the two could ever be seen in their beloved mask without the nation raining down on them. Kenzensho was back in control and creating the world he dreamt of. In the public eye, New Peak City was now the textbook example of a perfect city. However, what was not known to the public was the fact the criminals were running the town. His treasures were growing by the day as well as his powers. Sitting on his throne inside his penthouse, he knew that he had won. If by chance Night Dragon ever showed his mask again, he would easily destroy his enemy in the palm of his hands.

While Kenzensho enjoyed his throne, his son continued to roam the Jade Spirit Realm in search of a way back to his body. To Kenzensho and the world, Mayor Lee was lost in his mind. The truth of the matter was he was in a cocoon. The attack from White Rose revealed a weakness that he didn't plan for. He immediately retreated to the Jade Realm for power. He knew his father was running a major con on him to take over the Jade Army. Once he was left in the Jade Realm to take his father's place, Lee turned it into an opportunity to rise to his true throne. It was always a part of his plan, but White Rose sped up his time table. He wanted her as his prize. Turning her into his mistress and head assassin, he would publicly marry Maya Wollert for a fairy tale wedding that would seal his title of honor. As he continued to roam the Jade Realm, he found his general among the countless fallen soldiers of the Jade Army.

Looking at his Grandmaster in the Jade Realm, Taka yearned to be with his beloved and his master as they took their place in honor. However, with his demise, he was now a slave to the Shogun. Once he arrived in the realm, Taka was taken before the Shogun and given his punishment for failing. He was to serve an eternity as the personal slave and collector of the souls of the ill-fated. The Jade Realm was powered by souls of the evil and corrupt. No longer feared and revered, he was once again a hideous monster that gathered and feed the souls to the Shogun and the Jade Realm.

Lee Heto was an evil man but being the son of Leo Kenzensho, he learned the value of loyalty. Since his father was only loyal to himself, Heto learned the importance of his inner circle being loyal to him and being loyal to them in return. He gave the general his one wish to gain his loyalty and his power. Increasing his power with the addition of General Taka, Lee had his weapon of destruction. With Lopez, he had his weapon for law and order. With them at his deposal, his empire was sure and destined. He would control the people, their well-being, and their very lives.

As he roamed the Jade Realm, he could feel his powers growing. His mind began to fully understand the powers of the Jade Stone. While he was there, he also learned the truth. The truth that his adopted and biological fathers hid from him and Rick. The truth he was sure his brother was still being denied. Even in the Jade Realm, he could still use his powers to read minds and control weak souls. His powers were great, but his powers were no match for the Night Dragon.

In his last battle, he took his powers and formed them into a physical dagger that inserted his evil Jade powers into Night Dragon's body. Lee knew that was poison in a vessel of the Blue Heart Stone. With the Blue Heart Stone being apart of his DNA and coursing through his blood, he was sure that Night Dragon was finally destroyed.

The two powers introduced to his body without proper training was like drinking a gallon of the world's strongest poison. He found out about his miraculous reappearance that sent Taka to the Spirit Realm. However, Lee figured that was just the catalyst needed to initiate a fatal poisonous reaction. Lee felt the battle for life inside Night Dragon. He felt his life force slip away once he was trapped in the Spirit Realm. That was the only reason the Shogun never condemned his soul to the Jade Hell awaiting their evil spirits. As his powers continued to grow, Lee Heto knew it was time to take control of his empire once again. He studied the habits of his unholy evil master. Lee knew when to strike, but he just needed the right moment. It was time for the Shogun to make his way through the Realm. It was his daily task to wander through the Realm checking his domain.

However, Lee would make sure it was his last. As he normally did, he appeared before the Shogun to show his respect. Just as his master appeared, Lee hid his evil grin as she secretly formed anther energy dagger behind his back. Just as he walked up to his master and bowed, his master slightly bowed but was stabbed in the throat through. Falling back, the Shogun oozed Jade blood through his wound and his mouth. He fell back upon his throne, gasping to breathe. Lee let out an evil laugh.

Forming another energy dagger, he stabbed the Shogun into the heart. Lee smiled as his true plan to ascend succeeded. Just above the throne was the Jade Katana. A sword made of entirely out of Jade and the Jade Stone. The last of the stone was used to form the helmet he now wore. Taking the sword from its mantle, he held the sword in the air to absorb all the powers of the Jade Realm. Lee took the sword and swung a might blow that took head of the Shogun. As the body of the Shogun began to fade, his energy and power flowed to the Jade Stone upon his helmet. Once his body was completely dissolved into ashes, his helmet sat upon the ashes in front of his throne. Laughing at his success, he picked up the helmet and placed it upon his head.

Instantaneously, the Jade energy and smoke overwhelmed Lee and surrounded his entire being as he laughed. Once the energy faded away along with the smoke, Lee stood tall and strong, draped in Jade Shogun armor. Holding the Jade Katana and wearing the Jade Samurai Armor, Lee proudly took his place as ruler of the Jade Spirit Realm. All the souls imprisoned in the realm were now under his control. He summoned Taka to stand before him. With his destruction of his body, the general lost all his earthly powers. However, with his new powers, Lee could change that. He needed a soldier for his bidding. Lee laughed as he proclaimed his new throne and powers. Slicing open the air, he opened the portal between the Jade Realm and Earth. It was time to claim what was rightfully his.

The sky turned black and lightening began to fill the atmosphere over the Royal Arms, the Jade Army's headquarters in New Peak City. The penthouse and everything within it were shaking. Suddenly a lightning bolt shot through the window between Kenzensho and Thorton. Falling to the ground, the two watched as the lightning bolt struck the throne and filled the room with electricity.

Thorton was fearful and ran for cover. Kenzensho, on the other hand, knew what was going on. The master finally over powered his son and used him to enter the realm of the living. Kneeling proudly at the presence of the Shogun, Kenzensho showed respect as his master entered the realm. When the lightening ended, a heavy smoke cloud surrounded the throne.

As it finally cleared, Kenzensho knew to signal his men to bow before the Jade Shogun. Standing next to the Shogun was Taka, in his human form and in traditional Samurai armor. The Shogun stood up and ordered his servants to rise. However, the smile on Kenzensho's face vanished as he looked into the eyes of his master. He recognized his son and fear entered his entire being.

"Surprised, Father?" Lee Heto said as removed his face plate. "You honestly thought that you were in control of me. You think your trick worked. I wanted to go into the Jade realm. Now bring my body before me."

"Yes, Master," Kenzensho replied. Ordering the men to retrieve his son's body from the other room.

"It was smart of you to have a body in a medically induced coma. The Press would not dare bother to bother the city's injured leader. With no body left for me to claim there was no way for me to get back once I was rejuvenated. Especially, since you are using my body. Do you think I am falling for any more of your tricks? I know you took the body of one the fallen soldiers and put it in my bed. You forgot the one flaw to your plan. I am your son," Heto said to his father.

Walking up to him, he looked at his father with a smile. Then in one brief and powerful slice of the Jade Sword, he split the air over his father in half. He used to Jade Sword to then trap his father's soul in the Jade Spirit Realm for all eternity. Heto's body was then incased in a huge Jade crystal like tube. Energy began coursing over the entombed body. Thornton looked on in fear as he worried about the master taking his vengeance. Taka laughed as he watched his former master get his deserved punishment.

The new Shogun walked back to his throne and took his seat. Pleased he ordered that he be left alone with his body and ordered that Lopez be brought in as well. It was time to fully unleash his plan and power upon the world. It was time that the Jade Samurai Army took complete control. Standing over his body, he knew that the delicate nature of his plan to control life, death, and eternity. He could finally get the one thing he wanted his whole life. He looked over at his body and extended his hand. To be the perfect being, he now transferred his powers and himself back into his body. Lightning bolts and sparks filled the room. When the room finally calmed down, Heto's eyes opened to reveal him in the Shogun armor. He sat up and stood to his feet. Now it was time to claim his prize.

THE TRUTH HURTS

Standing alone in front of the mirror, Rick looked himself in the eye. For the last six days, he locked himself away from the world. Since waking from the simulator, he and others we denied the truth. Since the moment he walked into his loft, he refused to leave. Maya and Adonai tried to get him to leave only to be refused. He even turned Maya away from his room. Locking his door, he hid away to get answers himself. Rick was still upset that his powers were stripped way due to the three months he was hidden away from the world.

To his amazement, he was surprised that the entire Dragon Temple didn't realize he was gone. He walked over to the window and look out of New Peak City. He had been home for three days, and nobody was aware. He set up a small cameras and projectors throughout his place there at the temple. Rick also took control of the hidden cameras his uncle secretly installed in his loft. He was able to know if, or when Maya forced her way in. He knew the woman of his heart was a fighter. She would not allow Rick to endanger his life after making his promise to her.

Rick Steele knew that everyone in his family was keeping a secret. It was time for everyone to realize why he Night Dragon. Since returning to New Peak City, he began seeking answers on his own. Before leaving the Dragon Temple, he took only the items he needed. Rick took sacred text, the metal block, the original Dragon Armor, and the sacred Dragon Blade.

All these items were respected but hardly any information was ever given. Before he left, he also downloaded all his health records, and any information collected while he was unconscious. He was back inside his loft apartment and the damage from the explosion was still evident. His lair was destroyed, but his home was still in perfect condition. Before building the lair, his loft served a perfect base of operations.

With a push of a button, the loft converted to his fully functioning cove of secrets and weapons. Hidden away from the world in plain sight, he could be the cop and model citizen. When the moon was out, he became the Midnight Beast. Building the lair at the end of his first year, he wanted to separate the two beings completely. Especially, when Maya and White Rose came back into the picture after years of being apart.

As he looked at his home town, he didn't recognize it. Out on the street, he walked around with sunglasses and a baseball cap. A different disguise to hide his face, he tried to merge with the people about while studying his prey. Instead of uniformed police, his city was under Marshall Law governed by Mayor Heto's Samurai Guard. Now deputized, they were the only law within the city. Rick fought his urges to retaliate when he saw the abuse of power and the cruel abuse on the innocent citizens of New Peak City. He was back to old habits.

Picking up supplies and provisions. Stocking up on what he needed, he only purchased bare necessities and nothing more. All that mattered to Rick was back at the Dragon Temple and the people surrounding him now. At one time he was the leader of the clan, and then he was unceremoniously pushed to being labeled a soldier and weapon of the clan. Everything was wrong, and all the blame was put on him.

Rick had no more connections within the city. He was believed to be dead as both of his personas. The moment he revealed that he was alive would prove fatal for those who knew. He gained more of an understanding from the simulator than what was intended. He kept the subtle message Kuroi gave him close in mind. To make sure that he was not found alive by the clan, he left by foot and took off in his personal plane that was hidden from the Temple. The only person to know about the plane was his mother.

It was her private plane that she used in secret to travel back and forth with Rick and Maya to the hidden location of the White Rose Clan. Since her death, the clan retreated to an even more secluded location that Rick didn't know on purpose. He supplied every need they had and set them up with unlimited resources. Rick respected them and refused to allow them to be labeled as only assassins for hire.

Rick Steele for the first time was lost. He was accustomed to being alone, but this time it was a forced isolation. He had to leave everyone he loved in that temple to save the city that needed him. Sadly, it appeared to be too late. The other night he witnessed his most dreaded enemy ascend. He began to study his prey and set up cameras. Rick even setup a hidden supply post for the day he could attack the Jade Samurai. He watched the lightning storm begin to form only around the penthouse.

Rick immediately knew what was happening. He watched as his so-called brother destroyed his biological father. This time he reached a level more powerful than any other foe he has faced. Then, Rick watched as Heto merged his Jade Shogun essence with his body. The combination created the ultimate weapon and his failure. Now he had no chance of fighting the Shogun without ascending himself. It was then he felt doubt for the first time in his life. Retreating to his loft, he readied his weapons, but he questioned his reasons why.

Since returning to his loft, he fought with the fear and doubt from deep within him. He spent the entire day unable to sleep or eat. Pacing and thinking about his life, choices, and the challenge before him, Rick wanted to be true to himself. He wanted to let it go, grab his sword, and put on one last fight. Even if he somehow won, he was going to die. He looked at his medical records and found that the merger of the Jade and Heart stones only speed up his demise. It was now attacking his entire body without tapping into his powers.

Looking further into his records, he found that his father and Kuroi discovered a way to turn off his powers. It was found that sitting in the moonlight charged his body, but it only prolonged his life. His loft had a skylight that he loved but it became his lifeline. Rick took a seat in his favorite chair and sat underneath the skyline. Pondering his choices, he could not deal with the visitor he was about to have. He heard them fifteen minutes ago when they first climbed onto the roof. He could tell by their footsteps their height and weight. He was worried when he heard the gun cock and application of a silencer. His sword was in the closet and along with the rest of his gear. With everything going on, his safety was the last thing on his mind. When he took his seat, he finally got the confirmation of his would-be attacker.

"How long did it take you to know I was gone?" Rick asked.

"I saw that look in your eye. How did you know it was me?" Maya asked

"I know your walk, the way you breathe, and the coconut oil you use in your natural hair," he told her.

"If you know so much then tell me why I brought this gun?" Maya asked as she pulled her gun.

"To fulfill your true mission," he told her. "You want to be the title that my mother still holds. You have killed and made a lot of money by using my mother's name. You want to be the White Rose and lead the clan. Can't do it if the Night Dragon is still running around policing you."

"You don't understand," Maya said. "I love you, but the White Rose is all the family I have left. After my parents died, the White Rose took me in when you were too busy keeping secrets and fighting the world. I needed you. The Clan loved me, just like your mom did."

"I love you," Rick replied. "Why the hell do you think I literally spent my life away from you or tried to keep shit from you. You are my reason to live and the reason I fight. I rather have you safe and alive then in danger loving me. I am a magnet for death to the ones that love me."

"You have people that love you," She told straight. "I only wanted you and you pushed me away. If you loved me, you would have made it work. My father made it work. Your grandfather and every man before him made it work. Don't give me that crap." Maya demanded.

"My father didn't do anything to make things work. It was my mother. It was my mother that created your clan when my parents divorced. My parents never slept in the same bed. My mother finally told me the truth. That is why she was murdered," he told her.

"Well, I guess the truth dies with you," she told him as she took aim.

A single tear began to fall as Maya looked at Rick within her sights. Rick released a single tear as well. There was no need to fight anymore. He had no more fight left within. With his lover's gun pointed at him, he knew there was no end for the viscous cycle. Her truth mission was to kill him. To claim her crown, she had to slay the king. Lie after lie was told to people. Each lie was transferred into someone's truth.

Looking at everything going on since before he was born, his entire life as a lie itself. Looking her in the eye, he knew that this was the end befitting a ninja. To die by the hands of the one he loved was more meaningful than failing his beloved city. He reached inside his shirt pocket and removed a ring. He placed it on the table in front of his chair and sat back. Looking her in the eyes, he wanted her and her tears to be the last thing he saw. Suddenly the muffed sound of gunfire entered the room as she fired three rounds into his chest.

Disappearing into the night, Maya grabbed the ring and a duffle bag out of the closet just before leaving the loft. She hated the orders she was given, but they were her orders. They were vital to the survival of innocent people. Escaping to an awaiting van, she closed the door and looked into the eyes of Adonai. He grabbed her hand and ushered her inside while closing the door. He made sure to remove her camera from her body armor.

Pulling out the memory card, Adonai uploaded the video into his computer. Once the video uploaded, it was sent to the Dragon Temple.

Kuroi was sitting at the computer. He ordered the hit by his Rick's own team. It was clear were loyalties lied within the clan.

As they drove off into the night, Maya sat in the front passenger seat as Adonai drove. Her eyes were full of tears, as she cried her pain out. She was running away from the one man she loved. All for the sake of orders, she fired point blank, center mass into the heart of the one man made just her. She remembered the final words of her mentor, Rick's mother as she looked at the ring she took. Maya recognized the ring as his mother's wedding band. She had not seen the ring in years. Upon closer investigation Maya found an inscription, "3 Into 1". Thinking about to those final words, Maya finally made the connection with the inscription. Maya repeated those final words to herself:

"There is one who is your equal, and one that will be your opposite. They will be the same man. He is the man that is made for your heart. He will love you and protect you. That is the man you never let go of."

As they drove off into the night, she made it clear they had to get out of town before they were spotted. She only told Adonai to get them out of New Peak City. Maya didn't care how or by what route. As they made their way to the highway, their only concern was to escape to the next mission. The orders they received were direct and ongoing. They had to continue to the next mission in order to survive and save the lives of their love ones. Looking at the city in the view of the mirror, Maya knew that she would bring her fury down on those responsible for her actions. She had to find out who was in control. Her new mission in life was to find out who was in control, so she could personally put her hands on them. As of right now she only cared about her flight to Japan.

It had been fifteen minutes since Maya left the loft. The plan was working, and he just freed himself from the eyes of the clan. He knew that the true mole inside the clan would have planned for his escape. The virtual simulation was his warning. Creating a plan of his own. He wore a special vest that gave the illusion of a kill shot. He knew his team and their habits. Rick knew the path that Maya would take and where she would aim. He knew his friend Adonai as well. His friend was the only one that could turn off the surveillance cameras that Rick monitored from the loft.

Rick was fully aware of the surveillance on him and the tracker on his mother's plane. Whomever was calling the shots knew both Maya and Adonai would be the only people in the world who could get close enough to pull the trigger. This staged death was his only why to find out the truth. There is a traitor in the clan, his master refused to help him ascend, and his enemy gained mystical powers that he had no way of defeating. Rick had to get answers for everything. He walked over to the closet to find the armor was gone. That is what he expected to find.

Now he worried of the great stress and pain placed upon Maya and Adonai. With the thought of killing their friend in cold blood weighing heavily on their minds, He could see by Maya's reaction that she was torn between her place as head of the White Rose Clan and her love for him. He could believe that Adonai would ever agree to his murder. He knew something great was going on to drive their friendship and brotherhood to be destroyed by betrayal.

Pushing a lever on the back wall of the closet, a panel opened to reveal a hidden staircase. Not even Adonai knew about this secret. He walked down the stairs to the apartment underneath. It was his hide away from everyone. It was a safe house that not even Adonai could find. He pressed a button that closed and sealed the secret door from the loft. Once the door closed steel plates snapped into alignment and sealing the door. Locking himself away, Rick Steele knew that isolation is what he needed to figure things out. Opening the closet door into the cozy apartment, he could finally feel peace.

Rick was not surprised at the swiftness of his current murder attempt. It was proof that he was close to answers. He peeled off his blood-soaked shirt and tossed it into an awaiting garbage barrel. Removing his vest, and pants, he put all his things into the garbage barrel. He held nothing else of value as he tossed a match on top of his clothes and placed the lid on top. Rick put on a clean pair of jeans and sleeveless t-shirt. He walked over to his bed and sat down.

Reaching for his favorite stress reliever, Rick grabbed his guitar and strum a few cords. He needed to figure things out. There was one thing he was missing. As he strummed away, his mind began to wonder. He could feel peace come over him as his eyes got heavy.

Within moments, he was asleep and dreaming. In his dreams, his mind could see everything and everyone. The entire situation played itself out right there within his mind. Realizing the truth of the matter, Rick immediately woke from his dream state. He knew that it was time to train. To seek the path that was destined for him, Rick had to stop being what everyone wanted him to be. It was time to stop living up to the status of the Night Dragon and just live as the Night Dragon.

Sitting up from his bed, Rick placed his guitar next to the bed and stood up. He walked over to the Dragon Blade and the sacred book of his family. He looked closely at them both. It was the detective within him that found the clue he needed. It was the Dragon symbol imprinted on the cover was the identical match of the handle of the blade. He took the handle and inserted into the imprint on the cover. Once it was in, he heard a small click. It was then cover came off to reveal the complete truth.

Realizing what everything was all about, his mind became clear with the truth. Rick could feel the anger and rage coursing through his veins. And now it was time to end the war. Reading the truth written by the original Night Dragon, Rick knew he was the key needed. The foreign blacksmith wrote in his own words the truth behind his search. He was not looking for an alien meteorite. He was searching for the three pieces of the Dragon. The stones are the remains of the sacred warrior that merged mystic powers, alchemy, and mutated superhuman abilities. The

Night Dragon is the protector of the Blue Heart. It was the same story that was pass down through the family bloodline. It was then that he realized that it was a blueprint. He looked at the way the words were written. It was a simple fact that every member of the family had to learn three languages. Three native tongues were required of the Night

Dragon Clan. Three was always the magic number. It was time to see what was truly going on.

Rick grabbed the block of steel and walked over to his forge. He began to heat the forge and begin from scratch. Thinking of what he discovered, he looked back at the handle and realized something. He picked up the Dragon Blade. The handle was now loose. He twisted it open to find the three Stones. They were never just rocks, but powerful gemstones. It when then he made the ultimate discovery. Taking the stones into his hands, a massive surge of energy overtook Rick as images flooded his mind. A brilliant light began to overshadow Rick and a strange portal began to open right then and there.

Relieving the truth before his eyes, he stepped into the portal and disappeared in the blink of an eye. Within a mere couple of seconds, he was back in another flash of light. However, he was not the same. His shirt was burned and ripped apart. His jeans were in the same state. He moved towards the forge and was more convinced of his plan. Rick still had all three gemstones in his hand. He walked over to the forge and placed them all with the block of metal into the melting pot.

Rick then walked over to the middle of the apartment and removed a loose floor board. He pulled out from the floor a five more blocks of metal. He picked up the blocks and took them straight to the melting pot. It was time to be who he really was. He caught a glimpse of himself in the mirror as he removed more secrets from is hiding spot. He had molds that he had been creating for most of his life. Being a proud member of the Steele clan, he learned the family's original profession, blacksmithing.

It was also his knowledge of metal and physics that helped him to design the brilliant weapons and gadgets Adonai made. He was determined to be his own man and now was the perfect time. Turning on a special ventilation system, he began to heat the melting pot at extreme levels of heat. Rick walked over to a large cabinet and unlocked it.

Revealing the Dragon sword and Armor, he grabbed the items and took them to the melting pot. Everything of the past had to be used to create the warrior he wanted to be. For years he tried to merge the use of traditional and modern ninja weapons and gadgets. He tried to bring compromise, but it was time to stop pleasing his clan and others. Looking at his designs and the ideas in his head, Rick began changing every design. He erased all ideas of the suit being powered by the Blue Heart stone.

No more depending on his powers. It was time for Rick Steele to step into his own. He walked over to his desk and began to sketch out a new design. Adding guns and other useful components, Rick created a new being named Night Dragon. He immediately began building molds and mocking up the cutout of the new suit. Focusing on his ninja heritage, he threw away the armor that was more designed for a samurai.

Striping away the previous designs of his fathers, he wanted it to be tactical, stealthy, agile, and say boldly, Rick Steele. Pulling material from storage, he found a cloth like material with steel, titanium, polycarbonate, kevlar, carbon fibers, and the three stones. Rick began testing for the perfect mixture of those elements. As he worked, he pulled up his own surveillance cameras on his laptop. While he worked, he studied his prey.

When he needed air, he would leave through a secret exit that would let him out into the building next to his. He was fortunate to own both buildings. When he was out in the world, he always wore a disguise to avoid being recognized. Other than gaining supplies, Rick was still gaining intel on what his enemy was planning. He knew the real Lee Heto. There was no way Lee would rip a hole through dimensions, destroy his father, and kill endless people unless he had an endgame.

The fact that he now carried endless supernatural power terrified Rick. However, Rick knew that his powers were still limited. While Rick was studying when he began his isolation, he questioned why Heto had not struck his first blow to take over the world. While he continued to ponder this question over and over, Rick spotted the Samurai Guard. They set up a checkpoint for anyone that heading towards city all. It was announced that the Mayor was hosting a press conference since awaking from his coma. He knew something was up. Today he was disguised as an old man with a cane. He didn't have any weapons on him, but he was wearing the prototype suit under his clothes. The perfect time to test if it were detectable.

Once he moved past the checkpoint with ease, Rick followed the crowd surrounding City Hall. He watched as the Samurai Guard surrounded the platform and covered every possible vantage point. Rick took the opportunity to study their methods and manners. Spotting the Mayor emerge from City Hall under heavy guard, Rick had to hold back his anger. He listened to the lies of the Mayor and grabbed his cane tightly. Wanting to leap from the crowd, Rick wanted to introduce the new and Improved Night Dragon.

Rick watched as the evil Mayor painted a vicious picture of Night Dragon and White Rose on a murdering spree. At that moment, he learned the answer to his question. The Mayor introduced his next major project to give the people true protection. He presented a new city within the city…Jade Palace City.

Promising a safety and prosperity, Jade Palace City would be a major urban improvement on their crime riddled city. The city would increase economic growth and major technological advancements that would bring new life to their community. It was then and there, Rick realized what was going on. Without delay he made his way back towards his hidden apartment. However, before he could leave, he had to send a reminder. He used his phone to play with the security cameras surrounding City Hall. Turning them off, he then played a voice message over the sound system.

The Mayor and his men tried to hide their fear while searching for voice. While the guards searched, Rick made his way close to Commissioner Thornton. Pointing out a man in black he saw inside City Hall, he secretly placed a tracker on him. When their backs turned her ripped off his disguise and left it for them to find in his place.

"It was time to make sure the Jade Samurai meet the Real Night Dragon," Rick proclaimed as he found his way inside on of the news vans.

Grabbing the footage from the press conference, he finally made his way home. Rick made sure he was not followed nor leaving a trace of his presence. He entered into his hidden abode and got to work. He began analyzing the footage while working on the on improvement to his suit. Rick realized the end goal for his enemy and the fate of his dear people of New Peak City. They were the bargaining tool. Lee Heto was trying to bring the Jade Mystic Dragon back to life.

Now that he contained the powers of the Jade Shogun, he still was not all powerful. Soon he would require the souls of mortals to sustain his powers and his own life. It did not matter if he had the powers of the Blue Heart Stone anymore. All Rick Steele cared about were the innocent people of New Peak City. He checked the melting pot and found the stones and the metals were still solid and barely up to temperature. Frustration appeared as he pounded a table with his fist. Everything was against him. Rick quickly regrouped as he sat down at his desk. He needed the new weapons, but the people needed him more. Remembering his heritage, he refused to bow down to circumstance.

Rick decided that he would fight on for the people. He stood up and walked over to another cabinet. Opening the door, he revealed another cache of swords, guns, and other deadly weapons. It was time to go to war. With part of the new suit done, he grabbed a tactical, bulletproof vest and a gun belt. He made major alterations as he found a way to merge the two into one piece along with his sword sheath. He normally carried a single katana when most sword masters carried two.

As Night Dragon, he normally depended on his powers to compensate for the extra blade in battle. With all of that he observed since his returned, carrying guns and a single katana was enough. With additional weapons and his lack of powers, Rick had to keep everything light and portable. As he worked on his new idea, he thought about the family argument over Traditional and Modern or American Ninjas. He already decided to carry twin modified 1911 9mm pistols with extended silver tipped barrels for accuracy. The days of traditional duels and sword fighting were gone.

Spotting the weapons of the Samurai Guard, Rick noted that only squad leaders and officers carried sword. The foot soldiers all carried military grade weapons including a side arm and rifle. With the look of military soldiers, Rick got an idea that more dangerous and advanced weapons where in store as well. He remembered his last battle with Heto and the Samurai Guard officers. Somehow Heto was able to merge supernatural powers and advance tech to upgrade himself and his men. It was time to focus on the mission and not if he looked the part of a traditional ninja.

As he worked on into the wee hours of the next morning, Rick looked over at the tv and noticed a familiar face. It was the truck driver from the docks. He reached for the remote and was in tears when he heard the full story. A drive-by shooting took the life of his little girl as she played with friends at the neighborhood park. Rage began to take over his entire being at the news. Rick knew that the man was set to testify at hearing about the failed weapons deal next week. Proof that the Mayor was coving his tracks.

It was time to go to war. The blood of the innocent flowed in the street a river. Seeing the little girls face on the news was the final straw. Rick promised her as Night Dragon and as himself that she and her family would be safe. Tears began to fall as he realized that he broke his promise due to his thirst for the ultimate power to vanquish his enemy. In a since, he became just like the samurai he hated so much. He turned back to his work and further prepared for war.

Once everything was laid out before him, Rick began the task of piecing together his new uniform. As he worked, the weather outside began to become slightly violent. It was the beginning of heavy thunderstorm. As lightening flashed across the sky, he received the inspiration he needed. He finally had an idea to heat the forge. He rushed to gather tools and pieces of metal cables. Rick rushed to setup the rigging with the hope that nature would provide the heat he needed. He kept track of the storm that was to last all day. Due to his building being his base of operations, there was a lightening rod attached to the top of the building to protect the satellite dishes and special antenna he used.

Within less than hour, Rick had his special cables setup and connected to his forge. He only had to wait. The weather began to settle down just minutes after setting everything up. He was heartbroken and upset. As he gave up hope, Rick turned away towards his bed. Suddenly, there was a brilliant flash and monstrous roar of thunder that shook the building. Lightening struck the rod and sent a huge surge of electricity through the lines. All the energy met the forge with a brilliant flash of light. Rick was thrown back and slightly blinded. However, he could not turn away from the sight. He made his way towards the forge and smiled as he saw the stones melt and form around the metal he placed inside the pot.

Grabbing isolated gloves, Rick quickly got the hammer and began to pound away at each piece of metal. It took three weeks to do what normally took months. He had a fire within him calling to be set free. While forging something out of this world, he spent that time training. He started from the very beginning and never let up. He had to learn to fight on his own without mystic powers.

As his work moved along with great improvement, so did his skill. It was finally ready when Rick took the sword of his creation out of a special case. Taking the sword in his hand, he walked over a pillar in his apartment. It was made of steel and concrete and very solid. He had begun the task of moving his things out of the apartment earlier in the week. Bit by bit, he only grabbed what he needed. It was time to test his swordsmith skills on this new blade.

With one smooth but powerful slash, the sword cut through the pillar as if it were air. The pillar didn't buckle nor shake. Rick smoothly place the sword into its sheath and proceeded back to it case. Once he closed the case, he made his way to the secret exit and closed the door. As he descended a hidden stairwell, he heard the crash of his apartment imploding on itself. When he reached the moving truck awaiting him, he hopped into the driver seat and pulled out into traffic. He watched in his rearview mirror as the smoke and dirt filled the air from the collapse of the top two floors of his building. He made sure nobody else was in the building months ago before his fall from public sight. He made his way through traffic with a firm determination.

Pulling into a corporate building garage, he used an access card to enter the highly secure building. He was already wearing his disguise and making his way to his next appointment. Parking the truck in front of a garage door, he hit the button on a remote to open the door. After the door closed, he quickly made his way to a private elevator. Ascending to the top floor, he removed his coveralls to reveal an expensive, well-tailored three-piece suit. Just before the door opened, he added the key part of the disguise.

Rolling out of the private elevator, a middle age man appeared in a wheelchair. Rick hid his true age and features with make up and a mask. We wore gloves to cover his hands and to add to the character of the known germophobe. Changing everything about himself including his race, the energetic and proud black man was now a cruel, cold Asian scientist confined to a wheelchair due to his work as a weapons builder.

At Blue Steele Technology, he was made the head of the company when Richard Sr. was put in charge of the family company. He was running the company and supplying the weapons manufacturing department with gems of destruction. Daniel Akiko was an engineering mastermind. He also was a black-market dealer that dealt with every known gang and criminal mind in New Peak City. He was the middle man that would set up deals and collect the finders fee. He never sold Blue Steele Tech, but he always knew who had what and where.

Building a throne of power, he was the arms dealer that wanted the ultimate customer, The Jade Samurai. Now the fish he always wanted was waiting in his office. Arriving in perfect timing, Akiko greeted the Mayor as he entered his office. Mayor Heto stood and greeted his new best friend. Having supplied the Jade Samurai with the information to capture and ruin his greatest enemy, the Night Dragon. While the Jade Samurai built their criminal empire, Akiko helped to build their infostructure and advance technology. He wasn't privy to their top secrets, but Akiko knew enough to make his riches.

Now he met with the man that could give him the biggest contract the company has ever had. The Mayor's secret business was also the largest under the table black market deal that will seal his destiny. With money coming in from both sides, he could justify expenses and mixing inventory. Akiko finished off the deal with a toast of champagne.

As the Mayor, Thornton, and the Samurai Guard left the meeting in smiles, Daniel Akiko was happy that his planned worked. Holding all the cards, he sealed his office with the push of a button. He removed his mask to become Rick Steele again. It was time to bring the truth out to the world one piece at a time. It took fifteen years, but his plot to gain access to the Jade Samurai and the traitor in his clan. Rick removed the rest of his disguise and quickly put on his uniform. It was time to take back his city.

Creating Daniel Akiko at a young age with his friend, Adonai, Rick Steele created the mean-spirited engineer to create their dream weapons and tools all while building a bridge to the underworld. Gaining information from the gang leaders and criminal masterminds, he created a unless caseload of convictions that would rain down justice on every criminal except one. The Mayor was his true target. Becoming Night Dragon once more, he felt and looked totally different.

The Night Dragon uniform was now sleek and stealthy while being completely fearful. He stripped away his tech-friendly persona and combined his police and military tactical training. The one-piece body suit was form fitting connected with the special vest and gun belt harness he created. Now that he moved into the corporate tower, Night Dragon now had the access to an endless supply of weapon ammo and technology that would help him in his own man army. The very last piece was his mask. He put it on then made his way to the private elevator to ascend to the roof.

On the roof, Night Dragon looked over the edge while carrying the same case from before. He opened the case and presented him with his new weapons. The Dragon Katana laid next to twin 1911 9mm modified pistols. A matching pair of gauntlets sat next to an array of shuriken and throwing discs.

Finally, there were four remaining pieces of his new uniform. Night Dragon continued to suit up as he left the remaining four pieces inside the case. He stared at the remaining pieces and pause. Night Dragon took out the eye visor and face mask pieces. He then retrieved a custom dagger and placed it in a sheath inside his right boot. The final piece was the most important piece. When the stones melted, Rick made a major discovery.

The Stones received their power from the diamonds within them. Respectively colored by the stone that surrounded them, the black, green, and blue diamonds were the true source of their mystic powers. He took those diamonds and formed a medallion. Night Dragon put the medallion on and tucked it away inside his vest. He was finally ready. Night Dragon looked over the edge to spot his next target. His orders to deliver Blue Steele Tech weapons to the Samurai Guard were being followed to the letter. He now had his ride to their training base.

As the rain began to fall, the clouds unleashed a heavy storm. Night Dragon saw it as perfect cover. He climbed on top the ledge. Running at top speed to build momentum, he leaped to the next building. The landing was rough but silent. Working without his powers was different and strange. However, Night Dragon had only one thing in mind…The Destruction of the Jade Samurai.

He continued to move along the rooftops and follow his own company truck. Night Dragon made his way to the checkpoint heading out of the city limits. When the trucked stopped, he silently made his way onto the truck. Hiding in silence, he kept a mental note of his whereabouts. After an hour and a half of driving, the truck finally stopped at the front gate of the training facility. Night Dragon hid a tracking dot on the truck just before leaving the truck upon inspection.

Leaping over the gate, he hid behind a huge truck. While guards went through the shipment, Night Dragon began to investigate the former Police Academy now turned into the Samurai Guard training grounds. Moving through the shadows, he observed how the Mayor destroyed the proven school of law enforcement into an evil foot soldier factory. He continued to observe when he spotted a familiar face. It was Lopez, still badge up from her battle with White Rose. He began to follow her as General Taka pushed her wheelchair.

Using the night and rain to cover his tracks, Night Dragon followed behind the two as they met the Mayor and Thornton. Due to his changes, Night Dragon made didn't rely on the technology of his last uniform. He had to rely on his own skills. He did manage to keep a small digital camera in his utility vest. He made sure to turn off the flash and sound. He moved in closer to take pictures. Night Dragon followed them to their meeting place in the heart of the training campus. It appeared that it was time to unleash his full plan before his generals.

Night Dragon stood in the shadows as he watched the Mayor unleash his true self and Samurai Shogun Regalia. It appeared that the evil city leader had his hands in everything. Not only was he a master of the mystic dark arts, but also a criminal mastermind. As he ordered the newest weapons to be showcased, he unveiled his plan of domination. Night Dragon hid in rage as he listened to the plan that would send the Mayor into the ultimate power.

He heard enough and had to return to his ride out. Making his way back across the training facility, he made sure to move in silence and avoid detection. Moving in full stealth, he was pause by a familiar smell in the air. He immediately recognized the perfume and followed the smell to the source. As he moved closer, Night Dragon heard a faint humming coming from the barracks. He moved in closer to see. Climbing onto the roof, he made his way to a partially open window.

The humming turned into singing, and he knew the voice from a long distant memory. Doubt began to take over his mind. The only way to ease his thoughts was to look in. As he looked in to see a silhouette behind a curtain changing, he opened the window to climb in. He moved closer in great shock as the voice created endless memories of his past. Without further delay, he pushed back the curtain to find the truth sitting in front of a vanity mirror.

"No!" Night Dragon said as he walked up closer. "How can this be?"

"Surprised my son," his mother said with a devilish grin. Then she fired to muffed shots with a silenced 9mm Colt 1911.

Night Dragon was hit in the center of his chest. The bullets didn't penetrate his new uniform and armor, but they did knock him down to the floor. Before he could move his mother grabbed a taser and put it to Night Dragon's neck. At first, he resisted, but he felt weak and dazed. He started to lose consciousness and fell back onto the floor. Just before his eye closed, Night Dragon got one final look at his mother. She smiled just before delivering a viscous heel kick to his face.

To Be Continued In…
The Call to WAR!